Operation Minerva

By: **John F. Simpson**

A Rubric Publications Book

Operation Minerva

ISBN 0-9755099-1-8

Printed in India

First Edition May 2004

http://www.rubricpublications.com

This book is dedicated to the officers and men of the Green Berets who fought and died in secret battles no one ever knew of in places no one ever heard of, some of whom, still lay where they fell.

I would also like to dedicate this book to my wife JoAnn who has put up with my moods through some tough times and with whom I have spent countless good times.

JoAnn, I love you.

Operation Minerva

Published by
Rubric Publishing, Inc.
7040 W Plametto Pk Rd, Ste 4, PMB 542
Boca Raton, Florida 33433-3483

PROLOGUE

The tubular frame of the nylon-web seat was cutting off the circulation in Dawson's legs and the bulk of the equipment strapped to his body was smothering him. The heat, the confinement, and his pre-mission anxiety were causing waves of nausea to pass through him. He fought for a breathe of air as he leaned back, shifted his body around, and tried to relieve some of the pressure on his chest. He forced his right arm up between the rucksack resting on his knees and his chest pack. He took a deep breath and sighed in relief as the pressure on his chest was reduced and the feeling of nausea eased. The 150 pounds of combat equipment strapped to his body felt like a giant body cast; every movement was a fight against the cobweb of straps and the weight of the gear. He thought of what a relief it would be on the ground where the load would be trimmed down to a scant 105 pounds. After a few minutes his right arm began to ache, one of the straps was cutting the circulation. He took a deep breath and exhaled. Then, after taking one more deep breath, he pulled his arm out of the webbing and the suffocating pressure returned to his chest. He looked around the aircraft, trying to find something to keep his mind off his discomfort. The crew chief's Playboy magazine finally made its way down the line to him, but the red lighting in the aircraft destroyed the subtle shading and sensuous skin tones that made Playboy's girls so spellbinding and gave the pictures the drab quality of amateur bedroom snapshots; he soon lost interest.

He tried mentally to inventory his equipment; however, his head was so cluttered with thoughts; random thoughts, wild thoughts, about the mission, about the rigorous requirements of the escape plan. In an effort to gain control, he thought of Genie, he could easily recall her scent, but when he tried to create a picture of her in his head, his mind refused to cooperate. He looked around the aircraft and wondered if anyone else was having the same difficulty in concentrating. Everyone looked calm to him. As he closed his eyes again, his thoughts flashed to Pat in Savannah:

Well, today is the day I've been dreading, she thought, it's finally here. I just hope I can keep my promise to him and not fall apart. She pushed the bed covers down with her feet, threw her leg over Dawson, and began to rub his bare back. "I love you, honey," she whispered, thinking he was asleep and not really wanting him to hear. "We've had a good year; its been the happiest year of my life."

He turned and looked at her. Her eyes, normally a soft powder blue, were red with sorrow. A tear fell from her cheek and splashed on his shoulder. He, too, had dreaded the inexorable approach of this day; he knew when he moved into her apartment that this day had to come. He remembered the talk they'd had on the evening prior to his moving in:

"Why don't you move in with me?" she asked bluntly, "You love my large apartment and you're constantly complaining about the BOQ[1]."

"I can't think of anything that would make me happier than having you at my side each night as I fall asleep; unless, it would be having you at my side each morning when I wake up."

"Well, why not then"? she asked impatiently. He answered her question only after considerable hesitation,

"I feel that...that I'm cheating you, cheating you out of time that could be used in finding a permanent mate."

"Oh, Christ! I can't believe you said that."

She took his hand and pressed it to her mouth.

"Honey, I've already had a permanent mate, and was as miserable as hell. I've had security, respectability, society, and position. What I want to try now is a little happiness. You've given me happiness this past year by making me feel beautiful, by making me feel free, and by making me feel loved."

His thoughts were interrupted when she tried playfully to push him out of bed.

"Are you going to run today, soldier, or just lay here and goof off?"

---

[1] BOQ - Batchlar Officer's Quarters

Operation Minerva

She tried to get away after pushing him with her foot but she wasn't fast enough. He grabbed her by the leg and, as she fought her way off the end of the bed, she lost her pajama bottoms. She screamed with laughter as she scrambled to her feet and through the covers over his head. She had no panties on and she knew that the sight of her bare butt would compel him to chase her. In a desperate lunge to grab her before she escaped through the door, he became tangled in the covers and fell to the floor. She ran down the hallway and was half way through the living room when he pulled her to the floor; after a few seconds of struggling, she was pinned down.

"Now you're going to get it!" he said.

"Oh, I hope so!" she answered, feigning a thick Southern accent.

"No, no," he said, "not that."

Immediately she knew what he was going to do and struggled in vain to escape.

"You can't get away from me," he said, laying on her and holding her wrists.

He started working his way down on her as she continued to struggle. After positioning himself between her legs, he pulled her pajama top up with his teeth, exposing her belly button; then he inhaled as much air as his lungs would hold, placed his open mouth over her belly button and blew as hard as he could. She screamed with laughter and begged him to stop.

Dawson was jerked back into reality by a sharp command from the jumpmaster:

"Stand up!"

Operation Minerva

The command, amplified by a bullhorn, and given from such a short distance, exploded in his ears. He was having a hard time making it to his feet from the deep contour of the web seat until he got a helping hand from the two sergeants flanking him. Six men were going to jump tonight; a captain, a first lieutenant, a sergeant first class, two buck sergeants, and Dawson. Dawson was the black sheep of the team, the oddball, the man that (according to the regulations) didn't belong, couldn't belong. However, here he was, an integral part of the team. And, like the rest of the team, he was waiting for the next command. As he waited, his mind drifted back to Pat:

He stopped blowing and started kissing her belly. He could feel her body relax; he also became aware of the heat of her thighs around his chest. He rose up on one elbow and looked at her. Her waist-long golden-blond hair was laying in sensuous profusion on the grass-green carpet, like rays of sunlight around her head. She looked like a succubus or wood nymph, he thought, captured by a satyr and about to be seduced in the grass. He unbuttoned her pajama top and uncovered her breasts...

"Check equipment!" the jumpmaster commanded.
Again, he was pulled from his thoughts. This time the bullhorn even drowned out the sound of the aircraft's engines.
"Your altimeters," the jumpmaster continued, "should be indicating thirty-two thousand feet at a setting of two-niner-point-niner-five. Your opening altitude is two thousand feet indicated; set your automatic opening

device to one thousand feet indicated. The time is now nineteen-fifty-five ZULU[2], zero three fifty-five local."
The jumpmaster made an equipment check of each man and then took his place beside the door.
As Dawson awaited the next command, he once again thought of Pat:

"Are you ready to go?" she called.

"Just a second honey," he answered.

Moments later, he appeared in the door dressed in his summer uniform. From the soles of his spit-shinned jump boots to the top of his green beret, he was the epitome of the professional soldier. Decorated with a rainbow of combat ribbons, glistening silver jump wings and brightly polished brass insignia, he looked like he had just stepped out of a recruiting poster.

"How do I look?" he asked.

She didn't look at him or answer him. She stood motionless, looking out the window. Then, he could hear the stress in her voice as she began asking him safe questions. Questions not related to their relationship or her despair.

"Do you have your airline ticket?"

"Yes."

"Your orders?"

"Yes."

"Your money?"

"Yes, Mommy," he said, laughing at her as she went down her mental checklist.

---

[2] ZULU - Greenwich England time. The time used coordinate all military operations.

The tears started to come again as she looked at him and realized that the time had come and that he was really leaving.
"I'm sorry," she said. "I know I promised not to cry but I just can't help it."

He gave her his handkerchief as she looked away for a moment to compose herself. "Oh, god, don't get yourself killed," she sobbed. I know you may not be coming back to me but, I love you and I want you to live."

Dawson, lost in his daydream of Pat, did not notice the one-minute warning light when it came on; neither did he notice the jumpmaster as he opened the jump door nor was he aware of the fresh clean smell that entered the aircraft as the wind flushed out the smell of gun oil, new equipment, and the stench of vomit.

"Stand in the door!" the jumpmaster ordered.

The sound of the bullhorn was now subdued by the pounding wind that gushed through the open door. The jumpmaster repeated the command.

"Stand in the door!"

The last command jolted Dawson back to reality. He knew that the execution of the next command was the point at which there was no turning back; the thought sent an icy chill down his back. Everyone moved to the rear of the aircraft; the Captain was first in line. All eyes were on the yellow warning light over the jumpmaster's head; all eyes, that is, except Dawson's. Dawson was thinking about the Captain and the Captain was thinking about snow, snow and December, and of Boston:

Operation Minerva

Boston looked so clean, so quiet, and so peaceful under its heavy blanket of fresh snow on that Sunday; that Sunday when he left for his first tour of duty in Vietnam.

"I have placed your luggage in the limousine, Captain. Will that be all, sir?"

"Yes, Franklin, thank you. Has Mother come down yet?"

"No sir, I don't believe she has."

The Captain went into the living room to wait for his Mother and to enjoy the soothing warmth and sound of the fireplace. As he stood there the life-size painting over the mantel seemed to demand his attention; his eyes reluctantly returned to the painting again and again.

"Turn around and let me look at you, my Captain," his Mother said.

He turned and looked at her.

"The General would be so proud of you. You look just like him."

She walked over beside him and looked up at the painting.

"Someday your portrait will be added to that canvas," she said, putting her head on his shoulder. "A third generation general, from General Alex Lowenthan Coxe to General Vincent Chase Coxe to General Alex Hull Coxe. That is something to be proud of son."

As the Captain stood in the jump door, he looked up towards the front of the aircraft at Dawson and then up at the warning light overhead. Only a few seconds had passed, but to the jumpers, it seemed like hours since the one-minute warning light had come on.

Operation Minerva

Dawson noticed the Captain looking back over the stick[3] and gave him a thumbs-up. Dawson was worried about the Captain. Why had he vomited? Of all the soldiers he had known, the Captain was the one with ice-water blood when it came to executing a mission. Is he worried about the mission or is he sick? God, I hope he isn't sick. We would have to cancel the mission. Dawson looked at the light. What is the hold-up? Why is it taking so long to get a green light? Maybe the mission has been canceled. Maybe we were... there it is. It's on!

"Go!" roared the jumpmaster, as he pushed the Captain out.
Everyone heard this last command - without the bullhorn. As Dawson grabbed for the sides of the door to throw himself out clear of the aircraft, the force of the wind caused his left hand to miss. He didn't have time for a second try and the fear of hitting the aircraft flashed through his mind; however, he could feel the jumpmaster's hand on his left shoulder pushing him straight out, away from the aircraft.
"Good luck!" cried the jumpmaster as Dawson plunged into the darkness.
For a few seconds he was suspended in a dark, weightless, soundless, dimension. His close encounter with disaster in exiting the aircraft caused his mind to flash-back to an incident that happened to him in the airport in San Francisco:

---

[3] Stick – A group of associated jumpers.

"Mommy, mommy," the little girl said as she took Dawson's hand, "this man is dressed just like daddy! Is he going to go to heaven too?"

Dawson looked up just in time to see a young Mother burst into tears as she snatched up the little girl. An older woman approached him and begged his pardon for the little girl's actions.

"My son was a Green Beret," she said, her eyes filling with tears, "he was killed in Vietnam. Candy only knows that her Father has gone to heaven..." she said, sobbing briefly, then dried her eyes and tried to continue. "She knows that she'll never see her daddy again."

She stated crying again and was consoled by her husband.

"Are you going to Vietnam?" he asked Dawson.

"No, I've had one tour in Vietnam. I'm on my way to Thailand. I'm sorry about your son, sir."

Dawson walked over to Candy and her Mother; he reached into his flight bag and pulled out his extra beret.

"Candy, your daddy gave me a present for you, he said he wanted you to always remember him."

With tears in his eyes, he placed the beret on her head.

"He also asked me to tell you that he loves you..."

"Join-up, Join-up!"

The Captain's command cut through the night air. There was no moon but the stars were bright and the air clear. As Dawson made turns to orient himself for the join-up he could see the dim glow of city lights on the horizon to the east. There was a small halo of light over Hanoi.

CHAPTER 1
August 1968
Savannah, Georgia

Jack Dawson was eager to return to Thailand. He needed more overseas duty to balance out his service record (to make him look good for promotion) and Thailand would be just as beneficial on his record now as another tour in Vietnam. To Dawson, Thailand was a land of eternal summer, populated by a gentle people who had developed a highly civilized culture. Most of all he appreciated that the Thais considered it a social discourtesy to touch or grab anyone, only relatives and lovers touched. His appreciation for Thai culture could be attributed to his having served in Vietnam, North Africa, and Iran where every step was a fight against the grabbing, shoving, and pulling populace. He anxiously checked his wristwatch. It was the third time he had looked at it in the past two minutes.

"I'll have you there on time," Pat said, "just sit back and enjoy the scenery."

"What scenery?" he said. "After you've seen one Georgia pine you've seen them all."

Neither he nor Pat talked as she continued to drive north on highway seventeen from Fort Stewart to the Savannah airport. Both, however, were thinking about the same thing - how they had met twelve months ago at the same airport where they would now be saying good-bye:

"Your car is ready Miss," the woman behind the counter said, handing her the keys, "you'll find the car in parking spot eight."

As she was rearranging the contents of her purse, Dawson walked up and asked for his car. Oh! god, she thought, Georgia is looking better all the time. She stepped away from the counter and instructed a waiting porter to take her luggage to the car. She could hear from the conversation at the counter that the soldier's car was not ready. This is my chance, she thought.

Dawson walked away from the rent-a-car counter in disgust. He had made arrangements yesterday in Los Angeles to have a car waiting for him and now, there was no car. He sat down and thought about what he was going to do.

"Mister Dawson, I think I may be able to help you."

At first, he thought she was the woman from Rent-a-Car. He was puzzled about how this woman knew his name, and then he remembered the nametag on his uniform. She was a petite young woman of about twenty-eight, long blond hair, just enough Southern accent to be sexy, and dressed with a noticeable degree of class.

"I was standing next to you at the counter; I'm afraid I got the last car."

He stood up and removed his beret.

"Are you going out to Fort Stewart?" he asked.

"Yes, I'm going to Hinesville and I would be happy to drop you off at the fort."

Operation Minerva

"Thank you, that will solve my immediate problem. I can worry about being stranded out there without a car later. Do you have any luggage I can help you with?" he asked.
"No, I have a porter taking my things to the car. He should be there by now."
As they walked to the car, he learned that her name was Patricia Walker, and the pale band of skin encircling the third finger of her left hand told him that she had, for one reason or another, just removed her wedding ring. She was going home, she said, to live with her parents until she could get a new job and a place of her own.
"Are you going to be stationed at Fort Stewart?"
"Yes, I'm going to be a recruiting officer for Special Forces."
"Will you be going around to the schools trying to get recruits?"
"No, we get our recruits from soldiers who have already proven themselves to be effective and dedicated professionals."
"Where was your last duty station?"
"Vietnam," he answered.
I wonder what this lady's objectives are, he thought. Is she a miss-goody-two-shoes doing her good deed for the day? She gave that porter a five-dollar tip, and that outfit she has on looks like it cost a bundle. She looks like she just finished posing for a fashion ad; except, she couldn't be a model - she's too short and her tits are too big. He continued to puzzle over the young woman as she continued to chatter away.
"How long were you in Vietnam?"
"One year, March of 66 to March of 67."

Operation Minerva

My god, she thought, I'm running out of ideas. Why doesn't he pick up the conversation? Is he going to make a pass at me or not? She stared at the road; the silence inside the car was annoying her. He doesn't have a wedding ring on, she thought as she glanced at her own hand on the steering wheel. Suddenly, she became aware of the white band of skin on her finger. Is that it? she asked herself. Does he think that I'm a married woman? A wedding ring has never stopped a man from making a pass at me before, let alone the shadow of a ring. In fact, I think some men are encouraged by a wedding ring. I think it gives them a sense of security that they won't get captured.

"Why are you returning home to live with your parents? Did you get tired of New York?"

"How did you know I was living in New York?"

"I saw your driver's license when you tipped the porter."

Well it's about time, she thought, maybe he's not retarded after all.

"I was married to a man who turned out to be very dull and lifeless. I was taken to New York and installed in his house like a fixture. No, not a fixture, I think I was more like a trophy. We were married on my twenty-first birthday. Then, after six years of no friends, no children, and no love, I discover he's queer. As it turns out, he was only dull and lifeless with me. I found out that he is considered a real blast among his friends."

Dawson was stunned. He didn't know what to say, how to answer. Then a flood of questions entered his mind.

"How did you find out about him? Why did it take you so long?"

Operation Minerva

"He didn't have any of the classical characteristics of a homosexual; he looked very masculine and rugged. Our social events included the governor, the mayor, and there was always a cluster of senators and congressmen around. I always thought his lack of interest in me was due to his intense involvement in his work and politics."

"How did you find out?"

"This is very embarrassing for me."

"You don't have to tell me."

"I have to tell someone, and I won't be able to tell Mom and Dad."

After a moment of reflection, she told her story:

"I was sick and confined to bed. My maid was staying at the house to care for me. On the third day of my illness, I developed a craving for some grape juice. My maid had gone to the store so I went to the kitchen myself. I thought that I was alone in the house. As I walked past my husband's den, I saw my maid's ten-year-old son on the couch. The back of the couch was facing the door and all I could see was his bare back. It looked like he was sitting on the arm of the couch. I was furious because I thought he had been swimming and was sitting on the couch in a wet bathing suit. As I approached, I saw his bathing suit on the floor and could hear muffled groaning. In the mirror over the fireplace, I could see that the boy was grimacing, his eyes were tightly closed, his left arm was stiff across the back of the couch, and clenched in his hand was a ten-dollar bill. As I moved closer, the mirror reveled my husband's head buried between the boy's bare legs. I felt like I had wandered into the twilight zone. I was completely dazed by the situation. I could not speak and I could not move. The

sounds that he was making over that boy were sounds of pleasure that I had only heard in the movies. After an eternity of time had passed, I regained control of myself and quickly, and quietly, returned to my room. Once in my room, I became sick to my stomach and lost what food I had managed to eat that morning."

"Did you tell anyone?"

"No, you are the only person, outside of my doctor, that has ever heard the story. I did write him a letter and told him that I knew what was going on. I told him if he contested the divorce, I would expose him."

"I wish there was something that I could say to you," Dawson said, *"that would help you; something that would make it easier for you. I pride myself in being open-minded and in my ability to accept people as they are; but, I will have to admit that homosexuality baffles me, I just can't understand how a man could desire another man, or a boy."*

"I'm afraid the ordeal required more mental elasticity than my brain was capable of, too. I had to spend the next three months in a sanatorium trying to understand." You poor kid, he thought, that's really a tough hand to deal a young Southern girl who was raised believing that all people were honest and that all men were gentlemen. *"Would you like to stop at the house for something to eat before I take you to the fort? My parents aren't home, they're in Canada on vacation."*

"Yes, I'd love to; I haven't eaten anything since I left San Francisco."

That was one year ago, he thought. Now, as he looked at her, he thought about how much she had changed. She was even more beautiful now than when they met. She was warmer, softer. She was happier and more confident now. He wanted to think that he'd had something to do with the change in her life. He loved her and wanted her, but he was not willing to give up his military career. She also had reservations about marriage, she still had ghosts wandering around through her head; and, every so often, an occasional demon would leap from the shadows of her mind directly into the middle of whatever activity they were engaged in. He thought of their tragic first attempt at sex.

"Do you like my apartment?" she asked. "They just delivered the furniture this afternoon." Dawson walked around the apartment and inspected every room.

"Nice, lots of room. I wish I had more room at the BOQ."

"Do you like the bedroom?" she asked.

"Yes, I like it."

She walked into the bedroom and sat on the edge of the bed.

"This is a brand-new bed," she said, running her hand across the new covers. "No one has ever slept here before; no one has ever made love here before."

She looked up at him and held her hand out. He had been waiting for the past two months for her to indicate that she was ready to try sex. That time had finally arrived and he was determined to introduce her into the real world of sex without frightening her or upsetting her. Slow, he thought, slow and easy. He took her hand and pulled her up from the bed and into his arms. She folded her arms across her breast and snuggled up to him. As he held her, she continued to cuddle and draw her arms in. He sat on the bed and she pulled her knees up and nearly

assumed a fetal position in his arms. He rocked back and forth on the edge of the bed as if lulling a baby to sleep.
"You don't have to do this, you know, not for me. I can wait for as long as it takes."
"I'm not doing it for you," she said. "I'm doing it for me."
"I'll go into the bathroom," he said, "that will give you time to get into bed."
He waited in the bathroom until the bedroom became silent, and then slowly opened the door. She was in bed with the covers tucked up under her chin. Her body was rigid, her arms down at her side, her legs and feet tight together. She was like a soldier at attention and frozen in ice. Dawson knew, from their many long talks, that she had never been with any other man except her husband. He knew that her parents had given her an unrealistic, unhealthy, Victorian attitude toward sex and her body. He knew that she had given oral sex to her husband but had never experienced it herself. He also knew that helping her develop a healthy attitude and appetite for sex was not going to be easy. She looked away from him as he dropped the towel from his waist and slid under the covers. She and her husband had always made love at night and in a dark room; she had never seen her husband without his clothes on. Today, with the late afternoon sun coming through the window, would be her first time in a lighted room.
"Why don't we just hold each other for a few minutes," he said, holding his arm up so she could slide in close to him.
She moved closer but their bodies were still not touching. He slid his left arm under her neck, placed his right hand on the lower part of her back and drew her close to him;

she was trembling. A hot burning sensation developed deep within his chest as the smell and heat of her body triggered an explosive passion that he had, up until now, been able to hide from her. He fought to control his emotions, to regain his composure.

"What's the matter?" she asked, "Why are you breathing so hard?"

She placed her hand on his chest and felt his heart pounding.

"My god, you're not having a heart attack?"

"No," he said. "I'm having a passion attack."

"What do you mean?"

He tried to explain the powerful emotions that the sight, smell, and feel of her beautiful body generated within him.

"I've always thought emotions like that were just movie make-believe," she said, "I've never felt that stirred by anything."

"What feelings do you get when you look at a man? What did you feel for me when you saw me at the airport; what did you think?"

"I thought you were handsome and I wondered what it would be like to kiss you. I like kissing."

"What do you feel or . . . how do you feel inside when we are kissing?"

"I feel happy!"

This is going to be harder than I had imagined, he thought. He could still feel tension in her body; she was not relaxing as he had hoped. He worked with her for nearly an hour trying to get her to relax. He stroked, massaged, and caressed her while trying to get her to think pleasant thoughts. Finally, she stopped wincing

*each time he fondled her breasts or ran his hand down
between her legs. He kissed her and asked if she was
ready now.*

"Yes," she said quietly.

*He tried to move as gently and gracefully as possible into
position; he did not want to frighten her or make her
tense. He took a deep breath and relaxed as he settled
snugly and comfortably between her legs. Suddenly he
felt as though he were sitting atop a bucking wild bull.
She was scratching, screaming, and thrashing around
like a cat with its ass on fire.*

*"What the fuck?" he screamed, rolling off her, and the
bed, to the floor.*

*As he lay on the floor checking his wounds, silence filled
the room. Slowly, he peeked up over the edge of the bed.
She had returned to her original position with the covers
tucked up under her chin, body rigid, arms at her side,
legs and feet tight together. She was lying dead still. He
stood up slowly and looked at her. She had an astonished
look on her face as she asked:*

*"What's wrong? What's wrong, you're asking me what's
wrong! You scratch all the hide off my back, knee me in
the stomach, scream and scare the shit out of me, and
then you ask me 'what's wrong'."*

*She pulled the covers over her head and began to cry. He
went to the bathroom. After a few minutes, he came out
and sat on the edge of the bed.*

"Let's talk about this." he suggested.

"What do you mean?" she asked from under the covers.

"Why did you attack me like that?"

She was quiet for a long time so he asked her again.

"Why did you act that way?"

Operation Minerva

*After a long silence, she angrily answered his question
and the tone of her voice expressed her indignity.*
*"That's the way I'm supposed to act, that's why! Don't
you know anything?"*
*"My god, honey, who told you that you were supposed to
act that way?"*
*"My Mother and my husband! Mother always told me
that a woman was expected to resist and my husband
liked for me to try and fight him off."*
*"I think that was a little more resistance than your
Mother intended," he said.*
*"Well, that's the way my husband liked for me to do it. He
could not make love to me if I didn't act like that."*
*"Pat," he said, "if you acted like that during sex with
your husband, he was not making love to you; from his
point of view..., he was subjugating you, he was raping
you."*

"Here we are honey!" Pat said, as she pulled up in front
of the terminal, "right on time, just as I promised." She
stopped the car and Dawson got out with his bags.
"I'll go park the car, and meet you at the ticket counter."
"I have a reservation on flight 305 to Columbus, Ohio,
my name is Jack Dawson."
"Yes, sir, I have your ticket right here. Will that be cash
or credit card?"
"Cash. Does this flight stop in Atlanta?"
"No, sir, this is a straight through flight."
The ticket agent handed him the ticket and directed him
to the boarding gate.
"You have fifteen minutes until boarding, sir."
"Thank you."

Operation Minerva

"Is everything set?" Pat asked, as she walked up to him.

"Yes, my flight boards in fifteen minutes at gate three."

He did not like long airport good-byes, and today's farewell was going to be especially difficult; he was relieved that the time was short. He had gained such control over any outward signs of emotion that now the only measure of his grief was the intensity of his headache; and now, as they approached the gate, his headache was building with each and every step. Just as he had solved the riddle of Patricia Walker during their year together, she had developed a deep understanding of the force that drove him in his search for success. He had come from a family of what he called 'professional underachievers.' Although he loved and respected his Father, he thought him too emotional, too soft, and too trusting.

He claimed that his Father was one of the most clever, ingenious men that he'd ever known. His biggest shortcoming was that he expected people in business to do the right thing, and businessmen almost never do the right thing, unless the profits just happen to fall on that side.

Pat loved Dawson and would marry him, but she knew that he was first, last, and always a professional soldier and was driven to succeed. She believed that his desire was to be there for the final event; that if the last battle of the world at Armageddon were scheduled in advance, he would be there.

"Well, I guess this is it," he said, "it's time for me to go."

He dropped his flight bag and took her into his arms; she started to cry. He had wondered what he would say to her when the time finally arrived. He wanted to tell her to wait for him, but he did not want her to waste even one day of her life waiting for something that may, or may not, take place.

"Have you ever heard the saying, 'as fish are taken in a net, so are men snared in time'?"

"No, I haven't," she said.

"Well, I think it applies to us. We all experience major events during life that alter the course of our existence. An event that causes a basic change in our philosophy, or an event that just makes us aware of things that we may not have seen before. Your event, I think, has happened and you are off on a new course; my event, whatever it is, has not yet occurred. I know it is out there somewhere waiting for me; I can feel it. I wish time had been more considerate with us; it would have been so beautiful if we had met after both of our events had taken place."

"I love you, Jack Dawson," she said, "I'll be here … I'll be here."

She stood on the observation deck and watched the aircraft until it was out of sight.

CHAPTER 2
Boston, June 1968

This would be his third tour of duty in Vietnam and Captain Alex Hull Coxe was apprehensive about returning; he had become, day-by-day and month-by-month, almost intolerably discouraged by the lack of leadership and the use of inappropriate tactics by the army in Vietnam. He had gone into Special Forces after his first tour with the belief that the Green Berets, if employed properly, were the only solution to the war.

Alex was the son and grandson of U.S. Army generals and the great grandson of a Scottish General who had served in the glory-ladened Blackwatch Regiment and he had heard war stories and listened to the tunes-of-glory all of his life. He knew at the age of six that he too would be a general. He loved the deep old traditions and consistency of army life and he loved being a soldier. Most of all he loved being a Green Beret and working with the men he considered the most professional soldiers in the army.

He studied Clausewitz at ten and understood that the first job of a good general was to understand the nature of the war in which he was engaged. By the age of fifteen he was deep into "The Art of War" by Sun Tzu; and, before going to West Point, he had studied Che Guevara and Mao Zedong on guerilla warfare. His independent study

Operation Minerva

at West Point on the French debacle in Indochina and their defeat at Dien Bien Phu at the hand of General Vo Nguyen Giap was the foundation of his discontent. Alex thought General Westmoreland was the biggest ass the U.S. Army had produced since Custer.

Two days before he was to return to the war, he and his younger cousin Vincent, a third year midshipman at Annapolis, were talking about the necessity of combat time for advancement to field and flag rank. However, Alex was trying to talk Vincent out of volunteering for duty in Vietnam. He tried to tell him how poorly the conflict was being handled, and that he should stay away from it.

"Don't give me that shit, Alex; so this is not a good war. As you've said yourself 'it's the only war we have."

"Well, I hope it's over before you graduate from the academy and flight training."

"Thanks, Alex. Now you're trying to treat me like you did when we were kids. Every time Mother and I visited, you would pick up all your soldiers and tanks and put them away, you never let me play. Alex, this is not your private war and you can't keep me out by picking up the toys this time."

"I know what your objectives are, Vincent. It's just that I don't think anyone is going to come out of this war looking good."

"That's easy for you to say, now. Just look at your career; you have combat time, combat command time, combat staff time and duty with the CIA. You've been decorated on the battlefield. Look at your uniform; silver star, bronze star, purple heart, army commendation medal, combat infantry badge, ranger tab, airborne jump wings and special forces. Now, look at my uniform! You know, Alex, when I stand next to you, I feel like a piece of shit! You're the one who should stay home, because you've got it all - right now. You're just risking your ass for nothing by returning to Vietnam. Your Mother is a powerful woman, Alex, she could get you a job in Washington before the sun goes down tonight."

"I know, but I keep hoping that it'll change. I keep hoping that one of our generals will read one of the countless books available on guerrilla warfare and figure out what they're doing wrong."

"Why don't you send General Abrams one for his birthday? He's going to take command before long, isn't he?"

"Yes, and I'm afraid that he's just as much a military illiterate about guerrilla warfare as Westmoreland. I've thought for some time now that Westmoreland's problem was that he wanted to follow Eisenhower and become president. He has done so many things that a general, who thinks about victory and his men, would not do; but, a politician who only thinks of re-election would not hesitate to do. I don't think they know what Santayana meant when he said that those who are ignorant of the past will be condemned to repeat it. We're making all the same mistakes the French made twenty years ago; and, in some instances, on the very same sites."

"I understand what you're saying, Alex; but the fact still remains, the shortest route between where I'm at and where I want to be is through Vietnam. When my Grandfather retired, he gave me his flag. Someday I'm going to sit in his chair as commanding officer of Fleet

Airwing Three, and his flag will fly over N.A.S. Norfolk
again."

Alex did not hear Vincent's last comment; he was deep in
thought about Vietnam. After a long silence, he
continued.

"I'd feel better about Vietnam if I thought we were
learning something, but we're not. The lessons each
officer learns either dies with him or goes home with
him, nothing is carried over. The periods of command
are so brief that by the time a commander discovers an
acceptable way to do something it's time for him to be
replaced. The best comment I have ever heard about
Vietnam was 'the U.S. Army has not been in Vietnam ten
years...it has been in Vietnam only one year - ten times'."

"Do you boys mind if I turn the TV on," Mrs. Coxe said,
entering the library. "I think the election returns are
coming in from California. I've heard that Bobby is
already ahead of Senator McCarthy. Are you staying for
the party tonight, Vincent?"

"I'd love to, Mary; however, I must return to the academy
tomorrow and I have a thousand things to do yet."

"Your Mother is going to be here, you know."

"Yes, I know. She's been talking about it for the past
week. She is convinced that Senator Kennedy will win
the California primary. I think Mother loves him even
more than she did the President, if such a thing is
possible."

Mrs. Coxe sat down in front of the TV as Alex and
Vincent walked out of the library.

"Good luck, Alex," Vincent said, as he extended his hand
to him.

Operation Minerva

Alex, the professional soldier, whose metal had been tempered and tried in the fires of war, grabbed Vincent, the ambitious novice, and held him in his arms for several seconds. Tears came to his eyes as he said good bye to Vincent.

"I'll see you when I get back, Admiral."

Television news coverage of the California primary was not continuous or extensive enough for the celebrants at the Coxe mansion; so, the party was in constant telephone contact with election headquarters in Los Angeles for the up-to-the-minute vote count. At one o'clock in the morning, with victory for Senator Kennedy assured, the Coxe celebration ended and everyone returned home confident that Robert Kennedy would be the next President of the United States.

At 3 a.m., the private telephone beside Mary's bed rang. The voice on the other end was Claire McLean, Vincent's Mother.

"Mary, my God, Mary... Bobby's been shot!"

"What?"

"Bobby was shot tonight at the Ambassador Hotel in L.A."

"Oh, God, no. Not Bobby, too. How'd it happen? Is he dead?"

"No, he's not dead. Turn on the all-night TV movie channel, the're talking about it now. I'll hold on."

Mary picked up the remote control device and turned the TV on.

"I've got it on now, Claire."

Operation Minerva

"If you'll bear with us for a few moments we should have an on-the-spot report from our affiliate station in Los Angeles..."

The TV went blank for a few seconds and then a noticeably shaken newswoman appeared. She was standing in a narrow, busy hallway. Her microphone picked up the sounds of grief and confusion in the background and the camera reported in vivid color the bewilderment and disbelief of the officials being interviewed.

"Shortly after midnight tonight, California time, an assassination attempt was made on the life of Senator Robert Kennedy. A campaign aide who was with Senator Kennedy at the time says that multiple shots were fired at close range and that the Senator was hit. Another witness has reported that he thinks one of the shots hit the Senator in the head. As many as four or five bystanders were hit during the shooting spree, all have been taken to hospital. The Senator was taken to the Good Samaritan hospital but we have had no word as to his condition.

The Senator was at the Ambassador Hotel this evening for a victory celebration. He had just won the California primary over Senator McCarthy. The assassination attempt was made as he left the ballroom through a kitchen passageway. We have no information at this time on the would-be assassin except that he may be an immigrant."

The newswoman continued to interview people who had been close to Senator Kennedy during the assassination attempt; Mary turned the sound down and returned to the phone.

"Are you still there, Claire?"

"Yes, I'm here."

"The world has gone insane, Claire. We're just getting over King's assassination, and now this. I can't think of any reason why anyone would want to shoot Bobby. I wonder if anyone has called Rose? She didn't go to California, did she?"

"I don't think she did."

"Well, if she does know about it, I'll bet she's enroute now."

"That poor woman."

A long silence fell over the line as each woman thought of the agony and burden that Rose had carried in the past, and now this new tragedy.

"I'll call you tomorrow, Claire, ok?"

"Good night, Mary."

She thought about telling Alex about the tragedy but decided against waking him.

Let him get a good night's sleep, she thought. I can tell him in the morning.

She turned the sound up on the TV and settled back into bed.

Alex would've been thankful had his Mother chosen to wake him, for he was having a marathon nightmare. He was running through the jungle, he had no weapon except his knife and he was naked. He could hear the Viet Cong chasing him, calling his name, and shots were ripping through the trees and undergrowth around him. His dream was like a wild trip through a horror-filled wax museum of war dead. As he ran around a tree he slammed into the dead body of Major Swanson, his B-team commander, hanging upside down in the path.

Operation Minerva

He was nude, his throat had been cut and he had been gutted like a hog at slaughter. Alex was knocked to the ground by the collision and in his panicked effort to get to his feet to run again, he became entangled in the major's intestines. He looked at the intestines as he fought to get free, they were covered with maggots. He was up and running again, harder and faster, but he felt his legs were delivering so much power that his body was too light to keep his feet on the ground. He had the feeling that he was floating and he couldn't float as fast as he could run if he could just keep his feet on the ground. Another turn, another dead mutilated buddy impaled on punji sticks. He could hear one of the Viet Cong getting closer and closer to him as he ran up a dry stream bed. The banks along the stream became steeper and higher until he could not get out; he was in a deep chasm. He was overcome with panic as he ran into a concrete wall that sealed off the gorge. He ran along the wall trying to find some way to escape, a large culvert appeared and he could see light at the other end - he started through. Near the end he could hear shots being fired into the pipe, he could not imagine why he was not being hit. He fell out of the pipe onto the ground; the pipe was about three feet from the ground and as he looked up at it he made up his mind, he wasn't going to run any further. He could hear the Viet Cong soldier coming through the pipe; he waited and, as the soldier stuck his head out of the pipe, Alex, using both hands on his knife, ripped the soldier's throat open. He felt the soldier's hot blood splash in his face and run down over his naked body. As he pulled the soldier from the pipe and took his weapon, the soldier turned into a doll with sawdust spilling from a tear in its neck. He threw the doll down and looked at the rifle in his hand, it had become a toy. He started to run up the hill.

Up, up, he thought, I must get to the top. At the top of the hill the ground disappeared from beneath his feet and he began to fall, and fall, and fall.

"Alex, Alex, wake up." His Mother had to shake him several times before he opened his eyes. He was covered with sweat.

"You were screaming. What were you dreaming?"

"I'm sorry, I was having a nightmare. I must have been making allot of noise to wake you, Mother."

"I was not asleep, honey, I was watching TV. Come downstairs with me and we'll have some hot chocolate. I have something I must tell you."

Alex was stunned by the news of the attempted assassination. He couldn't imagine why an Arab immigrant would want to kill Bobby Kennedy.

"I can remember going to the Kennedy's when Father was alive. It was a birthday party and I remember Father playing football, everyone was having such fun. I wanted to play, but Father said that I was too little and that I'd be stepped on. I don't remember who the party was for; there were so many children there."

"I think the party you're remembering was for Teddy. That was the only time your Father ever agreed to play football, and I think he only did it then to satisfy the Ambassador."

The hot chocolate was beginning to relax Alex and make him sleepy, so he excused himself and returned to bed.

Operation Minerva

The news the next evening was being delivered by one of his favorite newscasters, Constance Ashley Armstrong, his childhood sweetheart. ˙ Her family had been in Germany with the State Department at the same time that Alex's family was there with the army. Alex had gone, under much pressure from his Mother, to a birthday party at the Armstrong house. It was her thirteenth birthday; when she walked into the room, the swish of her skirt, the smell of her perfume and the stunning combination of her dark eyes, cool white skin, and fluffy black hair falling over her bare shoulders changed his life forever. He loved her from that day on. And now, she loved him too.

"Are you going out with Connie tonight, Alex?" his Mother asked.

"Yes, I'm going to pick her up at eight."

"When are you two going to get married? Do you know how much a woman with her public image and influence could do for your career?"

"Yes, Mother, I know. The trouble right now is that our two careers aren't compatible. We will be married in three or four years."

"Good evening, Captain, Miss Armstrong is in the library."

"Thank you, Carol." Alex walked into the library and found Connie reviewing a video tape of her evening news.

"I've got to come across with more...more confidence and authority? Don't you think so?"

"Honey, if you had any more confidence or authority you'd be intimidating your viewers."

"Do you really think so?"

"Believe me, you're the best."

She stood up and put her arms around him.

"Let's not go out tonight, I'll have Carol fix us something to eat and we'll have a very quiet, intimate supper in my room."

"I only want to be with you," he said. "It will be good to have some time alone."

They ate and talked for nearly an hour, then retreated to the sofa with a bottle of wine. He put his left arm around her and began to unbutton her blouse with his right hand. He slipped her bra strap off her shoulder and exposed her left breast. He loved her breasts, he often referred to them as 'two one-hundred-meter ski jumps' because of the way her nipples turned up on the end. He cupped her breast in his hand and took the nipple into his mouth. She put her arms around his head and supported him like a mother suckling her baby. She started to become excited and her breathing became heavy as she unzipped his pants and put her hand inside. Upon reaching her goal, she squeezed his penis and suggested they would have more room on the bed.

"Before you take off your clothes," he said. "I have a request."

"I'll do anything you ask, honey, you know that."

"Keep your skirt on but take off your panties and hose." She kicked her shoes off and removed her hose and panties.

"Ok, now what?"

"This is something that I have thought of night after night while sleeping on the jungle floor. It was something to keep me from going insane, something to hold on to."

"I'm ready," she said. "Just tell me what you want me to do."

Operation Minerva

"Stand here and spread your legs apart."

"Ok, like this?"

"Yes, perfect."

He sat down on the floor in front of her, turned around and laid back placing his head between her feet. She leaned forward and looked down at him.

"Do you like what you see?"

"This is the most beautiful sight I've ever seen. A picture of this should be on the cover of TIME."

"I can think of a good caption for the shot," she said, "Do you know who this public (or should I say pubic) figure is?" He ran his hand up her leg and traced the line that separated her legs.

"Now, sit on my face."

"Ok, I like this more and more as we go along."

She had a full skirt on and it filled with air and encompassed his head and shoulders as she lowered herself over him. She squatted for a moment, trying not to put too much pressure on him as he worked his tongue up between the folds of her vagina. Her excitement began to rise and her legs became weak, so she placed her knees on the floor and leaned forward over his body. She thought he was going to eat his way right up into her stomach. Her excitement was building to the point where she had to do something. She laid down on him and took his penis into her mouth. The total sensation of having her beautiful ass wrapped around his face and having his penis buried in her throat was more than he could stand; he had a sudden and violent climax. The sensitivity of his penis and testicles became so acute that she was driving him through ecstasy and into pain. He tried to get away from her but she would not stop sucking on him.

"Stop!" he cried. "You're going to kill me." She stopped sucking but continued to hold his penis in her mouth. He relaxed.

"Let's take a shower," he said, "and then try this once more on the bed."

The next morning he was awakened with the tragic news that Robert Kennedy had died. His Mother was watching a special report on Good Morning America when he walked into the library.

"This is a nightmare," she said. "We'll all wake up soon and find that this is just a bad dream."

"Mother," he said. "The longer I live, the harder it is for me to distinguish my nightmares from reality."

They watched TV until Franklin came in and told them that breakfast was served.

Alex spent his last day at home in his room. He listened to Scottish pipe music, looked at his mementos from the academy, his collection of toy soldiers and, as he had always done, talked to the big painting of his Grandfather. The painting showed his Grandfather in his finest military dress and holding his favorite weapon, a sword that Alex now held in his own hand.

"Grandfather, why is it, when I read your letters and papers, that your objectives always seem so clear, your direction so steady, your resolve so firm. Was war so much simpler then. I'll bet you never came home to cries of 'baby killer'. I'll also bet that no one ever spat on you, not while you were carrying this sword anyway. I wish you could be here so we could talk about this. Some times I feel that I am really doing something worthwhile; other times I feel that I'm wasting my life. Lately, the wasting-my-life feeling is winning."

Operation Minerva

He fell asleep on the bed thinking about his grandfather.

That afternoon Connie drove him to the airport. He liked to be with her in public because everyone recognized her and that made her happy, he liked to see her happy. He was always proud to be with her, the man who she had chosen to be with; she could have anyone, but she had chosen him.

At the gate, since she was such a public figure, they had to be careful how they said good-bye. He had kissed her and held her in the car. Now, he would just kiss her on the cheek.

"Take care of yourself, Alex. I love you."

"I love you too, honey. Tear'em up on the six o'clock news."

At the end of the corridor he looked back and waved good bye to her.

CHAPTER 3
Newark, Ohio

Dawson was making this brief stop in Ohio to see his younger brother who had been in the Antarctic with the U.S. Navy on Operation Deep Freeze; they had not seen each other in nearly two years. His Father, a deputy sheriff, was happy that his two sons would both be home at the same time. Dawson did not like Newark, Ohio. He did not like the factory workers who could not see beyond their next paycheck; he did not like the local politicians who could not see beyond the next election; he did not like the general populace who could not see beyond the county border. His favorite saying was "when visiting Newark, all outsiders are required to surrender their intelligence at the city line - this is to prevent the locals from being subjected to new ideas and thus becoming insulted."

"Mom," Dawson said. "Jim and I are going out for the evening."

"Have a good time boys," she replied.

Dawson and his brother made their first stop at a nightclub in Southgate Shopping Center in Heath.

"This ain't the best place to go, ya know," Jim commented, "if ya wanta get laid."

Operation Minerva

"I'm not necessarily trying to get laid," Dawson said, "I really came home to spend some time with you, Mom and Dad. So, if I get laid it's ok; and, if I don't get laid it's ok."

During the evening, Dawson became interested in a businesswoman named Veronica who was in town attending a real-estate conference at the inn next to the shopping center. She was ten years his senior, very sophisticated, very lovely, and gifted with a seductive voice. Her jet-black hair contrasted sharply with her low-cut, white-silk, sheath dress. After he had danced with her for the third time, he was convinced that she was not wearing anything else except her shoes. Each time they danced she became more aggressive; so, he asked her to join him at his table for a drink and she accepted. She sat close to him at the table and immediately began to rub her leg against his thigh. He placed his hand on her bare leg and stroked the inside of her thigh. As he worked his way up her leg, he noticed that the nipples of her breasts were becoming even more visible through her dress.
She flinched slightly as his hand reached its goal. He was right, she had nothing on except her dress and shoes.
"You don't waste any time, do you?" she whispered to him.
"I don't have any time to waste; I'm only going to be here one more day."
"I like a man who knows what he wants."
"Well," he said. "I like a woman who knows what she wants."
"My friends will be leaving at midnight. Would you like to come to my room for a drink after they leave?"

Operation Minerva

"Yes, I would, but, I must take my brother home first."
"Good, I'll see you at about twelve thirty."
She returned to her table and Dawson found his brother
at the bar. His brother had just made arrangements to
meet a woman at Suzie's bar on the east side of town in
twenty minutes.
"You can just drop me off at Suzie's. Jill has a car."
Dawson had borrowed his Father's second car for the
evening; it was an old De Soto with a push-button
transmission. His Father had warned him that the car
would occasionally malfunction and start with the
transmission in gear, and that before starting he must
always check to be sure that the car was in neutral. He
remembered his Father's warning and cycled the
push-buttons as he started the car; however, the car still
was not in neutral. The car leaped forward, jumped the
curb, and rammed into a light pole. One of the pole's two
lamp fixture came loose from the pole and crashed to the
ground beside the car.
"Holy shit! This damn thing is a hazard to life."
"I don't think anyone saw us," Jim said, "let's get the hell
out of here."
He cycled the buttons again until neutral was indicated,
started the car, backed away from the pole and then could
not get the car to go into drive.
"I'm glad no one is chasing us or we would lose our ass
right here."
He continued to cycle the buttons until the car started to
move. They looked around the parking lot as they left to
see if anyone had seen them hit the light pole, no one
had.

Operation Minerva

Suzie's Bar was just across the railroad tracks on East Main Street. Jill hadn't arrived yet so Dawson decided to go into the bar with Jim and wait for her. He parked the car across the street from Suzie's, facing west, back into town. They could hear the noise and music from Suzie's before they got out of the car.

"Sounds like they're having a good time in there," Dawson said. "Is it always that loud?"

"No," Jim answered. "It sounds like they may be a little worked-up over something."

As they were about to open the door, it slammed open and a man came flying out. Jim pushed Dawson out of the way and the man fell to the sidewalk.

"Friendly little place they have here. You're sure you want to go in?"

"No sweat, that happens once in a while in the best of bars."

They opened the door and walked in. The noise level and smoke concentration were beyond that which any rational human being could, or would, tolerate; however, before Dawson could protest, the matter became moot. Through the dense smoke they could see a wall of fighting, biting, and scratching drunks moving toward them like there had been a bomb threat in the bar. Jim and Dawson hit the door and jumped outside just in time to watch a fresh supply of bodies pile up on the sidewalk. They were laughing at the spectacle as the beer and blood soaked participants began to untangle themselves. The combatants, as they began to regroup for a fresh assault on the bar, became aware of the laughter coming from the two clean and, as yet, unruffled bystanders. Suddenly their mood charged, now they had a common enemy.

Operation Minerva

Dawson and Jim ran for the car. Dawson out-sprinted his brother and, reaching the car first, jumped in the driver's side and locked the door. Jim ran around the front of the car to the passenger side but could not get the door open. The drunks mobbed the car, pounding on the hood, top, doors and trunk. Jim ran away from the car and half the drunks followed him. He ran about twenty yards down the street, around a house and back, losing his half of the drunks. As he approached the car one of the drunks had managed to get the passenger door open. Jim slammed a hard right into the drunk's left ear as Dawson was ejecting him from the car. Jim got in and locked the door. There were drunks all over the car when Dawson hit the starter. The car was in gear and lunged forward, tearing loose the drunks. The acceleration caused Dawson to sink back into his seat, pulling his foot from the gas pedal and consequently decelerating the car. The deceleration caused Dawson to be thrown forward by the compressed springs in the back of the seat. His foot slammed to the floor again. The pressure on the gas pedal broke the accelerator linkage and jamming the gas pedal full down.

The car leaped forward onto the railroad tracks and into the side of a passing freight train. Only the front end of the car made it onto the tracks; the car was cut in two at the firewall. As the car was thrown spinning across the street, Dawson and Jim were thrown out. Neither was injured. The car came to a stop directly in front of Suzie's Bar. By this time all the drunks had disappeared. It was 3 a.m. when they got home and sat down at the kitchen table. The accident, police investigation, and having to walk home had caused Dawson to forget about his 12:30 date with Veronica. He did not remember her until he was almost asleep. He told himself that he would have to call her in the morning and apologize.

Dawson's Mother was preparing breakfast when he walked into the kitchen the next morning.
"Did you have a nice time last night?"
"Yes, Mother, last night was quite an exciting evening."
"What time did you get home?"
"About 3 a.m., I think."
"Your Father was on duty out at the lake all night. He said they had a lot of drunks and several fights. They should close those nasty places down if all they're going to do is fight. I'm sure glad you boys don't get into any trouble like that." Dawson's Father walked into the kitchen and sat down across the table from him.
"Good morning, Dad. Mom told me you had a hard night at the lake."
His Father looked at him with a slight grin, stirred his coffee and took a drink.
"I don't think my night was nearly as tough as yours. I saw the car this morning and read the report."
"We were lucky."
"What are you two talking about?" his Mother asked.
"We had a little accident with the car last night, nothing serious, no one was hurt."
Jim walked into the kitchen and sat down at the table.
"Do you have anything for a headache, Mom? I feel like I've been run over by a truck, or maybe I should say a train."

Operation Minerva

His Mother placed a glass of water and two seltzer tablets in front of him.

"How bad was the car damaged? I noticed it wasn't in the drive this morning."

"I don't think it can be fixed, Mom," Dawson answered.

"Well, that was a stupid car and I have told your Father several times to get rid of it!
How did the accident happen?"

"Mom," Jim said. "We were hit by a train and the car was cut in two."

"Oh, my god, you were hit by a train! The car was cut in two!"

She pulled a chair out and sat down at the table. "Get me a cup of coffee."

Dawson got up, gave his Mother a cup of coffee and finished serving breakfast.

"What time does your plane take off?" Jim asked.

"At thirteen hundred, when are you going back?"

"I have another week to go yet."

"I'll be in Thailand before you get back to Quonset Point."

"Are Mom and Dad going to the airport with us?" Jim asked.

"Yes, I think they're getting ready now."

The thirty mile drive to Columbus airport was punctuated only occasionally with light conversation. Dawson and his brother had endless escapades that they wanted to share but, with their Mother in the back seat, their stories would have to wait until another time. A broad smile crossed Dawson's face as he remembered an incident that had happened to his brother in New Zealand:

48

Operation Minerva

Jim and his girlfriend Peanuts had returned to her apartment after an evening at the EM[4] Club and were preparing for some rousing sexual activity. Peanuts had only a small cot in her apartment and both the steel side straps of the wire grid supporting the mattress were missing, this made the sides weak and the mattress frequently slid to the floor during sex. Therefore, it had become their custom to place the mattress on the floor before having sex. Since this particular night was unusually cold, Peanuts positioned an electric-coil type space heater off to the side, near the foot of the mattress. She also placed two cups of hot chocolate on the floor beside them; hot chocolate and sex had become a regular custom with the two young lovers.

Peanuts was a very small woman with a very big appetite for sex; once her fire was lit, it was almost impossible to extinguish it. They initiated their foreplay while sitting together, nude, drinking their hot chocolate.

She was half European and half Polynesian, her skin was a light honey gold and her hair was like threads of fine black silk. She weighed only 90 pounds but she was a ferocious tiger in bed. Their sex began slow and gentle; however, the tempo soon quickened and the tiger in Peanuts was released.

"I have never made love to Peanuts," Jim told Dawson, "in the conventional sense of the term. I always start out to make love to her but, somewhere along the way, I always wind up just hanging on."

---

[4] Enlisted Men

49

Operation Minerva

This encounter on the floor of Peanuts' apartment was, to this point, no different from the many previous encounters. However, during the match, in his effort to prevent her from exceeding the stroke limit of his penis, he stuck his foot into the unguarded red-hot coil of the space heater. He recoiled violently, slamming his penis deep into her and crying in pain. She thought he was having an extremely violent climax, and this elevated her sexual drive even more and drove her into near hysteria.

He tried in vain to free himself from her grip but the more he fought to get away, the harder she held on to him.

He finally managed to get to his feet, despite the fact that she was stuck to him like an octopus. As he jumped up and down on one foot and screamed with pain, she screamed with pleasure. As he hopped, he stepped on one of the cups, lost his balance and went crashing to the floor on his back. She was still stuck to him. He remained there motionless and quiet. He was totally exhausted.

"That was absolutely fabulous, honey," she panted. "I have never had sex like that before in my life."

Jim looked up at her and told her that she would most probably never have it like that again. At least, not with him.

Jim noticed the smile on Dawson's face and asked him what he was thinking about that was so funny.

"I was thinking about that story you told me last night about you and Peanuts."

"Is this a story that I can hear?"

"Not really, Mother."

Operation Minerva

"That's a shame; I haven't heard a good story in a long time."

To Dawson's Mother, a trip to Columbus was not complete without stopping at White Castle for a snack, so he had set time aside and White Castle would be their first stop. He knew that, to his Mother, a visit to White Castle was a visit to her youth. His Mother and Father had lived in Columbus when they were young and, late at night, after the movies, the young lovers would go to White Castle to eat, talk, and hold hands. He always enjoyed sitting at the little tables with his Mother and watching her face glow and her spirit rise as she remembered and related to him the activities of her youth. As his Mother talked, Dawson was looking across the table at his Dad and thinking about a conversation that he and Jim had earlier that day about their Father and their relationship over the years.

"Jim, you have a better relationship with Dad than I ever did." Dawson said.

"Why do you say that? I thought you and Dad were always close. I've always thought you were his favorite," Jim replied.

"Has Dad ever taken you fishing?" Dawson asked.

"Yes."

"He never took me fishing."

"Has he ever taken you hunting?" Dawson asked.

"Yes, you know he has."

"Well, he never took me hunting."

"Has he ever taken you camping?"

"Yes, you know that too." Jim replied, tiring of the questions.

Operation Minerva

"Well, like I said. Dad never did anything with me. He was always too tired or too busy doing something else."

"I never knew that!" Jim replied.

"I remember when Larry Swankie got an old Ford roadster. He and his Dad worked on it all through the winter in their garage. When summer came he had the best looking little hotrod in the city. All the girls went bug-shit over it.

"That was the same summer I paid twenty dollars for an old 34 Chevy that would not run. I worked on that car for weeks in the back yard. I was working under that big maple tree that used to be right outside the backdoor. The engine was frozen up so I had to completely disassemble it, rework the bearings and then put it back together again. Dad never touched that car. He didn't have the time. However, he did seem to find the time to go bowling with his friends. All he ever did that summer was give me hell about messing up the yard or give me hell about making noise. I talked Larry Swankie into lending me his welding machine so I could do some modifications to the body and Dad made me give it back because it caused static on the radio and TV every time I used it. Yes, Dad and I have had some great times together!" Dawson said sarcastically.

There were several moments of silence, then Dawson continued.

"Dad didn't hate me; he just didn't want to spend what free time he had with a teenage boy. When he was young, it was all he could do the keep a roof over our heads and food in our mouths. I understand that he had to have some time for himself."

Operation Minerva

"Well, all he does now is talk about you and how great you are!" Jim complained.

"Jim, I think it's all a matter of perspective. Dad has never been very successful at anything he has tried. He looks at me now and sees me as wildly successful because I have a college education - he only went to the sixth grade; I'm an army officer - he was an army private. I have been in ten different countries and served in combat in Vietnam – he has only been in Korea and he got there after the war was already over."

"I think I see what's going on inside his head now," Jim said. "No wonder he talks about you all the time. You have been successful at everything and he has been successful at nothing. He gets pleasure from your success. I guess if you can't be successful yourself, the next best thing is to have children who are."

At the airport, as he had planned, there was little time for contracted good-byes. He had four days before his international flight left San Francisco for Thailand; so, he planned to spend a few days in Reno before proceeding to the coast.

"Is this seat taken, Sister?"

Dawson asked, as he started to sit down beside a nun.

"No, please sit down," she replied, with a German accent. He didn't really want to sit beside a nun, but it looked like the only open seat.

"You are a Green Beret, are you not?"

"Yes, I am a Green Beret," he answered in German.

"You speak German!" she said excitedly, "Have you been stationed in Germany?"

"No, I was an engineering major in college and German was a required course. I have also gone to an army language school for German. I would like to go to Germany."

He paused for a moment, and then continued. "Maybe, after I get back this time."

"You will love it, I know, my country is so beautiful. I love the south, the mountains are so beautiful."

"What are you doing in the United States? Are you on vacation?"

"Yes, I am," she said. "But it is also a learning experience. I'm a school teacher. I teach English and American studies in a boy's school."

"I didn't know nuns did things like that," he said.

"I'm not a Roman Catholic nun."

"Well, the way you're dressed certainly fooled me."

"My name is Catherine, and I belong to a uniquely European religious sect."

"What are you going to do in Reno?" he asked.

"I traveled through the Eastern part of the states two years ago; so, now I'm investigating the west. Reno sounded like a good place to start."

They talked about the Green Berets, the war in Vietnam, Thailand, and finally John F. Kennedy. After lunch, he fell asleep.

"Sir, wake up sir, we're coming into Reno. Please place your seat in its upright position for landing."

The stewardess moved down the aisle, waking passengers and reminding them to put their seats up. He sat up and repositioned his seat. The nun sitting next to him was writing a postcard.

Operation Minerva

"Keeping your sisters informed about your progress?" he asked.

"Yes, and telling them about you."

He made no comment, just acknowledged with a smile and continued to look at her; he had not really looked at her before, he had not noticed how lovely her face was, or that she had violet eyes. He was captivated by the thought of meeting a woman with violet eyes ever since he first saw Elizabeth Taylor in the movies. He thought, 'wouldn't you know it? The first woman I meet with beautiful violet eyes has to be a nun!

At the terminal, he told her that he hoped she would have an interesting and educational vacation, and that he had enjoyed talking with her.

Early in the evening he came to the conclusion that Reno was not the place for him. He called the airline and made a reservation for the two o'clock flight the next day to San Francisco. He woke up the next morning at eight o'clock, got dressed and went to breakfast in the hotel restaurant. After breakfast, he sat for some time drinking coffee and thinking. On his way back to his room he passed the swimming pool and a female voice called out to him:

"Mr. Dawson, Jack, over here."

He turned to see who was calling him. There, sitting on the edge of the pool was a beautiful young woman with pale skin, large breasts, long black hair, and a small bright red bikini. She was waving her arm at him.

"Who the hell is she? I don't know anyone here."

He walked toward her and, as he got closer to her, he stopped, frozen in amazement.

"Holy shit," he said under his breath. "This can't be. Catherine?" he asked.

"Yes, don't you recognize me?"

"Well, I haven't seen too many nuns in bikini bathing suits. But then, maybe I have and didn't know it. How do you recognize a nun if she doesn't have her uniform on?"

"It's not a uniform," she said laughing. "It's a habit. Are you coming in?" she asked.

"No, sorry, I'm leaving on the two o'clock flight for San Francisco. I think I'll rest and watch TV until it's time to go. Thank you for asking."

Back in his room he kept peeking out the window at her and her bright red bikini,

"What a waste," he kept saying, "What a waste."

At 12:30 he called for a taxi to the airport; on his way out to the taxi he looked for Catherine but she was not at the pool.

"I have a reservation on the two o'clock flight to San Francisco; my name is Dawson.

"Yes, sir, Mr. Dawson," the lady said, flipping through a stack of tickets, "I have your ticket right here. Will that be cash or credit card?"

"Cash," he answered, handing her the money.

"Is lunch served on this flight?"

"No, sir, just a light snack."

He went to the USO lounge, drank coffee, ate doughnuts and tried to watch TV. A young soldier was trying to explain the TV program to his even younger oriental bride. As he looked at her, admiring her petite features and subtle beauty, she looked at him and smiled. The joy expressed in her smile and the innocence he saw in her eyes provoked a memory within him that grabbed his heart like an icy hand:

The fifteen-year-old Vietnamese girl who did his laundry and cleaned his quarters at Camp Evans disappeared one evening on her way back to her village. He could not find out what had happened to her. Several weeks later he saw her on the road and stopped to talk with her. She told him that she had been abducted and tortured by the VC because she was working for the Americans. They told her it was to serve as a lesson to the others. She would not look at him, she looked down at her feet and talked as she drew circles in the dirt with her bare toe. He asked her what they had done to her, but she was reluctant to talk. She kept looking from side to side to see if anyone was watching. As she fidgeted, he became aware that she was hiding the right side of her face. Each time the wind would blow, her hand would go up to prevent her long black hair from exposing her face. He asked her if she was going to come back to work for him. She became almost hysterical in her reply:
"No, No! I no can work anymore!"
She started to cry as she continued to talk. "I number ten girl now, me beggar. No can work. Now, I no can get married."
"Why can't you get married?" he asked, "What did they do to you?"
Crying and sniffling, she wiped her nose on her sleeve as she slowly looked up at him and brushed her hair away from her face. He was stunned by what he saw. He had been a soldier for a long time and seen countless victims of VC torture; however, this was different, she was a

young girl - not a soldier, and he knew her. He fought hard to keep his composure. He wanted to cry. He wanted to scream. He wanted to take this precious little girl into his arms and hide her, protect her, comfort her. He had seen this type of damage before; he knew exactly how it was done. The VC had heated a spike bayonet in the fire until it was red hot, then, mercilessly pushed the red-hot steel into the screaming young girl's right eye. Her concaved eyelid bore the unmistakable black triangular scar. He was choking inside, he could not talk. All he could think about was the panic and pain that this beautiful innocent little girl had suffered.

"I am not pretty girl now, not pretty girl now. No can get married."

This was more than he could bear, tears filled his eyes and ran down his face. He took his handkerchief out and dried his eyes. He wanted to talk to her, but could not. He wanted to help her, but realized there was nothing he could do. He wanted to tell her he was sorry and beg her forgiveness, but he was ashamed. As he dried his eyes again, he secretly reached into his front pocket, pulled out a roll of bills and hid them in his handkerchief.

"You are still a pretty girl," he said, drying her face. "I am sorry but this is all I can do."

"Be careful with this," he said, giving her the handkerchief. "Make it last a long time."

She continued to dry her face and then quickly added the handkerchief to the contents of her bag.

"Good-bye," he said quietly as he turned and walked back to his jeep.

The announcement of his flight over the PA system would have gone unnoticed if the sailor sitting next to him had not bumped him with his sea bag. He got up and looked for the young oriental girl - she was gone.

On the aircraft he found a seat by a window and sat down. Moments later a feminine voice with a German accent asked, "Is this seat taken, sir?"

"Sister Catherine! What the. . .what are you doing here?"

"I'm on my way to San Francisco - you didn't give me time to tell you this afternoon, you acted so strange at the pool."

She sat down by him and fastened her seat belt. He was very uncomfortable sitting beside her after the emotions that she had stirred up in him that morning as he looked at her by the pool. She was a paradox and he couldn't unravel his feelings about her.

"Sister, may I ask you a question?"

"Yes."

"Why does a beautiful young lady become a nun?"

"Do you mean me?"

"Yes, I mean you."

"I was never given a choice. I never had control of my life long enough to question my parents' decision and by the time I was ten years old they had me convinced that the only life for me was in the church." He looked at her and shook his head in sympathy.

"Why do you stay? Can't you leave?"

"It's not an easy thing to walk away from. . .my parents would die from shame if I ever left the church. But, most of all, I think I would miss teaching. I love teaching."

"Can't you be a teacher without being a nun?"

"Yes, but how would I do it? I have no money, no clothes, no friends outside our village. I would have to move to another village, or to a city. No, I'm afraid it's not an easy thing to do, not without help from outside."

"Have you ever talked to your Mother about leaving the church? If she knew that you were not happy. . ."

"If I ever so much as hinted that I was not happy with the church I think my Mother would die from heart attack."

"And I thought I had problems."

He sat looking at Sister Catherine in disbelief. The stewardess stopped at Catherine's seat and asked, "Would you like coffee or a soft drink, Sister?"

"Coffee, please."

"And you, sir?"

"Black coffee, thank you."

"Sister," he continued. "What are your plans for San Francisco?"

"I want to see Chinatown first, and after that I don't care."

"How are you going to get around?"

"I'll have to take a guided tour, they must have city tours."

"I'm going to rent a car at the airport Sister, if you'd like to, you can come with me; we'll see Chinatown together."

"You wouldn't mind taking me? This is all I have to wear."

"Sister, if you don't complain about my uniform, how can I complain about yours."

She laughed at his comment and accepted his offer.

Dawson got into the car on the driver's side, looked at Sister Catherine sitting beside him and said. "Grant Avenue, here we come; a nun and a Green Beret, I hope San Francisco is ready for this."

She laughed, then added, "If San Francisco isn't ready it's too bad - because we are here."

Operation Minerva

"There's a parking area," She said, as she pointed down
the street to the sign.
After parking, he walked around and opened the door for
her.
"Thank you, Mr. Dawson."
"Sister, please call me Jack. It might relieve some of the
tension."
"Well, Jack, which way do we go first?"
"It's your vacation Sister, take off in any direction you
want. I'll just keep you from getting lost."
Chinatown was unbelievably crowded; the sidewalks
were clogged with people. Dawson and Sister Catherine
were separated by the crowd twice and after the second
separation it took Dawson several minutes to find her.
"Sister," he said, "give me your hand. We are not getting
separated again."
He took her hand and started off through the crowd,
pulling her behind.
"Would you like something to eat?" he asked.
"Yes, and it would be nice to sit down for a few minutes
and rest."
He continued to plow through the crowd, she close
behind, until they found a small cafe.
"Is this place OK with you?" he asked.
"Right now, any place is OK with me. I must sit down."
Inside, she collapsed in a booth, took out her
handkerchief and blotted the perspiration from her face,
then told him:
"My feet are killing me!"
"Take your shoes off."
"You must be joking."

Operation Minerva

"No," he insisted, "American women are always taking their shoes off in restaurants, whether their feet hurt or not."

"How can I do it without people seeing me?"

"What kind of shoes do you have on?"

"Slippers, but if I kick them off, I'll not get them back on."

"Stick your feet up to me under the table, I'll pull them off." She blushed and tried to look nonchalant as she had him pull off her shoes.

"Oh, that feels so much better," she said, leaning her head back over the seat and stretching. "You run good interference Jack, did you play foot ball in school?"

"No, I was never much good at sports."

"What do you want to eat?"

"I'll have ... a hotdog and a coke."

"Oh! My god," he said, "you come six thousand miles to visit Chinatown and you order a hotdog," he laughed. She did not understand what was so funny.

"Don't they have hotdogs here?"

"Yes, yes honey, if ...," he stopped talking and looked at her.

"What is the matter?" she asked, looking at him.

"I'm sorry, Sister."

"Sorry for what?"

"I called you honey."

"That is an American term of endearment, is it not?"

"Yes, it is."

"I do not find it offensive," she said, looking at him and smiling. Now, why is it so funny to order a hotdog?"

62

Operation Minerva

"I would think that after traveling six thousand miles to visit Chinatown, you would want to try some Chinese food."

"Can't we do that later?"

"Yes, we will have supper at a good Chinese restaurant, but for now it's Cokes and hotdogs."

They sat and talked for half an hour; she was very interested in the Green Berets so he was doing most of the talking.

"Do you go to the movies, Sister?"

"Yes, certainly, why do you ask?"

"There is a movie in town about the Green Berets. Would you like to go this evening?"

"Is that the movie starring John Wayne?"

"Yes, it is, but it's on at a drive-in."

"Oh, that's wonderful," she said, sitting up and leaning over the table, "I've never been to a drive-in movie."

"Our next problem is finding someplace to stay tonight; do you have a hotel reservation for this evening, Sister?"

"Yes, I have the address here … somewhere." She dug around in a small black purse for the address. "Here it is," she said, holding the paper out to him.

"If we leave right away," he suggested, "we will have time to clean-up and eat supper before the movie."

She agreed and after he helped her on with her shoes, they set out to find her hotel. They stopped outside her hotel and he inspected it with a critical eye.

"How did you come to have a reservation at this hotel? Who recommended this place to you?"

"A travel agent in Nuremburg made my arrangements. What is the matter?"

"Do you see those ladies standing over there?"

"Yes, I see them."

"Sister, those ladies are prostitutes and I'll bet money that they're working out of your hotel. You're not staying here; you can come to the Holiday Inn with me."

He drove away before she had time to protest.

"But Mister Dawson, I do not have money to stay at an expensive hotel."

"Don't worry about it, Sister, I'll pay for your room."

They were silent for a while then she asked him, "Do you condemn those ladies for what they do?"

"Condemn?" he asked. "No, Sister, I don't condemn. I'm in no position to pass judgment on anyone."

"Are you not passing judgment on them by refusing to stay at that hotel?"

"Sister, I refuse to stay at that hotel because it is beneath my class; or, as you say in Europe, 'my station.' I know you have taken a vow of poverty, Sister, but I have not. I was born in poverty and I was raised in poverty. However, through hard work and education, I have pulled myself out of poverty and I will die, if necessary, to avoid returning. You would make a good social worker, Sister; we have been together only six hours and you have already uncovered one of my basic hang-ups."

They pulled up in front of the motel and he opened the car door for her and escorted her inside.

"I'm Mister Dawson, I have a reservation for tonight."

"Yes, sir, I have your reservation right here. How many nights will you be staying, sir?"

"Just tonight, thank you."

"Here is your key sir, room 214."

Operation Minerva

"This is Sister Catherine," Dawson said, introducing her to the desk clerk. "She needs a room also. Do you have one close to mine?"

"Yes, we do, she can have room 216, an adjacent room."

"Thank you, that will be fine. Is the dining room open now?"

"Yes sir, it is."

"Oh! My goodness," she exclaimed as she saw her room, "I've never... Oh! I've never seen anything so beautiful. With my budget, I have always had to stay in the cheapest hotels I could find. It's so big! And a color TV set too."

She ran around the room looking into everything and then jumped on the bed.

"If we hurry and get ready," Dawson insisted, "we can eat supper before going to the movie. Can you be ready in thirty minutes?"

"I'll be ready in twenty," she said eagerly.

"Sister Catherine," Dawson said, knocking on her door. "Are you ready?"

Her door opened quickly and the swishing sound of her habit followed her outside. Dawson also notices something else following her, the gentle fragrance of roses.

"Sister, you smell like a rose. Do you have perfume on?"

"Is it that noticeable? I didn't use very much. Do you think I should wash it off?" She started back into her room, but he grabbed her arm.

"Absolutely not!" he said as he led her down to the dining room, "I think the delicate scent of roses is very becoming."

Operation Minerva

Sister Catherine talked all through supper. She talked about her school, her students, her sisters, her parents, and about how beautiful her room was. Dawson began to believe she was going to explode with excitement when she started talking about going to a drive-in and seeing *The Green Berets* movie. She was like a child seeing the world for the first time. She kept asking him if it was time to go. She didn't want to be late.

"Two, please." Dawson said, handing the money to the ticket agent, "Is *The Green Berets* on first or second?"

"It's the first movie sir."

"Thank you," he said, pulling away. "This looks like a good spot, Sister, right in the middle."

"So many cars and so many people, where are they all going? How do they find their way back to their autos?

"They're going to the refreshment stand to get something to eat. Would you like something?"

"No, no, I couldn't eat a thing after that big supper we just had."

He laughed to himself at her statement because she had talked more than she had eaten. She was constantly bombarding him with questions about the movie. During one exciting scene she took his hand while talking to him; however, after the scene was over, she did not let go. She had taken off her shoes almost as soon as they had started and was sitting on her left foot with her knee pointed toward him. At first, she had the back of his hand resting on her knee; as the movie progressed, she shifted her position and he found the back of his hand resting on the inside of her left thigh. The heat from her leg was driving him absolutely insane. His heart was beating so frantically that he was sure she would notice the noise. He focused all his consciousness, all his attention, and all of his feelings to the six square inches of skin on the back of his hand. He could feel the muscles in her leg pull and flex as she laughed and shifted her body around in the seat. The sensations pouring into his brain from this single point of contact were maddening. He wanted to turn his hand over, but he was afraid to move. Then it happened, she moved and released his hand.

"I must find my handkerchief," she said, digging around in her pockets.

His hand was free; she had released it just a few inches above her leg. Should he drop it straight down where it had been? Should he turn it over? What would she do? He gently lowered his hand, palm down, onto the inside of her leg. He was engulfed with excitement as he slowly extended his fingers and thumb around her thigh. He waited to see what her response would be. Would she push his hand away, would she just ignore him, or would she give some indication of approval? He waited. Finally, she responded by placing her hand over his, pressing his hand tight against her thigh. His heart exploded with passion at the touch of her hand. He did not see the remainder of the movie. He sat with his eyes closed, head back and his total consciousness centered on the contact between their bodies. His hand was like a siphon, drawing heat and pleasure from her body to his. Neither Dawson nor Sister Catherine talked on the way back to the motel. When they stopped at her door, he told her that he had enjoyed the evening and that he would see her in the morning at breakfast.

Operation Minerva

He immediately undressed and took a shower. As he showered he could hear her shower running also. He knew that she was standing just a few feet away from him, in her shower, nude! He could close his eyes and see her standing there wet and slippery; the thought nearly drove him out of his mind with passion. He got out of the shower and tried to watch TV. Still, he could hear every move she made, every sound from her room echoed through his head. At last, her room was quiet. She has gone to bed, he thought. Then he heard a knock at his door; but, when he answered, no one was there. Again, he heard someone knocking, but this time he realized that the knocking was on the door between his room and hers. As he unlocked and opened the door the scent of roses filled his lungs. She was dressed in a black lace night gown that didn't quite cover the nipples of her large white breasts. She held her hand out to him.

"I thought we might watch TV together for awhile," she said, smiling.

He took her hand and led her into his room and over to the bed.

CHAPTER 4
Bangkok, Thailand

"Ladies and gentlemen, please have your passports ready for customs and immigration officials."
A very young, attractive and petite Thai girl made the announcement in English, German, and Siamese. Dawson would pass through customs without inspection; a benefit, he knew, of being an officer and a Green Beret. The airport had not changed; everything looked familiar to him. He made his way through the crowd and into the next room where he was met by another young Thai girl. This one wanted to help him with transportation to Bangkok, he declined.
Outside he walked to the military bus stop and got on a familiar Air Force blue bus.
After asking how long it would be before the bus would depart for Bangkok, he found a seat in the back where he could lay down for a while. The night air was warm and heavy with humidity; a light breeze paraded a multitude of smells past his nose, smells that triggered memories, memories of old friends, memories of some good times and memories of some bad times. He remembered Lieutenant Bill Johnson and a ludicrous adventure the two of them had in Bangkok two years ago. He also remembered that Johnson had been killed a few months

later while commanding a group of Nung mercenaries and Vietnamese Special Forces on a CCN FOB[5] team in Quang Tri, Vietnam. He thought again of their last night together:

"What the hell? They're locked up!" Lieutenant Johnson said, shaking the door. "Man, they must've burned rubber getting out of here, it's only five minutes past five. By god when they say be here before five o'clock they mean it. You know what this means don't you Jack?"

"Yes, It means that we're going to have to sleep with this equipment tonight!"

"Get back in the cab," the Lieutenant said, "and let's get the hell out of here."

The Lieutenant gave the driver a card with the address of their hotel. At the hotel they decided to share a room, they thought it would be safer for the Top Secret COMSEC[6] equipment they were delivering to Bangkok. The equipment was in two boxes; each box was a cubic foot in size and weighed thirty pounds. Lieutenant Johnson was signed for one and Dawson was signed for the other.

"You shower first," the Lieutenant said, "and I'll watch the equipment."

"What a hell-of-a-way to run a war," Dawson said, throwing his equipment on the bed. "You can figure out how we're going to eat tonight while I'm in the shower."

After both had cleaned up they decided to have supper in the hotel dining room - with their top-secret plain brown

---

[5] Command Control North – Forward Operating Base
[6] Communications Security

wrapped packages. They walked into the dining room wearing their short sleeved, light blue jump suits, shoulder holstered .45 caliber automatics, K-bars, and each holding a brown box under his arm. The hotel was full of tourists and the dining room was crowded; all eyes locked onto the two armed men as they walked in.

"Man," Dawson said. "I feel like a whore in church. I've never seen so many sweet little old ladies in one place before in my life, maybe we should eat in the room?"

"No chance, we can't do anything else tonight so we might just as well enjoy eating."

The hostess approached and motioned for them to follow her. She seated them at a large, round, white-linen covered table. The table was elegantly set with four polished silver place settings, crystal wine glasses, and candlesticks.

"You sit over there," Johnson told Dawson, "and I'll sit over here. This way I can see who is behind you and you can see who is behind me."

Dawson moved around the table, set his package on the extra chair and took his seat.

"Gentlemen," the waitress asked, "may I keep you packages for you?"

She made a move to pick up Dawson's package; he put his hand on top of it and told her that he would like to keep it where he could see it.

"What are you going to have?" Dawson asked.

"I'm going to have the best steak and the best wine in the house. What are you going to have?"

"I think I'll have the same thing."

"How do you like your steak?"

"Just wounded."
"Ah, a true Green Beret, I like mine raw too."
The waitress came and Lieutenant Johnson ordered the food and wine. The first thing to show up was a very large bottle of wine. The waiter poured a small amount of the wine into Johnson's glass. After going through all the required motions he accepted the wine. The waiter filled both their glasses and then vanished into the kitchen.
"Well," Johnson asked. *"How do you like it?"*
"It's very good. Where did you pick-up all your information about wine? You're not old enough to have drank that much."
"I guess you could say it's one of the small side benefits of being born to a French Mother. I've been drinking wine with my meals since I was old enough to sit at the table. My Mother says: 'a gentleman must know how to order wine and must be familiar with good wine'."
"You must've been paying attention because you've learned your lessons well. Your Mother would be proud of you. I haven't seen it done any better, even in the movies."
The food was slow in coming and the wine disappeared fast. Half way through the second bottle the food arrived, with still another bottle. Dawson was as drunk as a boot on his first liberty by then and well on his way to oblivion. His steak was tough and his knife dull so he proceeded to cut up his steak and eat it with his K-bar. Lieutenant Johnson, seeing his success also switched to his K-bar. They were now the center of entertainment in the dining room. Dawson was not a drinking man, his tolerance for alcohol was not as high as the lieutenant's. As he became more and more intoxicated the other guests

in the room ceased to exist. Fortunately, he was not in the habit of using abusive language so his loud talking was not too offensive to the other guests. His antics, however, proved to be hilarious. Upon leaving, Lieutenant Johnson threw his box up on his shoulder and started toward the door. Dawson got up, grabbed his box, and tried to follow the Lieutenant. However, he also grabbed the tablecloth. As he threw the box to his shoulder the tablecloth went over his head. The weight of the box and the confusion of being hit in the face with the table cloth was too much for him. He became unbalanced and went over backwards to the floor with the box, the table cloth, the dishes, and his chair. Every available waitress and waiter in the room was there instantly to help him back onto his feet. After helping him up and carefully positioning the box on his shoulder, one of the girls helped him to the elevator.

A sergeant, sitting next to Dawson on the airport bus, woke him from his dream and told him that they had arrived at his hotel. He got up, still drowsy and half-asleep as he removed his suitcase from the overhead rack and unsteadily tottered off the bus. A short summer rainsquall had just passed and the air was clean and fresh. He stood still, enjoying the cool breeze as the bus pulled away behind him. A small boy approached him and offered to carry his suitcase into the hotel. Dawson didn't think he was big enough to run away with it so he agreed. The boy struggled to get the suitcase up the stairs and across the lobby to the check-in desk where he immediately turned and held out his hand to Dawson. A big smile came over his face as Dawson dropped five

Operation Minerva

Baht[7] into the boy's hand. The boy pressed his hands together in front of him, as if in prayer, bowed to Dawson and ran back outside.

In his room, Dawson opened the window and looked out over Bangkok. The night air was still fresh and clean from the rain and the warm breeze that was stirring had a sweet scent. The city was lit-up in all directions for as far as he could see. The magnitude and majesty of the view gave him an emotional high; however, the smell and the sight of Bangkok also stirred-up forgotten names, faces, and memories of places he had not thought of for a long time. Dawson was always amazed at how a faint smells could solicit such vivid memories from his brain. He stood quietly and looked out the window for several minutes.

It must be around supper time in Georgia. He thought. Pat is probably eating. Mom and Dad are sitting at the kitchen table right now, drinking coffee. I'll have to go back to Newark after this tour and spend more time with them. Newark, Ohio, it seems so far away, light years away. Newark! What an asshole place to be from. A little city filled with little people who are more mercenary than I am, but they call it business, little people who are consumed with their self-importance. They're a bunch of ass-holes fighting and backstabbing their friends for a position in an isolated micro-orb. Jean is the only one in the whole damned town with any sense and I question her sanity for not leaving.

---

[7] 25 Cents

Operation Minerva

He looked out over the city again and took a deep breath, and again his mind was flooded with thoughts. He returned to another warm summer night that had just been washed with rain, his first night in Saigon. The date was August the 20th, 1966; it was 2100 hours on a very dark, warm, overcast night in Saigon:

"Sir! You may pass through," the gate guard said to Dawson. "But the rest of you will have to wait until morning."

"Why can he go into the city and not us?" a soldier protested.

"My orders," the guard said firmly, "is not t'let no foot traffic through this gate after 1900 hours except Green Berets. I don't know why! I didn't ask why! I don't care why! If you don't like it, go talk to the chaplain."

The grumbling disappointed crowd at the gate started drifting away as Dawson checked the directions to the officer's hotel one more time as he passed through the gate into the city. After leaving the security of the base behind, he soon became acutely aware of the dead silence blanketing the deserted streets. The long wet street glistened under the streetlights. The only movement, except for his, was the shimmering reflections from scattered puddles disturbed by the occasional breeze. He reached up, unsnapped the strap on his .45 and moved the strap out of the way. He checked his knives and tightened the harness; he pulled his beret down firmly onto his head and continued down the street, trying to stay out of the streetlights.

He walked slowly, but deliberately, his eyes constantly scanning every doorway and alley, his ears strained to detect the slightest sound. After walking two blocks, the silence was broken by the scream of a military police jeep speeding through the deserted street. A young MP in the jeep smiled and waved at him with his rifle as they went past. Dawson raised his hand to wave but the jeep was passing from sight around the corner. The silence became so intense after the jeep passed that he became aware that he could hear the echo of his own footsteps across the street. After another two blocks he came to the officer's hotel and quickly entered.

The clerk, who was of some nationality that Dawson could not readily identify, told him that all the single rooms were taken and that he must share a double.
"Well, war is hell," he quipped. "I guess we must all put up with a little inconvenience now and then."
"Here is your key, you are on the fourth floor and, I"m sorry but, the elevator is out of order."
Dawson openly laughed about the elevator as he took the key and started for the stairs. At the room he found that the key would not open the lock. He checked the number on the key - 405 then the number on the door - 405! He knocked on the door and was greeted by a grumpy middle-aged woman.
"I'm sorry," he apologized, "there must be some mistake. The desk clerk gave me this room." He looked at his key again and the door, "room 405."
"Don't worry about it," she said sharply. "That jerk must think I'm lonely, every night he sends a man up here to me. You can leave your bag here while you check on another room if you want."
"Thank you," he said, placing his bag inside the room, "I'll be right back."

Operation Minerva

Moments later, he returned with a key to 406, he thanked the lady in 405 for watching his bag and entered his room. Room 406 was a double room but he found, to his relief, that he was alone. He threw his bag on the bed and looked around the room; the room, even in its rundown condition, showed signs of once being one of Saigon's most luxurious French hotels. By examining what was left of the wallpaper, he could tell that it had been a fancy relief pattern that looked like the design had been birds. The white doors and woodwork around the room were, at one time, decorated with ornate carved designs which were covered with gold leaf; now, however, the door to the bathroom had the silhouette of a man on it, drawn with a black marker, and the entire door was peppered with countless knife wounds. The woodwork around the door leading to the hallway was scarred with the repeated installation and destruction of a chain lock that was, once again, ripped from the woodwork. The entry door, once beautifully decorated with a peacock, now hosted numerous useless locks, knife holes, and the initials of many of the rooms past guests.

On the dresser he found and advertisement for the "Roof Top Supper Club" that, according to the add, was open every night from 6 P.M. until 2 A.M.." He looked at himself in the mirror and commented: "Well, I don't look too bad for such a long hot flight. I think I'll wash up and have some chow."

About twenty minutes later, he opened the door to the roof and was surprised to find himself standing in the middle of a flower garden with fountains, pools and a marble terrace. A few meters away people were dancing to soft music. The dance floor was encircled by white linen covered tables, each ornamented with flowers and polished silver place settings. The smell of charcoaled steaks, beer, and lady's perfume filled his senses as he crossed the dance floor to a table near the edge of the roof. From this vantage point, he could see up and down the street in front of the hotel. The menu was more of a surprise than the garden. He ordered a rare filet mignon, baked potato with sour cream, asparagus tips and Portuguese rose wine.

About thirty minutes later, he pushed his plate away and sat back to enjoy the contented feeling that accompanies a full stomach and good wine. Just at that instant a flash of red light caught his eye. "A tracer," he said aloud, but to himself. He looked down the street to where he thought the tracer had come from. More tracers were fired. He could see and hear them ricocheting off buildings and streaking into the black sky. That's a 50 caliber. He thought. He shifted his chair around for a better view of the intersection. Just a block away, a fire-fight was taking place between an American military police jeep, equipped with a 50-caliber machine gun, and Viet Cong terrorists. At first, he felt a sense of urgency in the situation; however, he noticed that no one on the dance floor was paying any attention to noise of the gunfight on the street. He heard an explosion. A hand grenade, he thought. Again he looked at the couples dancing to the soft slow music and then at the men fighting in the street below. He sighed, shook his head in disbelief and sat back in his chair. He relaxed in the comfort and safety of his roof-top vantage point, drank more of his wine and observed the action unfolding before him like some strange make-believe stage

*production. He saw an MP fall under fire; he saw
tracers passing around and through one of the terrorists
as he tried to run across the street. Dawson would never
know that the young MP who had smiled and waved to
him from the passing jeep earlier in the evening was the
same MP who died in the street.*

Dawson's thoughts were pulled away from Saigon by
someone knocking on his door. "Just a minute," he
called to the persistent knocking. "Just a minute."
He opened the door and was greeted with a very hearty
handshake.
"Mister Dawson, I'm Captain Romero. The desk clerk
told me a new Green Beret had checked in and I thought
I'd welcome you to Bangkok. I was going to ask you if
you'd been here before, but I see by your Thai jump
wings that you have. Are you having any problems that I
can help you with?" he asked.
"The only problem I'm having right now is getting
something to eat; the desk clerk said just about
everything was closed."
"Well, no problem, I think we can take care of that. I
know several good places to eat around town that stay
open all night."
Captain Romero was a professional Green Beret with six
years experience in South East Asia. He was half-black
and half Puerto Rican, born and reared on the tough side
of Chicago. Romero was not generally liked by black
troops because he would not buy their 'poor boy
bullshit.' He was a self-made, self-educated,
self-supported college graduate and he believed 'If I can
do it - you can do it too.' He had a deep respect for men

that had proven themselves in combat. He had a preference for airborne troops in general, and the airborne rangers, to him, were second only to 'his' Green Berets.

The taxi stopped in front of the Mandarin restaurant. Captain Romero paid the driver and they walked into the dining room under the staring eyes of half a dozen oriental couples. Captain Romero ordered supper for Dawson and himself in flawless Chinese. Dawson was impressed and expressed his surprise to the captain. The captain explained that he was trained as a China specialist and had served for two years in Formosa as a military advisor.

The captain and Dawson spent the next hour telling war stories about their training days at Fort Bragg and reminiscing about old girl friends. Finally, the captain suggested they go to the Three Sisters Bar and finish off the evening with a drink. Dawson agreed and within minutes they were on their way in a taxi. The Three Sisters Bar was an old Special Forces hang-out and was affectionately referred to as the six-tits bar by the green berets. The bar was about half full when they arrived. Before they could even order a drink, a leg soldier walked over to their booth and started giving Captain Romero a hard time.

"Well, captain, I've been waiting all evening for you to show-up around here."

"Your vigilance had paid off, soldier. For, as you can see, I am here. Now, what's your problem?"

The soldier accused Captain Romero of messing around with his girl friend. It was obvious to Dawson, and to the captain, that the soldier was looking for a fight; however, the captain, in a cool and unbelievably emotionless expression, leaned back, looked up at the angry soldier and said, "I'm going to pose two situations to you and I want you to think very carefully about them. Right now you have the unpleasant, but not tragic, job of explaining to your friends that your girl friend has left you and run-off. Now, that's bad, bu t compare it with this situation. How would you like to have to explain to your friends that a nigger stole your girl friend and then mercilessly beat the shit out of you? Think about it carefully now!"

The soldier stood quietly for several seconds looking at the captain; then, without a sound, he turned and left the bar.

"Man," Dawson said, "you sure talked your way out of that one. He was bigger than both of us!"

"All it takes is a positive mental attitude," the captain said.

"And what if a 'positive mental attitude' hadn't worked?"

"Well, then, he would've just had to settle for a few days in a hospital. The rest would probably do him a world of good."

Captain Romero motioned to one of the girls at the bar and told her to bring two beers. She delivered the beer, collected her money and then sat down beside the Captain.

"You must be new," she said to Dawson. "I not see you before."

Dawson answered her question in Siamese, then asked her what her name was. She was delighted that he could speak her language and called her girl friends over so they could hear him speak Siamese.

"Well, I see you're not without your own linguistic accomplishments," the Captain said.

"Thai is an easy language to learn, much easier than Chinese."

"You speak Chinese too?" the second girl asked Dawson.

"No, but the Captain does."

"What dialect?" she asked.

"Taiwanese."

"My Father is Taiwanese."

At that point she began talking to the Captain in Chinese.

They ordered drinks for the girls to keep the house Mother happy. A Green Beret Sergeant in fatigues walked up to the table and spoke to the Captain. Dawson could tell by the greeting that they had been friends for a long time. The sergeant had his right arm around a little bar girl who was trying in vain to get him to leave the bar. She finally became tired and laid her head against his chest and closed her eyes. The Captain introduced the Sergeant to Dawson then invited him and his girl to join them for a beer. However, the sergeant said he had to get home before his Teelak[8] became suspicious. The Sergeant was assigned to the Team House in Bangkok and lived in a rented house next door. The Sergeant explained that he liked to slip out once in a while and that he used the excuse that he was on duty to cover his extra activities.

"She checks on me so I can't stay too long."

---

[8] Girlfriend

Operation Minerva

"Just a quickie, right?" the Captain said laughing.

Dawson saw the girl with the knife but didn't become alarmed until she raised it over her head and started toward the sergeant.

"Sergeant, look out!" he shouted, as he pointed at her.

The Sergeant turned just in time to see Mea, his Teelak, start her attack. She was not trying to stab him, she was after the girl under his arm. He sensed who her target was and covered the girl with his shoulder. Mea's thrust, once started, did not change course; she stuck the knife in the Sergeant's left shoulder. The knife didn't penetrate too deeply because the Sergeants body was rotating at the time of contact. The Sergeant stood up straight and released the girl from his arms, she promptly ran away. Mea began to scream hysterically when she discovered that she had stabbed her boy friend. The Sergeant reached over his shoulder, pulled the knife out and threw it to the floor.

"Will you shut-the-fuck-up, Mea," he said. "Well, Captain it looks like I've got to be going. Stop by the team house and see me when you've got the time, ok?"

He took Mea's hand and led her out of the bar.

"Well," Dawson said. "This hasn't been a dull evening. I'd forgotten how exciting it was around here?"

The bus ride from Bangkok to Lop Buri the next day was just as Dawson had remembered it - a kamikaze mission performed while packed in a sardine can. He could never understand how they could manage to get so many people, bags, produce, and animals packed into such a small container. Thai buses were always decorated with wild designs in multiple bright colors and then ornamented with brass, chrome, flags, and pin-wheels. Thai buses only had two speeds: stopped, and what ever it would do with the accelerator pushed to the floor. The Thai's lack of observance of basic highway rules, like driving on your own side of the highway, and the fact that everyone drove too fast, accounted for the fact that nearly all highway accidents in Thailand were fatal.

At Sara Buri the crowd thinned and the noise level dropped. A twelve-year-old girl and her Grandmother moved into the empty seats beside Dawson. They had not been on the road long before the old lady began to work on Dawson, trying to get him to take the young girl as his Teelak. Dawson pretended not to understand what the old woman was saying in Siamese so she gave it her best shot in English.

"She good girl, virgin," she said. "She not be with any man before."

"I can certainly believe that," Dawson said. "She's too young, too little."

"All Thai women little, she ok. Look, she beautiful." The old woman reached over to the little girl sitting between them and pulled up her skirt, she had no panties on. "See, she beautiful, yes?"

Dawson was embarrassed by the old lady's brass and thankful that no one was watching the proposed sale. He looked out the window and tried to ignore her; however, she would not be ignored.

"We come live with you," she said. "I clean, cook, shine shoes and wash clothes. She be your woman. Only 500

Operation Minerva

baht[9], ok?" He continued to look out the window and did not answer.

"Look, look her," the old lady said poking him. "She very nice."

Dawson turned and looked at her. The young girl was sitting on the edge of her seat facing him, her blouse was pulled open.

"She has nice ones, yes?"

The old woman was right about one thing, she did have nice ones. The young girl's breasts were the size and shape of half an orange. He looked into her eyes and got the feeling that she was quite detached from the activity taking place. Her eyes were dilated so he figured the old lady had doped her. He pulled her blouse closed and motioned for her to button it up. He was becoming irritated with the old lady's attempt to sell him the young girl's ass. He thought the only way to get rid of them was to turn the tables on the old lady. He decided to make a run on her and see what she would do.

"I do not like young girls," he said, "I like you. You be my Teelak."

The old lady looked at him and began to laugh while covering her beetle nut stained teeth with her hand.

"You crazy," she said, still laughing.

"No," he insisted, "I want you. Pull up your skirt and let me see what you have."

Without hesitation the old lady pulled her skirt up as high as she could and still remain seated. She also had no panties on!

---

[9] Twenty-Five Dollars

"Good," he said, "good. Now, let me see if you have nice ones."

Still laughing and without hesitation the old lady reached into her blouse and pulled out one of her breasts.

"Ok," he said, "put it away."

The old lady's attitude about the turnaround and her readiness to be the one in the bag made Dawson change his mind about her. She doesn't care who brings home the bacon, he thought, just so someone does. He reached into his pocket and pulled out a 100 baht note and gave it to the old lady.

"This is for you, but I don't want a Teelak, ok?"

The old lady took the money and smiled.

"Ok," she said. "Ok."

46th Special Forces Company,
Lop Buri, Thailand

At Lop Buri, he walked to the address Captain Romero had given him. The 'House for Rent' sign on the gate was in English. He walked into the compound and within ten minutes, and 4000 baht[10], he had a new two bedroom teak house; and within another two minutes, the old lady and the young girl were at his door. The old lady walked in as though she had just paid the rent instead of Dawson, and the young girl followed. Then another woman, who lived in one of the three other houses in the compound, also walked through the door without knocking.

---

[10] Two Hundred Dollars

Operation Minerva

"Hello," she said, "My name is Kim. I live next door.
I'm Captain Carver's girlfriend."
Kim was tall, too tall to be Thai. He thought she was
probably Chinese. She spoke perfect English and had
bright eyes and an intelligent face.
"Kim," he said. "Maybe you can help me out. I can't get
through to this old woman that I don't want her twelve-
year old grand daughter as my Teelak. Will you talk to
her?"
Kim started talking to the old woman as he walked up
stairs to unpack his bag. He did not have to check in
until tomorrow but he thought he might just as well get it
done today. Minutes later when he come downstairs Kim
and the old woman were still talking.
"What is she saying?" She mumbled and talked so fast
that I couldn't understand a word she was saying in Thai.
"She lied to you about the girl's age. She is seventeen."
"Why did she say twelve?"
"They are from Phitsanulok and if a girl is not married
and have children by seventeen they call her an old maid,
no good. She didn't think you'd like her if you knew she
was that old."
"Well, that still doesn't change my mind."
"They've got no place to go, she's an orphan, the old
lady's brother threw them out. They went to Bangkok to
live with relatives but couldn't find them and were out of
money when they met you on the bus."
"That sounds like a line of bullshit to me. Tell them they
can stay in the extra bedroom tonight but tomorrow they
must find something else."
"She is a lovely girl," Kim said. "She would make a good
girl friend for you."

Operation Minerva

"Look, I just don't like to do things that way. They can stay here for the night if they want to but that's all. I must go to Fort Narai now and check in, I'll see you later."

He checked in with the duty officer and then walked over to the officers club. He introduced himself to the few officers he found there and then returned to his newly rented house. Before he entered the house he could see steam coming from the kitchen and smell food. Inside he found the old woman in the kitchen cooking. She had taken some of the money Dawson had given her and bought food.

The young girl was in the shower. The old woman motioned for him to sit down, so he went to the couch to wait. The girl came out of the shower with her hair up in a towel. She was still wearing the same white blouse and black skirt. She sat down on a stool across from Dawson.

He became painfully aware, as she sat with her legs apart and moved around drying her hair, that she still did not have any panties on.

"What is your name?" he asked her in Siamese.

The girls eyes opened wide and she looked at him in disbelief.

"What is your name? He asked again.

"I am called Seadang."

Dawson was aware that Seadang was not her legal name. He knew Thai parents give their children temporary names until they are five or six years old and are expected to live. Seadang is Thai for Red and she was probably called "Little Red" by her parents. Many Thais use this short easy-to-remember name with friends and family throughout their lives.

Operation Minerva

"My name is Jack."

"Jack, Jack," she said. "I like that name, it is easy to say."

Seadang took the towel to the shower room and returned with a comb. Dawson had a fetish about women's hair and he could not let this opportunity pass.

"Let me comb your hair."

"A man combing a woman's hair?"

"Yes, I like to comb a woman's hair."

She sat down between his legs and gave him the comb. A big smile lit up the old lady's face and she clapped her hands when she peeked out of the kitchen and saw them together on the couch.

"Well, you two are much closer together now," Kim said walking into the house. "Have you decided to keep her?"

He was slightly irritated by Kim's habit of walking in without knocking; however, he made up his mind to wait and not protest until he became familiar with the customs established among the girl friends living in the compound. She did not give him time to answer her question, she just continued to talk.

"Would you and Seadang like to go to the movies with Ted and me tonight? They've got a good movie at MAG[11] house at eight o'clock."

"Seadang doesn't understand English and I would not be caught dead with her the way she is dressed. In that school outfit she does look twelve years old!"

"English does not matter; she'll enjoy the movie just the same. If you give me some money I'll get her some clothes that will let her look her age."

---

[11] Military Advisory Group

Operation Minerva

"I guess we have time for that," he said. "Ok."

"Will you buy me something too?" she asked.

"Yes, you can get something too. Make sure you get her some panties!"

"Good, first I must tell Ted."

Kim vanished through the door just as the old lady was placing the food on the table.

Dawson loved Thai food, and the old lady was an excellent cook; she had fixed the traditional Thai evening dish - fried pork, rice, and eggs in a one-dish meal and had supplied him with the hot sauce. He looked at Seadang across the room from him. How can I fight this? He asked himself. I have an old lady that cooks like an angel and a young girl who looks like one. I think I have just adopted a live-in cook and a would-be girlfriend.

When Seadang returned with her new clothes, she was laughing and talking so fast that Dawson could not understand her. In her excitement, she began to take off her old clothes right in the living room.

"Stop," Kim said. "You must make him wait and surprise him."

Kim took Seadang into the shower room with the new clothes. The two girls were laughing and having a wonderful time getting Seadang into her new clothes. Soon the door opened and she came out wearing a yellow mini dress, yellow shoes, and a yellow ribbon in her hair. He knew, by the degree of taste displayed, that Kim had selected the outfit. He asked Kim, in English, if Seadang had panties on - he did not know how to say it in Thai. A quick word from Kim and Seadang's dress was hoisted to expose a bright yellow pair of bikini panties.

"Good," he said." At least she won't catch cold now."

Operation Minerva

The movie was 'It's a Mad, Mad, Mad, Mad World' and Kim was right, Seadang loved it. Dawson became so enchanted by her laughter that he stopped watching the movie and began watching her. Her laugh was so delicate, feminine and innocent. As he watched her and took pleasure from the joy she was experiencing, her child-like laughter triggered a memory that he had managed to keep buried until now, a memory that struck him through like an icy sword:

During his last tour in Viet Nam he was visiting an A-Team that was having communications problems. The Team was stationed in a safe village just outside Saigon. He had solved their problem, an improperly terminated directional antenna, early in the afternoon. However, he could not leave until the helicopter passed through the next day. The A-Team was planning to show a film that evening, a new one that had arrived with him on the morning helicopter, so the night would go fast. The movies were shown outside and were always a big event for the villagers; they started to collect in the area before the sun had even gone down. Minutes before the movie was to start, a six-year old girl struggled with a box that she wanted to use as a seat. A sergeant, who had a good seat in the front, picked her and the box up and placed her on the ground in front of him. Dawson was sitting next to the sergeant when the movie, "The Marx Brothers at the Circus" began. The laughter of the little girl could be heard above everyone else. A few times, she laughed so hard that she fell off the box. During the second reel, the projector stopped and Dawson was asked if he could help find the problem.

Operation Minerva

He quickly determined that a surge in the power line had blown the fuse and the sergeant ran to get another. The little girl was standing on the box looking over the heads of everyone trying to hurry Dawson along with his repairs. As he stood there watching her jump up and down on the box, she disappeared in the flash of a blinding explosion. The sergeant and several others near the explosion were killed. Dawson was knocked to the ground, dazed. An investigation conducted later determined that the box the little girl had chosen to sit on was a time bomb. The sergeant had, unknowingly, positioned the bomb in the middle of the group.

Seadang's laughter pulled Dawson from his thoughts - she was laughing and pulling on his shirt. He had made it through his first tour in Thailand two years ago without a live-in girlfriend and had enjoyed a variety of overnight girls. Teelaks were trouble; they had a habit of interfering with the conduct of a soldier's duties. He had seen numerous careers ruined by personal problems, and the biggest personal problem a soldier can have is a girl friend who is not loyal to him and sympathetic to his calling.

During the walk home, Captain Carver told Dawson about a conversation he had had earlier that day with the commanding officer. He told Dawson that his reputation of being an officer who could 'get things done' had preceded him and that the commanding officer had a special job waiting for him. Dawson was happy to find out that there would be no delay in getting to work and wondered what the special assignment was. Dawson, although a signal officer, had proven himself capable of handling any problem, and men assigned to him were always eager to follow.

"I don't know exactly what the job is," Captain Carver said," but if I were you I would be ready to travel north... and soon."

"I'm always ready, I could leave right now."

"With that attitude, Jack, you'll get along just great with our new commanding officer. He feels that the most permanent ties a Green Beret should have anywhere, are his tent stakes - everything else must be fluid."

"He and I will love each other, because the thing I like to do most is travel and I like to travel light."

"Well, you'll think you've died'n gone to heaven here. We're always on the road. I'm off to Chiang Mai tomorrow and will be gone for six days."

Dawson and Seadang stopped in front of the old woman's bedroom. He opened the door and told her to go to bed.

At 08:00 the next morning he was standing in the Adjutant's office:

"Have you met the staff signal officer yet?" The assistant adjutant, Lieutenant Collins, asked.

"No, I haven't. Does he have an office in this building?"

"Yes, it's downstairs in the far end of the building. However, he should be here in just a few minutes for the morning briefing, you'll meet him then."

Dawson sat down at one of the desk and started to look through his 201 file, he wanted to be sure it was in order before giving it to the adjutant. He looked up when he heard his name mentioned and saw a very large hairy major walking toward him.

Operation Minerva

"Mister Dawson," the major said, extending his short stubby hand. "I'm the Adjutant, Major Zuvich. Come into my office."

The major was very loud and dynamic. He was also very friendly and shaking hands with him was like shaking hands with a guerrilla.

"The CO[12] has been waiting for you Mister Dawson; I hope you're ready to travel because you will be going to Trang as soon as we can establish your top secret CRYPTO clearance and cut your orders."

"I'm ready to go, sir. What's the problem in Trang?"

"Communications, we can't maintain communications, our ability to communicate changes with the weather and time of day. Everything is ok, then everything turns to shit."

"That doesn't sound like an impossible problem, Major. Has anyone tried to help them before?"

"Yes, we've had two specialists down there. As a matter of fact, I think one of them is still there. Major Savage, our staff signal officer will give you a better briefing, have you met him yet?"

"No, sir.

The major pushed a button on his office intercom and told his sergeant to find Major Savage. "Tell him his new signal officer, Mister Dawson, is in my office. Ask him if he has the time to come up and talk to us, also, tell him that this morning's briefing has been cancelled because the CO is not available."

---

[12] Commanding Officer

Operation Minerva

Dawson was not impressed with Major Savage. He was overweight, a bit on the sloppy side, and too meek to be a special forces major. During the briefing on the communications problems at Trang, Dawson got the distinct impression that Major Savage did not know what the hell he was talking about. This asshole, Dawson thought to himself, is a professional paper shuffler. That's the only way he could've gotten here. I know he's one of those assholes that could find a dog turd on his desk and, by shuffling paper around, convince everyone that it was a gold nugget.

Lieutenant Collins, the assistant adjutant, escorted Dawson around the post and introduced him to everyone. There were only ten special forces qualified warrant officers in the army and Dawson wanted to know all of them by name; so he was happy to be introduced to Chief Warrant Officer W3 Paul Kressevich. Paul was the signal CRYPTO officer, and Chief Warrant Officer W2 William Silverman, the signal officer he was replacing.

Dawson and Lieutenant Collins were having lunch in the newly completed officers club when they were joined by the Commanding Officer and the Deputy Commanding Officer. It did not take Dawson long to determine that the C.O., Lieutenant Colonel Mark Tucker, was overworked; and it did not take him long to determine that the D.C.O., Lieutenant Colonel Lafayette, was the main reason. The C.O., Lieutenant Collins and Dawson talked about the subversive activities of the Thai Cong; Colonel Lafayette talked about the discipline problems caused by Teelaks. Lieutenant Colonel Tucker explained some of the training problems he was having with the Thai Rangers in the north; Colonel Lafayette talked about the destruction of

morals caused by Teelaks. The C.O warned him not to
travel at night during his trip to Trang because there was
a danger of being ambushed on the highways; Colonel
Lafaytette talked about the danger to a young soldier's
career of having a Teelak.
Outside of the officer's club after lunch, Dawson
questioned Lieutenant Collins about Colonel Lafayette:
"What the hell is his problem? Is he always like that?"
"Yes, Jack, he is. I feel embarrassed for the man every
time he opens his mouth."
"Is he some kind of religious nut? All he thinks about,
evidently, is whether or not the troops have girl friends."
"You're lucky, Jack, you don't have to worry about him;
he's not in the review cycle for your OER*'s."
"Thank God for that!"
"It's the young staff officers who really get screwed. If
they have a Teelak they might just as well kiss their ass
goodbye because he nails them to the cross. He has
ruined several young officers that way. Colonel Tucker
tries to keep him under control, but he's not always
successful. "
Lieutenant Collins and Dawson spent the remainder of
the day in finance getting Dawson some money, and in
supply getting his equipment.

He returned home at 16:30 and found the old lady
cooking and Seadang, once again, in the shower. He went
up to his room, took his clothes off, put a towel around
himself and returned; he wanted to be next for the
shower. The old woman came out of the kitchen and
handed Dawson a package.
"What is this?" he asked her.

Operation Minerva

"This is what all Thai men wear when they are home," she replied. "Very comfortable, look good."

He opened the package and found a new phanung, the short version that men wear.

"Thank you. Thank you very much!" he said.

He was really taken aback by the old woman's actions since she had made herself at home in his house. First, she bought food with the little bit of money he gave her. Now, she has spent more of her money to buy him a phanung to wear around the house. After she returned to the kitchen he put on the phanung and called to her to look at him.

"Very good!" she said. "You beautiful man."

Seadang came out of the shower and smiled when she saw him in his new outfit. She offered him the comb and sat down in front of him. He sat for a few minutes combing her hair and enjoying the slight aromatic herbal fragrance her body had after showering with her Thai soap.

"You smell good," he told her.

"I am clean! That's why," she said in a matter-of-fact manner.

After his shower he told them that he would be going away for a while and that he would leave money with Captain Carver for the rent, food and spending money. He gave each of them 300 baht and told them to see the Captain when they needed more.

After he ate supper he walked out into the courtyard and wondered what Seadang was doing sitting on the ground. As he approached her from behind he could see that she had a machete in her hands and was chopping something. He was horrified when he saw that she was holding a coconut between her bare feet and chopping the covering off with the machete.

"Oh, my god!" he called to her. "Stop."

The sight so frightened Dawson that he was shaking.

He took the machete away from her and told her to never do that again! Then he took her into the house and made the old woman promise him that she would never let Seadang do that again.

"She could cut her little toes off!" he shouted. "She could hit her foot and be crippled for the rest of her life!"

He told the old woman that if she needed any coconuts opened to pay one of the samlaw drivers that were always parked outside their front gate to do it.

"They will do it for one baht and Seadang will not be missing any toes!"

He made her promise one more time that it would never happen again.

The next morning he was in Major Savage's office receiving his travel orders to Trang. At 08:30, Lieutenant Collins, called and told them to report to the commanding officer immediately. Dawson and Major Savage walked up the stairs to the CO's office and knocked on the door.

"Come in,"

Major Savage opened the door just a few inches and stuck his head inside.

"Sir, did you want to see Mr. Dawson and me."

"Yes, is Dawson out there?"

"Yes, sir."

"Good, come in here and sit down."

Major Savage and Dawson sat on the couch and Colonel Tucker sat in a large easy chair. Between the officers

Operation Minerva

was a coffee table set with fresh coffee, an assortment of cookies, toast and the remains of the Colonel's breakfast.

"I know you gentlemen would like some coffee," the Colonel said, pouring out a cup for the major and then Dawson.

"Thank you, sir." Dawson replied.

"Help yourself to the cookies, too."

After a few moments of silence, while the Colonel picked at his last piece of toast and jelly, the adjutant came in with a message for the Colonel.

"Thank you, Dick. This is just what I've been waiting for."

"Do you need anything else, sir?"

"No, Dick, that's all. Thank you."

"Mister Dawson, I'm going to have to postpone your trip to Trang; we've just been given a requirement to provide communications for a First Special Forces Group team out of Okinawa. They are going into Laos from a base camp at Nakhon Phanom. I do not know what their mission objective is or how long it will last, all I know is they want additional commo[13] support from us. Can you leave today?"

"Yes, sir, I'm ready."

"I want you to pick a good sergeant to go with you. Do you have anyone in mind?"

"No, sir. I haven't met any of the commo people yet."

"Take Sergeant Spasiano, he's good."

"Yes, sir, thank you for recommending a good man."

---

[13] Communications

CHAPTER 5
September 1968
Flintridge, Ohio

Lieutenant Patrick Deluca, his green beret cocked jauntily on his head and his uniform decorated only with new silver jump wings and a National Defense ribbon, looked out over the back yard. From his vantage point on the high back porch, nothing in the valley was hidden from his view. He could see the full length of the long graveled lane that stretched out across the green valley and disappeared into the darkness of the trees on the other side. He thought of all the times he'd stood there anxiously awaiting the appearance of his Father's truck at the tree line. He looked at the old, tired, red truck parked in its official spot by the corn bin down on the lane. As a boy, his Father's truck was a symbol of strength and security to him and the sight of it coming down the lane was always comforting. He could not imagine his Father without the truck nor the truck without his Father. He thought about that wonderful day, that first day, his Father let him drive it:

"Patrick, you're twelve years old today. Twelve years is when a boy becomes a man," his Father paused for a moment and then added, "and every man must know how to drive a truck. After lunch we'll go out to the west pasture and I'll teach you how to drive."

Operation Minerva

That day was such a high point in his life that to remember it, even now, flooded his mind with happiness. The telephone rang and before he answered it, he knew it would be his Mother.

"Patrick, if you don't hurry you're going to miss your Father's funeral."

"I'm starting now, Mother."

He didn't say good-bye, just hung up the phone. Patrick looked at the truck keys hanging beside the back door and remembered the day in 1955 when his Father put the nail there. Then he remembered the first time he got to take the keys down, that was in 1960, when he got to take the truck out on his first date. He picked up his suitcase and flight bag, took the keys down from the nail and walked out onto the back porch. The familiar screech of the screen door's rusty, spring-loaded hinges triggered a cascade of memories. He had always loved the back porch; it was like a tree house to him when he was small. He loved to play there when it rained because he was high off the wet ground and the overhang always kept it dry. It was his castle, his fort, a safe place that was high above danger where nothing could get to him. As the screen door slammed shut behind him, a feeling of loneliness and vulnerability engulfed him. It was such a final sound, a sound that he would not hear again for a long time, he was leaving for Vietnam after the funeral. He stopped in front of the truck and looked at the collection of items that had accumulated in the corn bin. His family had given up farming during his grade school years and the corn bin had become a storage bin, a place for things that were not needed but too good to throw away. The sight of his Mother's old butter churn stirred

Operation Minerva

vivid memories of a distant warm summer day and a smile covered his face. He was 13 years old that summer that his cousin Lewis came to visit. He remembered the fun, and the adventures, they'd had together:

"Patrick," his Mother called from the back porch, "go down to the corn bin and get my butter churn."

"OK, Mother," he answered as he and his cousin started racing down toward the lane.

At the corn bin, he explained to Lewis that the keys to the two doors had been lost and that the only way to get in was through the trap door in the roof. The two young boys easily scaled the sides of the bin and dropped to the floor inside. There were so many items of interest to them that they soon forgot what they had been sent for. After several minutes of looking at old tools, broken toys and a corn knife, the boys were reminded of their chore by calls from the house. Lewis found the butter churn under a work table. Several items packed in around the churn prevented it's easy removal so the boys grabbed the handle and gave a determined yank.

"What's that humming sound?" Lewis asked.

"I don't know," Patrick answered.

One more good yank brought the churn out into the open where it could be inspected. Patrick stuck his finger through the hole in the cover and opened it for a look inside.

"Bees," he screamed, "bees!"

Quickly he slammed the cover back over the opening. However, he neglected to plug the finger hole. The bees began exiting through the small hole with amazing speed; each exit was announced by a distinct sound, like

102

blowing across an empty jug. In their panic, the boys had
forgotten that the doors at each end of the bin were
locked. A trail of bees followed them as they ran for the
door. Remembering, upon approach, that the doors
couldn't be opened, each boy jumped and kicked the door
to quickly reverse his direction. Fighting their way
through the oncoming stream of bees, the boys made it to
the other end of the bin, up the wall, out the trap door and
finally to the ground. With the bees still hot on their trail,
they ran for the house. By the time they reached the back
porch, nearly all of the bees had either been lost or had
given up the chase. On the porch, Lewis pulled his shirt
off and half a dozen dead bees fell to the floor, he had a
corresponding number of stings. The bees had made
their entry through a small hole in the back of his shirt.
Patrick had been stung on the arms and neck. Both boys
found live bees in their pockets.

After an hours rest and some intensive first aid from
Mother, Patrick was ready to go after the butter churn
again. This time, however, he was wearing a long sleeve
shirt, gloves, a make believe bee-keeper's hat his Mother
had made from one of her old hats and a coal oil torch.

Once inside the corn bin, he lit the torch and opened the
churn. The bees flew directly into the flame, burned their
wings off and fell to the floor. Lewis, with no shirt or
shoes on, crept closer and closer to see exactly what was
taking place inside the bin. He failed to notice that some
of the bees had fallen to the ground outside after their
wings had been burned away. As he moved around to get
a better look inside, he stepped on a bee that was still
alive. As he screamed and jumped around on one foot,
he stepped on other bees, also still alive. The noise and

movement attracted a few of the remaining bees and once again he was off and running for the house. That evening, at the kitchen table, the boys drank cold milk and ate fresh, hot homemade bread soaked in the wild honey from the churn. Patrick's Father listened and laughed as each boy told and retold his own story of the adventure.

During the funeral, he saw Jennie Simross, an old high school girlfriend, sitting in the back of the church. She had changed considerably since he'd seen her last. He knew that she was living and working in Columbus, over the objections of her parents, and didn't expect to see her at the funeral. He also looked at her older sister sitting beside her. Dorothy had graduated two years before Jennie; however, she'd been a 'good girl' and stayed at home on the farm. He remembered them as good, clean, bright, fun-loving young girls. He and Jennie had dated for most of their senior year. However, nothing serious came of it. Upon graduation from Ohio State, he went directly into the army and never saw her again until now. He felt sorry for Dorothy, she looked almost lethargic sitting there in her plain brown print dress and dark blue cloth coat. He wondered as he looked at her if, under her bandanna, her hair still had that bright new-penny copper color the boys had always loved. Jennie was the talk of the church. Stories of her disregard for her parent's wishes had reached him, through his Mother's letters, at Fort Bragg. They didn't look like sisters now, Dorothy was dull and overweight; Jennie was bright eyed, alert and very smartly dressed. She was wearing the only fur coat in the church and the more he looked at her the more aware he was that everyone else was also looking at her.

Operation Minerva

He remained beside the grave long after his Mother, relatives, and other mourners had returned down the hill to the church. The sun had gone down behind the big ridge to the west and the temperature dropped suddenly. The wind now had a sharp, penetrating chill to it as it blew the brown, gold and red leaves around his feet and into his Father's grave. He felt more alone now than he had ever felt before in his life. He'd never thought about his Father dying, it had just never occurred to him. He was not old enough to die. He looked down into the grave and began to talk to his Father:

"Good-bye, Father, I'll miss talking with you. I'll miss your help, advice, and your implicit understanding of my problems. You've taken many secrets with you, secrets that you promised to tell me. I wish we'd had more time together. I'm a Green Beret now. You were right, it was tough, and I did feel like quitting. However, it made me remember the values you put into my head. I kept repeating to myself what you always said to me: 'a man never quits, a man always finishes his job, a man is always true to his beliefs, a man never lets his friends down, a man never forgets his duty'. I always wondered why you kept telling me those things. Now, I know. When I was at the point where I thought I could not go any further I could hear your voice and it kept me going."
He thought about his last night in the Panamanian jungle; his final test, an E and E^{14} problem that had lasted five days. He had wanted so much to tell his Father about it:

---

[14] Escape and Evasion

Operation Minerva

"Do you guys feel like staying here an extra day in their POW camp?" Patrick asked.

"That's a dumb-ass question," Lieutenant English said, "what pecker-head would want to be locked-up and tortured for another day?"

"Do you know how we can get out of it, Lieutenant?" Sergeant Walters asked.

"I started working on this problem while we were still back at Bragg. You remember that cute little redhead that worked in training? Well, she got me a map of this area, not the piece-of-shit map they gave us for this exercise, but a real map. Look at this. I've traced the map they gave us on the map that she gave me. What do you see, Sergeant?"

"Those cheating no-good bastards! Look at this you guys; no wonder they brag that no team has ever made it through this course, it's impossible!"

"Not impossible, Sergeant, just tough," Patrick said.

"What's your plan, Lieutenant?" the Sergeant asked.

"As you can see, those 'occasional wet spots' they told us to avoid are in fact two converging swamps funneling us into their trap. The swamps, here where we start, are five clicks[15] apart. However, ten clicks to the north at the PZ[16], the swamps are less than one click apart. Now, if I were the aggressor commander," Patrick said. "I'd concentrate my men between the PZ and this east-west jeep trail six clicks to the north of us. I'd also have patrols out around the two visual navigation points they

---

[15] Click = 1000 meters
[16] Pickup Zone

gave us, the radio tower and the water tower. The area
between here and the jeep trail I'd have only two
two-man teams for harassment purposes. The two main
roads to the east and west of the operation area are
patrolled by MP's, and to get caught there is an
automatic drop from the course, no one will do that. The
harassment teams below the jeep trail will, I think, will
be pulled up to the north when the aggressor commander
thinks we've cleared the first five or six clicks of the
course. That would put every available man he has on
the jeep trail, the funnel inlet to the PZ and the
navigation points."

"So, what do we do?" Lieutenant English asked.

"We stay right here and rest for about an hour, maybe an
hour and a half, and then we head west to the swamp.
The good map shows two bridges on the jeep trail. The
west bridge is about 200 meters long, the east bridge is
just a culvert. That tells us that there is a hell-of-a-lot
more swamp to the west then to the east. We wade into
the swamp until the water gets about three feet deep, then
we turn north. I think it'd be a good idea to stay away
from the main stream; if the aggressor commander is
really aggressive, he may have a patrol boat out. We
should have the bridge in sight by last light. After dark
we go under the bridge and continue until the light on the
water tower gives us a bearing of 050 degrees; then we
stop and wait for first light to enter the PZ."

"Lieutenant Deluca," Sergeant Walters said. "You've
really done your homework on this problem. I think it'll
work. No, I'm positive it'll work."

"If it doesn't work and some of us, or all of us, get caught
- we'll still have an edge."

Operation Minerva

"What's that?" the Sergeant asked.

"You're blindfolded as soon as you're captured and taken by truck to the P.O.W. camp. Now you're lost; you don't have any idea where you're at. Right? Wrong! You can see two red lights, the radio tower and the water tower. All you have to do is escape and run between the lights. Right? Wrong! Look at the good map. The P.O.W. camp is here, northwest of the PZ on the west side of the west swamp. Now, look two clicks to the northwest, a second radio tower and red light. From the P.O.W. camp you can't see the water tower because of the trees to the east."

"Those rotten bastards," Sergeant Walters said. "You escape, thinking you're running into a safe zone, and you walk right back into their hands again."

"My plan worked, Father. My estimate of the aggressor commander's tactical plan was exact; we even spotted a patrol boat on the stream south of the bridge. By ten o'clock my team was at the PZ, all we had to do was wait for morning. The P.O.W. camp was only about five hundred meters from us. We could hear gunfire, a loudspeaker playing V.C. music and propaganda, recorded screams and mock executions. The P.O.W. camp at the Panama survival school is well known and feared by most trainees. As we sat around and waited for morning, my men got restless:"

"Lieutenant," Sergeant Walters said, "I don't feel good about this."

"What do you mean?"

"I mean that I don't feel good about sitting here safe and sound while my friends are being tortured only five hundred meters away."

"What'd you suggest?"

"Is there anything in the rules about rescuing people from the camp?"

Lieutenant Deluca looked at the Sergeant for a moment and then they both began to smile.

"You know, Sergeant, I didn't read anything for or against rescue - I think it's open to us."

"Good," the Sergeant said. "How do we do it?"

"Lieutenant English," Deluca said. "We're going to rescue the men from the P.O.W. camp. Do you want to help? "What do you want me to do?"

"Take your five men and circle around to the northwest of the camp. When you're in place, cause as much noise as you can for about one minute; then move west about five hundred meters and repeat the performance, then move into the deep swamp to escape. I'll take my five men and go to the camp. We'll look for a good escape point and when you attract their attention we'll help the men through the fence."

"My plan worked again, during the first diversion we helped nine men escape. They came under the fence three at a time. For each three men, I assigned one of my men to lead them to safety. During the second diversion six more men escaped to safety before I was captured by the aggressors. I soon learned that my captors were indeed hostile aggressors. I had thought the aggressor force was made up of, and controlled by, school cadre; it was not. The aggressors were Regular Army troops who caught this assignment as a shit-detail[17]. The Captain in charge was an Engineering Corps officer that thought he was going to Panama to play with the locks. The aggressors and the aggressor commander in particular, approached the assignment with a vengeance. Their capture rate had been about 93 to 99 percent. I crucified their egos by hacking their captured count to a record breaking low of 25 percent. Thirty men would be picked up on the PZ at sunrise, the largest number ever. And, for the first time, not just one team, but two would be picked up without a loss. My captors were not happy with me, Dad:"

"You think you're a real smart-ass. Don't you Lieutenant?" the aggressor commander screamed at Deluca. *"Throw this piece of shit into the garbage pit*, Sergeant, I think we have a quitter here. He looks like a pussy to me. This won't take long."*

"I was taken to the pit, my hands tied behind me, and thrown in. A safety rope was tied around my chest to prevent accidental drowning. The bottom of the pit was rounded, so it was hard to stand. Each time they jerked the rope I would slip and go down to my knees. They would make me scream out my name, rank and serial number, and while I had my mouth open they would jerk on the rope. They were determined to get me to quit:"

"Pull that piece of shit up here so I can talk to it," the aggressor commander said.

---

[17] Not a desirable assignment.

Operation Minerva

"I was pulled from the pit and washed off with buckets of water. The commander told me that I had only been in the pit for 20 minutes and that I had another 3 hours to go. I had, in fact, been in the pit nearly 2 hours and time was running out for the commander. All of my cloths were taken and I was tied to a post in the middle of the compound. Vietnamese soldiers, assigned to the school for cadre training, dressed as Vietnamese school girls, danced around and taunted me. The aggressor commander came out and walked around the stake, looking at me. The commander taunted me."

"You know, girls," he said. "He don't look like a Green Beret to me. I think he's in the wrong place, he's lost. Maybe he's part of the exercise the Brownies are having down the road. He looks like a Brownie. He has a cute little ass. Maybe I'll take him into my tent and fuck him. No, I couldn't do that," he said holding his nose," he stinks too much. Throw him into the box until daylight."

"The Vietnamese danced around the box I was in while music blasted from nearby speakers. Every few minutes the commander would try to get me to give up and quit. I almost quit, Father. It was fun while I was outsmarting them and winning. But, the reality of what is expected of me while I wear this uniform became clear when I was captured. During the few hours of my captivity, I made a vow, and that is: I will never be captured again."

"Patrick," Jennie said. "Everyone wants to see you before you go. Why don't you come down to the church?"

"I don't want to; but, I guess I should."

She took his hand as they walked down the hill. At the church, he accepted the condolences of the sincere and exchanged the proper amenities with the curious. After most of the congregation had cleared the church, she pulled him into a secret hiding place they had used when they were children. The small cubical was the result of a design flaw in the church remodeling plans; now, heavy curtains hid the error. He became aware of her perfume first, then as his eyes adjusted to the darkness, he could see her standing quietly in front of him.

"Do you remember?" she asked.

"Yes," he replied.

She was referring to the first time they had kissed, it was on a Wednesday night after prayer meeting. Their parents had stayed after church for a board meeting.

"It was so exciting, then. I think it was the chance of getting caught that made this hiding place so much fun, don't you?" she asked.

"My excitement came from being with you."

"Well, what if your Father had caught us?" she asked.

"Dad knew, I told him."

"He didn't tell you to stop?"

"No, he said it reminded him of the times he and Mom had hidden in the trees and kissed when they were young." He put his arms around her, held her for a few moments, and then kissed her.

"You were always so gentle," she said. "You were the only boy that I could really have fun with. I could relax with you. I knew that you wouldn't grab my breasts or run your hand up my dress the first time I let my guard down. My dates with other boys were marathon wrestling matches and by the time I got back home I was worn out and my cloths were a mess."

"Not all the girls I dated appreciated that."

"Yes, I know, but I did."

112

"We'd better join the others," he said. "Or we may be discovered yet."

"When are you going back?" she asked.

"Uncle Frank is taking me to the airport after the funeral. "My flight is at nine o'clock this evening."

"I'm going back to Columbus this afternoon. Let me take you."

"Do you live close to the airport?"

"Yes, I'm right on East Broad, not three miles away. We could have supper together."

"That sounds like a good idea. Where's a good place to eat?"

"We could go to the Desert Inn; it's not as fancy as it once was, but the food is still good."

They talked about how being independent had changed their outlook on life and how it had altered how they look at other people. They talked about her older sister and how her family's Victorian ideas, and the church, had suffocated her spirit and strangled her desires.

"I've tried to get her to come to Columbus just to visit a few days, she's afraid. She won't leave home without Mom. If I hadn't escaped when I did, I'd be the same way."

She was right about the Desert Inn, it had lost much of its class; however, the atmosphere was pleasant and the food was good. After they were finished eating they went into the lounge for a drink. The jukebox was loaded with early sixties music that reminded them of their high school days. They selected several old favorites and began to dance; they were alone on the floor. Early in the evening it was decided that he would use up the two days of grace on his travel orders, delay his flight and spend the next two days with her. Her small efficiency apartment was on the top floor of a building that had been one of the old city's exclusive apartments. Her one window faced west and provided a good view of downtown Columbus.

"It's not much, but it's all mine!"

"You certainly have an impressive view," he said, looking out over the city.

"You know," she said. "This entire west wing used to be one apartment. My little room here was part of a penthouse that had three bedrooms, each with its own bathroom, a kitchen, a dining room, and a foyer that was bigger than this room. The dining room would seat 30 guests and the living room had 17 windows and a fireplace."

"How'd you come to know so much about this place?"

"There's an old woman down the hall that has lived here for 30 years. She has the only remaining original apartment in the building. She and her husband moved here from New York in 1937 and she's never left the state since that time."

"What does her husband do?"

"He's on the state museum board or something like that. I know he collects antiques; their apartment is full of beautiful things."

She reached up and turned on the high, wall-mounted TV set, made him comfortable on the couch, opened the folding wall that hid the kitchenette and made some coffee. She placed a tray of cheese, crackers and green olives on the coffee table and settled down beside him.

"I must confess something to you," she said. "Your being here is not a casual coincidence. I planned it, every

114

move. I started working on it as soon as I heard you were coming home."

"I'm glad your plan worked; it's good to be here with you. You're even more beautiful than I remember. When I saw you at the church today I wanted to be with you. However, you must know that I feel different about things now. Now, I do want to grab your breasts and run my hand up your dress."

"I was hoping you would."

He pulled her closer to him and gently bit her on the neck.

"Oh," she sighed. "You have changed. The boy I knew didn't bite."

He nibbled on her neck and then her back as he unzipped her dress and unhooked her brassiere. Her dress and brassiere fell from her shoulders as he put his arms around her and cupped his hands under her breasts.

"Oh, boy," she said, taking a deep breath. "I like the change. Did you learn this in college or in the army?"

He didn't answer; he just turned her around to face him and pulled her legs up onto the couch. He held her in his arms and took her breast into his mouth. Her small, pink nipples were hard and she was breathing heavily when he ran his hand down inside her panties.

"Let's get into bed," she suggested, squeezing his hand between her legs.

He unfolded the couch, undressed and climbed into bed while she prepared herself in the bathroom. In a few minutes she appeared beside the bed in a shorty nightgown made entirely of black lace. He could tell that she had no panties on. She got into bed and cuddled close to him.

"We forgot to turn the TV off," she said.

"It does spoil the effect, doesn't it?" he said. She got up and walked over to the TV.

As she reached up to turn the set off, the shorty nightgown was pulled up to her waist. He smiled when she dropped her arm and turned around.

"What are you smiling about?" She asked.

"You are absolutely magnificent." He told her.

She smiled as she got back into bed with him.

Operation Minerva

CHAPTER 6
Vietnam
April 1969

At the Studies and Observation Group (SOG) Headquarters in Nha Trang, South Vietnam, a top-secret briefing in the SOG war room was about to start; the Operations Officer opened the briefing:

"Gentlemen, this briefing is top secret. You may not take notes except on the serialized blank paper provided in your planning guide packet. Sergeant Cook," the Operations Officer ordered, "hand out the planning guides and collect the receipts."

While the Sergeant carried out his orders, the Operations Officer continued:

"This initial briefing will be general in nature and will supply the necessary background information required for the planning of a successful mission. Your assignment, gentlemen, is to select personnel for the mission, to determine the type and amount of equipment required, and to recommend a training curriculum. The Commanding Officer will be in momentarily to personally brief you on the mission."

"Gentlemen," the Operations Officer said, "the Commanding Officer."

Operation Minerva

Everyone in the room came to attention and quietly awaited the Commander. The Group Commander mounted the platform:

"Be seated, gentlemen." After the noise of rustling paper and shifting chairs died down, the C.O. continued. "We have been asked to perform one of the most daring, and dangerous, missions in this war."

The Commander paused for a few seconds as if giving his comment time to make its way around the room.

"This is the type of mission the green berets were meant for. Before I get into details, I must again remind you that this is a top secret NOFORN[18] briefing. All participants in this operation will be U.S. citizens and selected from Special Forces troops."

Instant approval of this bit of information was indicted by the sighs of relief that echoed through the room. The Commander paused and motioned toward the back of the room. A tall, lean, civilian dressed in tailored jungle fatigues with no markings joined the Commander on the platform. Most of the officers in the room knew the identity of this visitor. He was Mr. Smith, an official at the American Embassy in Saigon, and an agent for the CIA. The Commander introduced Mr. Smith as an intelligence advisor from G2 and that he was going to give some background information for the mission. Mr. Smith was not concerned with social or military amenities; he just pointed to an organization chart and started talking:

---

[18] No Forign Nationals

Operation Minerva

"The top slot in the organization of North Vietnam belongs to the Central Committee of the Lao Dong (Communist) Party. All controls (Political and Military) ultimately come from the Central Committee. The Reunification Commission directly controls the National Front for the Liberation of South Vietnam. The Military Command is responsible for the military training of troops deployed into the South. The intelligence organization that is the counterpart of our CIA is the Central Research Agency. This agency directs the training and extensive undercover activities of double agents and special intelligence agents assigned to VC[19] units. This, gentlemen, brings us to the objective of your mission, the training of covert agents by the Central Research Agency."

He removed a black cover from a large map of North Vietnam; a bold red TOP SECRET NOFORN was stenciled across the top left and bottom right corners of the map. He picked up a pointer and continued:

"At Xuan Mai, 25 kilometers west of Hanoi on Highway 6, there is an elite North Vietnamese spy school operated by the Central Research Agency. This school is phase one of a two-phase training program that prepares covert agents for infiltration into Burma, Laos, Thailand, Cambodia, and South Vietnam. Phase two of the training program for operations directed into South Vietnam, Southern Laos, and Cambodia takes place at Dong Hoi. Dong Hoi is located on the coast 80 kilometers north of

---

[19] VietCong

the DMZ and is the gateway to the Ho Chi Minh trail into South Viet Nam."

He was like a robot in his presentation. He had no facial expressions, no excitement and no humor. He was a computer programmed only to give this briefing. He didn't even look at the map as he pointed to different cities, rivers, roads, and mountains; but he was always on target. He paused in the briefing and uncovered another map, then continued:

"Phase two, for operations directed into Burma, North Laos and Thailand is conducted at Moc Chau on Highway 6 between Hanoi and the Plaine of Jarres near the Laotian border. Your mission objective is to observe and photograph phase two operations at Moc Chau for possible identification of graduates that may be headed for Thailand. You are also charged with identifying any foreign influence that may be present at the training facility."

He stopped as abruptly as he started and asked if there were any questions. No one in the room made a sound so he nodded at the group commander and walked out. The Commander remounted the platform:

"I have proposed a HAELO[20] drop approximately 15 kilometers from the objective; delivery and pick-up will be handled by a special Air Force team out of Udorn, Thailand. The drop aircraft will be masked as one of a flight of attack aircraft making a raid on the out-skirts of Hanoi. The pick-up point is an isolated area near the Laotian border. My general guidelines are to select two

---

[20] High Altitude Exit Low Opening

Operation Minerva

teams of six men each. Follow the planning guide in selecting personnel. Only one team will go in, the second team will be used to replace any training casualties on team one; or, if there are more than three casualties, team two will go in. All training will be conducted in Thailand and all men will wear the 46th Special Forces unit flash. The code name for this operation is Minerva; the code name is classified Secret, keep it secret. We have two weeks training time and one week for administrative requirements and travel, so gentlemen, get busy!"

The Commanding Officer stepped off the platform and the room came to attention.

As the Commander walked out of the room, the Operations Officer mounted the platform:

"Gentlemen give me your attention please! This is Lieutenant Blair, our air liaison officer. He will spend the next three weeks with us to coordinate our efforts with the Air Force. I am sure you are all anxious to hear about the duties of this next Air Force Officer: This is Lieutenant Genie Francis, an air photo intelligence officer. She has been working in photo intelligence for eight months and was the first to recognize the target area as a possible site for the school. From now until the operation is executed we will receive daily aerial photographs of the target area. Lieutenant Francis will be available to you and later to the team to answer any questions that may arise on the interpretation of aerial photographs of the target area."

The officers in the room, five majors and two lieutenant colonels, immediately began to digest the information presented. After about forty minutes of study and talking, the group decided to separate into two committees; one for selection of personnel and one for selection of equipment. Each Lieutenant Colonel headed a committee of two Majors. The remaining Major was assigned a special duty, photographic equipment. Both committees agreed to have a joint meeting at 1600 hours on the following day to present their ideas for consideration. Major Wood, in charge of photographic equipment, doubted if he could have any hard information on his project in such a short time, he was excused from the meeting.

At 1600 hours the following day, Colonel Adams, in charge of personnel selection, was the first to speak:

"We have selected two Captains, two Lieutenants, two Senior NCOs, and ten   Sergeants. Only the officers and Senior NCOs will be discussed in detail. Sergeant Cook, will you hand out the folders now? Sergeant Cook has prepared detailed resumes on each of the sixteen candidates for us. Thank you, Sergeant, that will be all."

"I'll be outside, Sir, if you need anything else."

"First, we have Captain Alex Coxe, our selection for command of team one: He is a graduate of West Point and was the top man in his class at the Special Warfare School. He is on his third tour in Vietnam as a Green Beret and served with the CIA for several months during Operation Phoenix. He has always enjoyed an out standing rapport with his men. The enlisted men of his last unit gave him a plaque inscribed, 'To Captain Alex Coxe, the only officer in the U.S. Army that we would follow on a raid into Hell'. Any question, suggestions or complaints?"

Operation Minerva

All of the officers in the room indicated approval of Captain Coxe.

"Good!" said the Colonel. "Now, for the executive officer of team one." The Colonel turned to the next page: "First Lieutenant Patrick Deluca, graduate of Ohio State University, ROTC[21], OCS[22], and the Special Warfare School, he is a language specialist. This is his first tour in Vietnam and ..."

"Colonel," someone interrupted.

"Major Wood," said the Colonel. "Do you have something to add?"

"Yes, Sir," he said. "I know Lieutenant Deluca and he is very young and. . ."

"He's almost 24," the Colonel said, cutting Major Wood off.

"Yes, Sir, I know," said Major Wood, "but he looks like he's 18 and he often has pangs of self-consciousness when working with older more experienced men."

"Major," the Colonel said. "I sometimes have pangs of self-consciousness when I am working around old, crusty, jungle-hardened Green Berets, and I'm older than any of them. Let me read you a part of a letter-of-commendation given to Lieutenant Deluca by his OCS Commander: 'Candidate Deluca (now, Lieutenant Deluca) has set a new school record in the jungle warfare tactics phase of our training program.' I think that is a good recommendation and I have more if you want to hear it?"

---

[21] Reserve Officer Training Course
[22] Officer Candidate School

Operation Minerva

Once again, the officers in the room indicated their approval - except Major Wood.

"Next," said the Colonel. "We have Sergeant First Class Samuel Applewhite. Sergeant Applewhite is a black, professional soldier. He has three tours in Vietnam and three tours in Thailand. He is a 6th Degree Black Belt in Karate and an instructor of hand-to-hand combat. He is an intelligence specialist, speaks Vietnamese, he is a graduate of the Special Warfare School, the Thai Ranger School, and the Jungle Survival School in Panama. He has served with Captain Coxe on previous missions. They have an unbeatable record of success. Are there any questions?"

"Colonel, what if these men will not volunteer for this mission we have."

"Major," he asked. "How long have you been with SF[23]?"

"About three months," he answered.

"Well, Major, let me tell you something about Green Berets. They love three things. They love to fight, they love to drink, and they love to screw, not necessarily in that order."

The Colonel's comment triggered off several seconds of rowdy laughter.

"Not one of these men will turn down the chance to go on this mission, in fact," he added, "they would fight you for a position."

The Colonel continued to discuss the personnel selected for the mission and by 1800 hours he had completed his

---

[23] Special Forces

presentation and an agreement was made to adjourn until the following day.

After the other officers had gone, Colonel Adams called the C-Team Headquarters to locate Captain Coxe. At 1830 hours Captain Coxe walked into SOG headquarters and asked for Colonel Adams; the two officers were old friends, they had worked together during the Phoenix Project. They sat in the war room and discussed the mission at length and the Colonel presented Coxe with the list of men selected and approved for the mission by the committee.

Captain Coxe examined the list for several minutes, then asked the Colonel if he could make a special request.

"Sure," said the Colonel. "What is it?"

"Well," the Captain said. "There is a very special trooper that I would like to have on my team."

"That shouldn't be any problem," the Colonel replied.

"Yes, Sir, it may be." The Captain paused for a few seconds then added, "You see sir, the man that I want is a Warrant Officer."

"Oh, I see what you mean. . ." There was a long silence while the Colonel walked around the room scratching his head. "Is this man really worth the extra trouble? You know what a stink this is going to cause?"

"Yes, Sir, he is and I do."

"Write his name down and where I can get in contact with him. I'll see what I can do."

"Thank you, Sir," Coxe said.

The next day at 0900 hours, Colonel Jackson, head of the equipment committee, took the platform:

Operation Minerva

"Gentlemen," he said, "this briefing will be in the form of an Intelligence Estimate with our recommendations on each area followed by an open discussion to provide for recommendations from the floor."

Colonel Jackson opened his folder and started:

"Operation Minerva, Intelligence Estimate, Classification - TOP SECRET NOFORN.

First, the Mission: Observe, photograph, identify, and record operations at the special school at Moc Chau, North Vietnam in a effort to identify operatives headed for Thailand. Major Wood," said the Colonel, "has the necessary information on the photographic equipment and will cover that portion of the briefing, Major Wood."

Major Wood took the platform and began:

"I have contacted Mr. Smith at the Embassy in Saigon and Military Intelligence for help and direction in the selection of the photographic equipment. This is what we've come up with: Three black Nikon FTN SLR camera bodies with 50mm, 100mm, and 1000mm lowlight lenses; ten rolls of ASA 125 film, ten rolls of ASA 400 film, twenty rolls of ASA 1200 film, and ten rolls of high speed infrared film; two tripods, assorted filters, cable releases, and a small repair kit. According to the CIA and MI this should take care of any photographic needs."

The Major indicated to the Colonel that he was finished and the Colonel returned to the platform.

"Are there any questions or suggestions about the photographic section?"

The Colonel glanced around the room, there were no indications of disagreement so the Colonel continued:

Operation Minerva

"Next we have observation: For daylight observation we recommend the standard 7 x 50 binoculars, two each; for night observation, two starlight scopes with repair kits. We also have included a metascope for detection of any IR[24] radiation."

"Colonel," Major Elliott interrupted. "May I make a suggestion?"

"Please do, Major," insisted the Colonel. "That's why we're here."

"Sir," the Major continued. "Those binoculars are heavy as hell and impossible to hold still for any length of time unless you have something to rest them on."

"So, what do you suggest?" the Colonel asked.

"I suggest we include a tripod for the binoculars or an adapter so one of the camera tripods can be utilized."

"That's a good suggestion, Major," said the Colonel. "You take care of the problem and report your progress to me by 1600 hours tomorrow."

"Yes, Sir," replied the Major.

"Second," the Colonel said, returning to his briefing. "We have the Area-of-Operations:

The weather forecast for the area is 80 to 90 degrees during the day and 60 to 70 degree nights; no rain is forecast except for the usual seasonal short showers. This, we feel, will require no more than a sleeping bag liner and poncho for adequate protection."

The terrain in the AO[25] varies from flat lands in the East, to 8,000-foot mountains in the West in Laos; cover and

---

[24] Infrared
[25] Area of Operation

Operation Minerva

concealment should be no problem; however, we suggest a small camouflage net be included if possible.

If the HALO drop places the team near the selected area, there should be no major obstacles in their route, each man should be able to carry up to 100 pounds of equipment and still be able to move freely, we also feel that 100 pounds should be considered a maximum."

"Third," the Colonel said, as he paused to take a drink of water, "we have the Enemy Situation Report: This is not a heavily guarded area. The largest force, numerically, is the Civilian Village Defense Force; however, they are not very well trained and are poorly equipped. The next largest threat, the biggest threat, is the NVA[26] regular troops in the area, about thirty of them. The last, and I think least, threat to our men is the local Cong An (secret police), they usually just give the locals hell.

Fourth, Enemy Capabilities: Reports from rescued pilots and informants indicate the troops in the area stick to the main roads, footpaths, main waterways, and other clear trails. There are almost no vehicles in the area of operation, and the nearest helicopter is 45 minutes away."

"Fifth, Conclusions: The weapons to be used by the team should be enemy weapons. The distinctive sound of an M-16 would give away team position too readily and unnecessarily attract attention to inadvertent individual encounters; furthermore, if needed, ammunition can be taken from dead enemy troops - or stolen."

---

[26] North Vietnamese Army

Operation Minerva

The Colonel closed his folder and asked if there were any questions.

"How about communications?" one of the Majors asked.

"Communications," said the Colonel, "has been taken care of by the CIA, and that is all I know about that subject."

CHAPTER 7
The Team

46th Special Forces Company,
Lop Buri, Thailand

Dawson stopped in front of the DCO's[27] door and checked his uniform.

"Thank Good he called so early in the day," he said to himself, "or, knowing how this asshole is, I'd have to go home and change my..."

"Did you say something to me, Sir?" a sergeant asked as he passed in the hall.

"No. Sergeant, I'm just mumbling to myself."

"Is there anything I can help you with, Sir?"

"Well, maybe, do you have any idea why the Colonel wants to talk to me?"

"No, Sir, I don't. I've been lucky so far this morning; I haven't been in there yet...rots-a-ruck, Sir!" the Sergeant said as he continued down the hall.

Well, Colonel asshole, what do you want me for this morning? He thought, as he took a deep breath and knocked on the Colonel's door. Colonel Lafayette served with the 82nd and the 101st Airborne Divisions during the 'real war'; this was how he always referred to WWII,

---

[27] Deputy Commanding Officer

and he always called Southeast Asia 'a game room for boys.' After a brilliant start as a young airborne officer in WWII, winning the DSC, a silver star, a trunk full of bronze stars, and nine awards of the Purple Heart, Colonel Lafayette's military career cooled and stagnated almost as fast. He was now a very old man and very senior Lt. Colonel who was bitter and envious of young officers.

"Come in!" a voice commanded from the other side of the door. He stepped inside, closed the door, briskly snapped to attention and saluted.

"Chief Warrant Officer Dawson reporting as ordered, Sir," he said in a loud but not strained voice.

He held his salute, waiting for the Colonel to recognize him. Finally, the Colonel looked up from his desk and returned the salute.

"At ease," the Colonel said, then returned his attention to the papers on his desk.

Dawson stood quietly in front of the Colonels' desk watching him shuffle papers. What a flaming asshole, he thought; I wonder how long you have to practice to become the perfect asshole. The Colonel opened his center desk drawer, searched out a paper clip, meticulously tapped the papers on their edges until all were even, then placed the clip carefully in the upper left-hand corner. As he placed the papers in his out box, he again tapped the edges even and then aligned the new arrivals with the papers already in the box.

"Mister Dawson," he asked, as he leaned back in his chair, "why do you refer to yourself as Chief Dawson and not Mister like all other warrant officers?"

Operation Minerva

"Sir," he said. "Mister is for civilians, I'm not a civilian, I'm a professional soldier."

The Colonel opened his center desk drawer and pulled out a 201 file. Dawson could see his name and serial number across the top as the Colonel laid the folder down and started to leaf through it.

"You have a very interesting and varied background, Mister Dawson," the Colonel said, emphasizing the Mister.

"Yes, Sir,"

What the hell does he want? He thought, why does Colonel asshole have my 201 file?

"How long were you in the Navy?"

"Ten years, Sir."

"Why did you change over to the Army?"

"Rank and money, Sir," he replied in a cold matter-of fact tone.

"Why didn't you try for a warrant officer position with the Navy?"

"Sir, with the specialty I had in the Navy, to become a warrant officer was to be sentenced to a life of permanent sea duty."

"How did you get your warrant in the Army?"

"Sir, I wrote the Department of the Army a letter and enclosed a resume."

"You wrote DA and gave them your resume? How long did it take for you to get an answer from them?"

"Six weeks, Sir,"

"Six weeks!" the Colonel shouted. "Are you telling me that they offered you a position as a warrant officer on the strength of your resume in just six weeks?"

"Yes, Sir, that's right."

132

"What the hell did they do, send your fucking bars to you through the mail?"

"No, Sir," he replied calmly. "I had to go from Quonset Point Naval Air Station in Rhode Island to Fort Devens, Massachusetts and be interviewed by a board of Army officers."

The Colonel ignored his comment and started talking:

"I received a message today from the Embassy in Bangkok. The message was in 'Commanders Only' code and requests that you been given the opportunity to volunteer for a combat mission. It says that you will be under the command of a Captain Alex H. Coxe."

The Colonel stopped talking, got up and walked around the desk. He stood in front of Dawson for a while, looking at him.

"The message," the Colonel continued, "does not have your rank indicated, only your name with no service number. I notified the Embassy that you were a Warrant Officer and to please advise. I received a very terse reply that the Embassy knew your rank and that they expected your answer within the hour. The CO[28] is in the states for two weeks and there doesn't seem to be anyone here that knows shit about your past; so, why don't you tell me, what is it with you and the Embassy? Why are they so interested in you?"

"Well, Sir, I've done some work for them in the past and I guess they like the way I do things."

"What have you done for the Embassy," the Colonel asked.

---

[28] Commanding Officer

"Sir," he replied. "I'm not at liberty to discuss the subject."

His answer noticeably irritated the Colonel.

"Sit down, Dawson," he said, pointing to one of two lounge chairs separated by a small coffee table; the Colonel sat in the opposing chair.

"How old are you?" the Colonel asked.

"I'm thirty two, Sir."

"I wish I were a warrant officer," the Colonel said.

"Why, Sir? You make a hell-of-a lot more money than I do."

"Yes, I do, Mister Dawson, but money isn't everything. People don't look at you and ask themselves why you are only a warrant officer grade W2. A warrant officer can be fifty years old and be a warrant officer grade W2 and no one gives him a second look; however; be a fifty-year-old Lieutenant Colonel and see how many people stare at you. They stare at you, and you know they are asking themselves 'I wonder where he fucked-up? He must have really fucked something up to be frozen at 50'."

The Colonel continued to talk as Dawson sat emotionless looking at him and thinking. You poor bastard; this thing is like a cancer eating your guts out. Jesus, if this is the way he looks at life, it's no wonder he is such an asshole with everyone. Old man, how long have you been torturing yourself like this? I'll bet you have an old lady at home that gripes at you all the time because she is not a general's wife, doesn't she? The Colonel had stopped talking but it was a few seconds before Dawson was aware of the silence, then he asked the Colonel:

"Sir, why don't you retire? Go home and go fishing or golfing and forget all this bullshit!"

"I would, Chief," the Colonel said. "But it's like having a mistress that you can't live with and can't live without; I love the Army, it's been my whole life, I have nothing else."

He called me chief, Dawson thought, he actually called me chief; I wonder if he meant to or if it was just an accident?

"Well, shit, Chief, I didn't call you in here to talk about my troubles. What's your answer? What do I tell the Embassy? Do you volunteer for this mission not knowing what it is?" He looked at the Colonel for a few seconds and then answered. "Yes, Sir, I'll go."

The Colonel stood up and walked over to the door.

"I'm going to S2 for a minute, we'll talk more when I get back." The Colonel pointed to a cooler and told Dawson, "Help yourself to a Coke."

"Thank you, Sir," he replied as the Colonel closed the door behind him.

Dawson pulled up into the courtyard of his house and as he was chaining his motorcycle to a palm tree, Seadang appeared on the balcony drying her hair. The white silk pasin[29] wrapped around her waist was decorated with bright tropical flowers. A perfect complement to her honey-golden skin, he thought. As he looked up at her, she threw her head back and let her waist-long hair settle around her shoulders. She picked up her comb and ran it

---

[29] A Thai version of a sarong.

through the silken strands. He leaned back on his bike and looked at her.

"My god," he said aloud, but to himself, "What else could a man ask for in life? I live in a tropical garden paradise in a country blessed with eternal summer and I share this garden paradise with an old woman who is a wonderful cook and a beautiful young girl who treats me like I'm a rock star."

She stopped combing her hair and leaned on the low railing with both hands.

"What you look at?" she asked.

"You!"

"You talk crazy; you have seen me many times."

"Yes, I have." He answered. Then asked himself, "Have I …, really?"

"Go inside, food ready."

After he had eaten, he sat back and started to read some magazines he had brought with him form Bangkok. Seadang sat across from him and said, "You must go away again, yes?"

"How did you know?" he asked, looking at her, "how did you know?"

"I can see it in your eyes. I can always tell when you must go away and leave us."

"Yes," he said, "I must go away again ... for a long time. I will be gone for five or six weeks this time. I'll pay the rent and give you additional money to live on while I'm gone. If you need more money, Captain Carver will have it for you. Ok?"

"When do you go?" she asked.

"Tomorrow," he said, looking away, unable to look at her, "Tomorrow."

Operation Minerva

The old woman and Seadang always got depressed when Dawson had to go away so he would never tell them until the last minute. He did not know if they were afraid that he might get killed and they would have to find a new home or if they really missed him not being there; or, maybe both.

Special Forces Camp B4636
Southwest of Nakham Phanom, Thailand,

A communications trailer located near the S2 office served as an operations center for team one. Inside the trailer Captain Coxe, the commander of team one, was conducting a terrain study with Lt. Francis and SFC Applewhite, the senior enlisted man on team one. Lt. Deluca, the XO* of team one, was reviewing COMSEC procedures with SFC Tamashiro and SFC Lovejoy. Sergeant Cooke entered the trailer and handed the Captain a message. After reading the message, a smile crossed the Captain's face. He looked up and spoke to the team:

"Men, I just received the name of the final member of our team. He'll arrive at 1700 hours today on the mail run from Udon. I personally requested Chief Dawson be..."

"Chief," interrupted Lovejoy, "I hope by Chief, you mean he's a god-damned Indian."

Lovejoy was a Puerto Rican with a constant chip on his shoulder; however, he was a tried and proved Green Beret of exceptional ability. He didn't make friends easily but once you were a friend you were a friend for life.

Operation Minerva

"At ease, Lovejoy, and let the Captain finish!" Applewhite ordered.

The Captain walked over to the table where Tamashiro and Lovejoy were working and placed his hand on Lovejoy's shoulder.

"Let me tell you about Jack Dawson: I first met him at group headquarters in Nha Trang about two years ago, he had just finished training at Bragg after entering the army from the navy. We had two Viet Cong terrorists that had been captured in the city the previous night. We interrogated the two men for thirteen hours without success and were about to give up on them. Chief Dawson came up with a beautiful idea and we decided to try it. He suggested we take the two up in a helicopter and tell them they were going to be thrown out if they did not give us the coordinates of an arms cache known to be located in a cave somewhere on Hill 235. The prisoners were blindfolded and pushed aboard a helicopter. We flew around for a few minutes and interrogated the two men; they would not answer any of our questions, so we told the senior man that we were going to throw the junior man out. Our hopes were that the senior man would have more information. We pushed the first man out and you could hear his scream fade as he fell from the helicopter. Now, before you get too excited about it. When we pushed him out we were about 20 feet over the bay and a boat was ready to pull him out of the water as soon as he hit.

So, Dawson and I grabbed the second man and started pushing him slowly toward the open door. We held him in the door momentarily so he could feel the air circulating around him; we asked one more time if he would talk. He said no.

On our cue, our Vietnamese interpreter began screaming that we should 'throw the Viet Cong bastard out' and began kicking him in the back trying to force him out. The prisoner started screaming and begged us not to throw him out because he would tell us everything we wanted to know. The helicopter flew us to an area identified by the prisoner. We were flying low and slow trying to pinpoint an area for a team insertion. Suddenly, we were being shot at from all directions, the prisoner was killed immediately and one door gunner was wounded. The helicopter was losing power and the pilot said we would have to land. We landed in a very steep area. The pilot could only put one skid on the ground. He told us to jump out on the down hill side and run like hell; he said the aircraft would turn over as soon as he let it go. After we cleared the area, the pilot jumped out and threw himself flat on the ground on the up hill side of the air craft. The helicopter rolled over on its side and caught fire.

The pilot, co-pilot, two gunners, Dawson, and I were stranded on a Viet Cong held mountain. The co-pilot had transmitted a mayday call so we expected help within minutes. We knew the aircraft fire and smoke would draw every VC in the area so we decided to get away from there as fast as possible. The air-crewmen had never been on the ground before so Dawson took the lead and I brought up the rear. We had seen a clearing in the woods before we crashed so Dawson was taking us there so we could be picked up. Contact was made almost immediately with five Viet Cong who, I think, must have wanted to capture us alive because they did not open fire on us, but attacked in hand-to-hand combat. Now, Dawson always carries three knives, two Gerber Mark II fighting knives and a standard issue K-bar; he always quips that he has two to throw and one to go. Well! Dawson silently wasted two of the Viet Cong with his throwing knives before we were fully aware of the attack, then he killed a third in hand-to-hand combat with his K-bar. The helicopter crew killed one and the last of the five attackers ran away. Well, to cut the story short, one of the pilots directed a rescue helicopter into the clearing with his survival radio and we got the hell out of there."

"So, he's good with a knife. Does that qualify him to go on this mission?" asked Lovejoy.

"Chief Dawson," the Captain continued, "is a communications expert, a qualified Green Beret, a demolition expert, a sniper, SCUBA qualified, a photographer, and a master at survival, escape, and evasion. He has attended the U.S. Air Force desert E&E[30] school in Arizona, the U.S. Navy arctic E&E school out of Whidbey Island, Washington, and the U.S. Army jungle E&E school in Panama; and …, he has never been captured. I think Dawson is qualified to go with us."

A deep silence settled over the room for several seconds, then Lovejoy asked,

"They didn't give this dude a serial number like 007 did they?"

---

[30] Escape and Evasion

Operation Minerva

Lovejoy's comment filled the room with laughter and the Captain suggested they get back to work. Somewhere in the northeast section of Thailand, an Army helicopter, on and ash-and-trash mission set a course for B4636. Aboard the helicopter, sitting on the deck and wedged between two large mail bags, Jack Dawson was thinking about his next assignment. I wonder what Captain Coxe has hold of now? It must really be hot for that message to be delivered through the U.S. Embassy. A secret message with nothing in it that you wouldn't normally say over the phone and transmitted in "Commanders Only" code, I don't think this is going to be an R&R[31]. Where are we going … Cambodia, Laos, North Vietnam, China? Maybe we are going to kidnap Ho Chi Minh! He laughed to himself.

"Hey, Sir!"

The crew chief leaned over the mailbags and shouted as he pointed out the door to a small group of buildings located some distance from a small lake.

"The Camp."

Dawson sat up and looked out as the aircraft circled the camp waiting clearance to land and a smoke to indicate wind direction. Camp B4636 looked clean and well organized, almost like a Boy Scout Camp. A jeep emerged from the camp and raced to an area that been cleared and marked as a helipad. One of the men popped a yellow smoke grenade and the pilot, observing the surface wind, started in. As the helicopter was hovering for touchdown, Dawson could see Captain Coxe standing

---

[31] Rest and Relaxation

about fifteen meters from the helipad shielding his eyes from the rotor wash and trying to keep his beret from blowing away. Dawson jumped out as soon as contact was made with the ground and ran over the Coxe. The two shook hands and started to walk up to camp. The Captain asked the driver of the operations jeep to take Dawson's bag to the team OP trailer. No mention was made of the mission during the long walk up the hill. Both men wanted desperately to get on with the business-at-hand but the necessity for secrecy dictated postponement, so they talked of old friends and other times.

Coxe stopped momentarily in the vestibule of the operations trailer and briefed Dawson.

"Lieutenant Deluca, my XO[32]., must go to Bangkok in the morning to give the brass at the embassy a briefing on our operations plan and, I hope, bring back approval. I thought it would be good for him to practice his presentation in front of a live audience and at the same time he can brief you."

As the Captain opened the door to the briefing room, Lieutenant Deluca called the team to attention.

"As you were," the Captain said, entering the room. "Lieutenant, are you ready?"

"Yes, Sir!" Deluca replied.

Coxe walked over to the table were Dawson had already taken a seat with the team. "What was your decision on the weapons section of your briefing?" asked the Captain.

"I decided to keep it in, Sir!" replied Deluca.

---

[32] Executive Officer

Operation Minerva

"Good! Let's hear it," said Coxe.

During the briefing, Lieutenant Francis could not keep here eyes off Dawson. She had visions of a much bigger man from the story the Captain had told; she had also pictured him as being rough and hard looking; she had even foreseen scars on his face. He had none of these characteristics. She guessed from looking at him that he was about five-foot eight, maybe one hundred forty pounds, and about thirty years old. How could this little man with soft blue eyes and gentle features hide such a killer tiger inside? She mused and was intrigued by the ambiguity. Lieutenant Francis' interest in Dawson did not go unnoticed. Captain Coxe, observing her actions, jotted down a short note and passed it to Dawson. Dawson looked at the note,

"Don't look now, but I think Genie has the hots for you."

After reading the note, he folded it and pushed in down into the "burn only" trash can at his end of the table. After a short pause he looked over at Genie. Her face turned red as they looked at each other for just and instant.

My God, Dawson thought, a young lady that blushes. I haven't seen a woman blush in 15 years.

Dawson was totally captured by Genie; he was flattered that a young woman at least ten years his junior, should express even the slight interest in him, especially with all the young studs running around camp.

After the briefing was over, Captain Coxe introduced Dawson to each person in the room. However, he introduced Genie last, and for a good reason, he invited her to accompany Dawson and him to the club for a drink. She accepted immediately. The club was empty so the Captain acted as bartender. After Dawson and Genie started talking freely, the Captain found an excuse to leave them alone.

"I think the Captain is playing Cupid," Dawson said, looking down into his drink.

"Do you mind?" Genie asked.

"No, I need all the help I can get."

"I can't believe that," she said.

"Well, it's true, I'm just not too aggressive with ladies. I need to know a woman is interested in me before I'll approach her. I don't handle rejection well at all."

"As good looking as you are," she said, "I would think the girls would always be after you."

"I haven't noticed any lines forming up. I think most women like men who are more glib and sophisticated. And, I have never been much of a competitor. For me to really have a good relationship with a woman she must not only be physically attractive but mentally attractive. I must be emotionally involved with her and that requires time and time is something that I normally do not have."

Dawson sat staring into his glass for several seconds, then said:

"Excuse me, I didn't mean to wander off."

"Sounds to me like you're afraid to make a commitment," she said in a joking manner.

"No. Well, maybe," he said.

 "Let's talk about you" he said, straightening himself up in his chair and finishing off his drink.

She thought for a while, then said:

"Well, I'm here with you, and not with any of the other men that have been hitting on me. That should tell you that I like older, more experienced, quiet men who do not feel they have to prove themselves. I don't like men that go pole-vaulting around the room screaming like Tarzan at the sight of every female."

"You blushed when we were looking at each other in the briefing room. I haven't seen a woman blush in years."

"Don't let my blushing deceive you," she said. "I blush from embarrassment not innocence. I got that from my Mother, she is fifty and still blushes."

They sat quietly for a few moments sipping their drinks. She put her hand on his and said:

"May I ask you a question?"

"Sure, go ahead."

"This may sound dumb but why do you do what you do? You know what I mean …, the mission. Do all you guys have a death wish?"

He did not have to think about his answer because he'd been asked this same question many times in his career.

"I do what I do for two reasons: First, I like it. Second, I'm good at it."

"Don't you worry about dying?" she asked.

"Green Berets have a saying, 'If I don't get killed today, I have nothing to worry about, and if I do get killed today, I still have nothing to worry about.'"

The club was starting to fill up and the drunks were getting rowdy, so she invited him to her BOQ room for another drink and some private conversation. In her room they listened to soft music and talked until one o'clock in the morning.

"We both have a lot of work waiting on us in the morning," he explained. "I should be going". She walked him to the door and stood close to him, invitingly close.

Operation Minerva

He took her in his arms, kissed her neck and ran his face and fingers through her hair.

"God, you smell good."

"Tabu," she said.

He kissed her and held her a moment longer, he thought, I'll bet I could go to bed with her right now; but, maybe all this is not really what it seems. He kissed her again, said goodnight, and went to his room.

The next morning the team met in the operations trailer for a conference. The Captain was early and had an outline of the topics for discussion listed on the chalkboard:

1. Infiltration and Assembly
2. Movement to Observation Post
3. Movement from Observation Post
4. Exfiltration
5. Equipment
6. Personnel
7. Communications
8. Rules of Engagement
9. Intelligence Estimate Summary
10. Escape and Evasion--Rally Points

"I have listed," the Captain started, "ten major points of discussion, I could have listed fifty if I had wanted to get into the minutiae; however, we only have a few days left to iron out our problems, divide the duties and hold the necessary training. The primary duty assignments will be as follows:

Mr. Dawson and Sergeant Lovejoy will take care of photography, Lieutenant Deluca and Sergeant Tamashiro will take care of communications. Sergeant Applewhite and I will be working with Lieutenant Francis on a constant updating of the area intelligence."

The Captain paused, turned some papers over and continued.

"Three nights this week and three nights next week, we will have 'full team' night maneuvers. Sometime during the next nine days, we must work in weapons qualification and have Sergeant Applewhite give us a refresher course in hand-to-hand combat. Let's see now, what else do I have?"

The Captain paused once again and searched his papers.

"Oh yes," he said. "Mr. Dawson and I will work out our escape and evasion procedures. He will give a briefing one afternoon next week on our E&E plans in conjunction with some tips on the finer points of E&E. We have a lot to do men, let's get with it."

CHAPTER 8
Trouble At Our Door

The club door slammed open and a sergeant shouted:
"Grab your shit, men. The village at the bottom of the hill is under attack by Thai terrorists."
The camp's quick reaction force was assembled in minutes and on their way down the hill. They moved as quickly as possible. However, they were alert and expecting an ambush at any time. The Commander placed the camp on red alert and all available men were ordered to the perimeter. As Dawson was running out of the BOQ with his gear he saw Genie with an M-16.
"Where are you going?"
"On the perimeter," she replied.
"Ahhhhh," he cried, as though he were in pain. "Have you ever shot an M16?"
"Yes, when I was in boot camp."
"How long ago was that?"
"About four years ago. Why?"
"I would feel better if I knew you were safe. You are too important to our mission to get yourself wounded. Please, come with me."
He grabbed her hand and took her to the operations trailer.

Operation Minerva

"Sergeant Cook, bolt this door and don't let anyone in without positive identification."
"Yes, Sir!"
"Please stay here where you'll be safe, Ok? Do it for me?"
"Okay," she said, "I'll stay here."
He pulled her hand up and pressed it hard against his face, then he turned and vanished out the door. She stood motionless, her eyes fixed on the closed door. The noise from the other side made her think of another time in her life, when she was fifteen, that she was pushed behind a door for her safety. She was in Jamaica with her Mother and Father when the news of the Little Rock riots hit the local papers and radio. Her memories were so vivid that she could feel the hot Jamaican sun on her body, feel the confinement of the small area behind the door, smell the stink of the urine soaked alley. She remembered the little pink sundress that she was wearing and that she had gotten blood on it because the rough wall had cut her back. Her hands recalled the memory of the hot steel door shaking and thumping and pressing her violently against the course texture of the wall. Then, a warm flood of emotion overcame her and tears filled her eyes as she remembered the sight of her Father as he pulled the door away; he was covered with blood. When the disturbance broke out, she and her Father were walking on a side street; her Mother had stayed at the hotel. At first they had no idea what all the agitation, screaming and marching was about. They went into a small souvenir shop and were told by the owner that they should return to their hotel immediately, that they would be safe there. They tried to avoid the crowds by using small back

streets and alleys. Just a few hundred feet from the hotel three men cornered them and began shouting obscenities. Her Father told them that they were English, not American. Two of the men believed the story and started to turn away, the third, however, wanted to see some proof. Her Father was an Air Force officer and had been stationed in England and still had his international drivers license. He did not believe these men could read, but he handed it to them. The third man was becoming more and more agitated. He grabbed the billfold from her Father's hand. "Let us see what money you have. English or American?" The sight of American money set all three into a rage. They accused them of being Yankee bigots and racists. One of the men suggested that they rape her to 'pay back the white racist' for what they were doing to their American Negro brothers. Then the third man pulled a large switch blade knife from his pocket. Her Father shoved her behind a steel door that was propped open, grabbed a broom handle from a trash barrel and faced the three men. The first to go down was the man with the knife.

He broke the broom handle over the man's wrist and then jabbed the broken end into the man's face. As the man grabbed his face her Father kicked him in the testicles. A backhand with the broom handle caught the second man across the face. A sidekick to the knee combined with a sharp blow to the neck with the broom handle knocked the third man to the ground.

The second man grabbed her Father in a bear hug from behind. The first man pulled a piece of wood off the building and aimed a blow at her Father's head. Half way through the stroke her Father jerked his head to the side and bent over; the blow caught the second man on the forehead and he crumpled to the ground. At that point, the police that had been dispatched to guard the Americans at the hotel arrived and captured all three attackers.

She found out later in life, from her Father, that the three men were actually young hoodlums taking advantage of the situation to rob tourists. Since the day of the attack, she thought that her Father was the bravest man in the world. She had always had the idea that she would never get married until she found a man just like him.

Another warm flood of emotion filled her breast. This time it was one of excitement and eagerness as she thought about Dawson.

"Are you the man I've been waiting for, Jack Dawson?" she whispered, still looking at the door.

Halfway to the village, the Thai QRF[33] Commander split his force into three teams. He and four American advisors, plus ten Thai rangers circled around to enter the village from the north. The Thai executive officer with a similar force would enter from the east and a smaller blocking force of ten rangers was sent to secure and hold the only remaining access to the village - the south footpath. After the Commander's team (to the north) and the blocking force (to the south) were in position, the Commander gave the order to enter the village. At first, the village looked deserted. However, the Commander's team found the bodies of five government troops assigned to protect the village. They had been killed by

---

[33] Quick Reaction Force

surprise attack, probably by someone they knew. The soldiers had been eating supper around their cooking fire. One soldier that had been sitting close to the fire had thrown his left arm up to protect his head from his killer's machete; his hand had been cut off as the machete slashed through to his skull. As the dead soldier lay on his right side, his arm still up in a protecting gesture and resting his head on a stone, his eyes were wide open as if staring at his severed hand simmering in the hot grease over the fire.

The two main teams joined forces in the center of the village where they found the village mayor and two school teachers that had been tied to trees and executed, each had been hacked and tortured with machetes, then shot 30 to 40 times each. The mayor's wife was lying at his feet. She had been stripped nude, her legs forced wide apart, and her pelvis split with a machete. She was still alive as the team entered the village square. The Thai Commander ordered his medic to give her something to kill the pain, 'so she can die in peace,' he said. As the medic was giving her a shot, a brief fire fight broke out to the south, seconds later the blocking force radioed that they had killed three terrorists trying to escape through their position, the Commander ordered the blocking force bring the dead men into the village for identification. In the mayor's hut the team found the only living member of his family. His eight-year-old daughter had been saved because her Mother had thrown her into a hole and covered her up. The team found her sitting in the doorway of the hut rocking her little sister. Her sister had been killed with a machete blow to the shoulder that had cut off her left cheek and ear. The sight was more than the QRF Commander could handle. Tears came to his eyes as he picked the little girl up in his arms and told her:

"You'll be my daughter now, I have all boys and my wife has always wanted a little girl. You can live with us in the safety of the camp."

He knew he could not leave her in the village because the terrorists would be back to kill her as soon as they found out she was alive.

The three terrorists who were killed trying to escape were identified as farmers who lived in the outlying areas of the province. They said they had seen them in the village market selling rice, chickens and pigs to the villagers.

About one hour later the terrorists made a harassment attack on the camp; however, there were no casualties in the five-minute firefight. After the perimeter was secured, Dawson returned to the operations trailer for Genie.

"I didn't know they were having any terrorist problems here," she said. "I thought Thailand was safe!"

"That is one of the best kept secrets I know of. The American public has no idea what's going on here and I don't know why Washington doesn't tell them. Most of the Thais are indifferent to radical politics due to the absence of any critical socioeconomic tensions that can be exploited. However, China, by way of Laos, is trying to convince the Thais in the North East that they are unhappy. And, it would seem that they have a few recruits. We've had Special Forces troops killed here fighting with Thai and Lao terrorists. Each time, they're retroactively transferred to Vietnam and added to Nam's

KIA* list. My Mother cut out a newspaper article and mailed it to my APO[34] address in San Francisco. The article, in Time Magazine and written by a leading reporter, said that there were 'absolutely no Special Forces troops or CIA in Thailand.' My Mother's note on the article asked 'Where are you?' I had a tough time convincing her that I was, in fact, in Thailand."

"I don't understand," she said. "Why we should keep all this terrorist activity quiet?"

"I don't understand either," he replied. "Thailand is going through some of the early stages of communist development similar to Vietnam. Still, the biggest deterrent for Communism in Thailand is the fact that the Thais are, for the most part, happy and satisfied with their life and with their government. You can't incite people to revolt who are satisfied. You must first convince them that they are really not happy."

He walked her to the BOQ then headed for the B-team operations center. Captain Coxe and Lieutenant Deluca were there when he arrived.

"Has the QRF force reported in yet?" he asked.

"Yes," the Captain answered. "They have the village secured and are going to remain there until morning. The Thai Commander is going to station a permanent team of rangers in the village to prevent this from becoming a habit."

"You don't think it had anything to do with us?" he asked.

"No," the Captain said. "I don't think so."

---

[34] Army Post Office

Operation Minerva

"Do you think it's over now, I mean for the night, anyway?" he asked.

"Keep your weapon handy, the camp Commander has warned us that they sometimes try to infiltrate the camp after their harassment attacks. "

"What a hell-of-a-way to run a war," he mumbled to himself as he left operations.

On the way back to the BOQ, he saw a figure moving slowly through the shadows. Dawson walked past then circled around. He could tell by the size and build that the man he was about to grab was a Thai. He moved silently up to within one meter of the figure then made a small noise, on purpose. The terrorist turned around just in time to catch Dawson's jump boot in his face, he went down instantly and did not move. He carried the unconscious terrorist back to the operations center and called the Operations Officer outside.

"Is this one of your terrorists?" he asked.

"Where did you find him?"

"He was sneaking around the supply building."

They blindfolded the prisoner and took him into Operations. The Operations Officer told his radioman to notify the Royal Thai Special Warfare Center in Lop Buri that a Thai terrorist had been captured inside the wire.

"Ask them what we should do with him. Also, notify the camp duty officer that we have captured a terrorist trying to get into the supply building. Suggest to him that he should search the area because there may be more."

Once again Dawson started for the BOQ and a night's sleep.

CHAPTER 9
The Night Jump

American air base near Udorn, Thailand, One week before Operation Minerva.

Captain Coxe and Captain Kenny, the commander of team two, had their teams lined up in two columns waiting the signal to board a C-130 for the last training night jump. Each commander made a last minute inspection of his team. This was the third night jump and last chance to practice mid-air assembly to ensure a tight LZ[35] formation. For safety reasons, a water drop was chosen for the last training jump. A water drop would reduce the chances of injury on this last jump and would prepare the team for a possible inadvertent landing in the Song Da (Black River) in North Vietnam. The pilots had not boarded the aircraft but the crew had the APU[36] running, the interior red lights on, and the ramp down. Inside the aircraft a USAF[37] loadmaster and an army jumpmaster were checking the aircraft to insure it was safe for the jumpers. Team one would jump first from the starboard side, and fifteen minutes later team two would jump from the port side. Drop time was 0400 hours, the

[35] Landing Zone
[36] Auxiliary Power Unit
[37] United States Air Force

same time as the mission was planned for to duplicate expected lighting of sky, ground, and horizon over the objective near Moc Chau. A blue station wagon pulled up in front of the aircraft and three Air Force officers in flight gear got out. Two officers boarded the aircraft and climbed to the flight deck. The third officer walked back into the cargo compartment and spoke to the loadmaster.

"Do you have the logbook?"

"Yes, Sir! Right here." The loadmaster picked up the log book and handed it to the pilot.

"Have all the gripes been worked off?"

"Yes, Sir, flight line radio maintenance was here before we were finished refueling and replaced the DME[38] indicator and the number two UHF[39]."

"Are the troops ready to go?"

"They're waiting on us, Sir."

"Very good, load 'em up," he said as he turned and walked forward to the flight deck.

The loadmaster, cupped his hands around his mouth to direct this voice and overcome the noise of the APU[40], shouted from inside the aircraft at the waiting troops.

"Load up, load up."

In the cockpit, surrounded by the warm glow of red instrument lights, the pilot sat down in the left seat and stretched his arms over his head. He yawned and then with a deep exhalation and look of drowsiness spoke to his co-pilot. "You know, Fred, I have always thought

---

[38] Distance Measuring Equipment
[39] Ultra High Frequency radio
[40] Auxiliary Power Unit

that Green Berets were crazy. Well, this proves it. Anyone who would jump out of an aircraft at 28,000 feet at 4:00 a.m. has got to be crazy as hell."

The loadmaster, in the cargo compartment, called the pilot to report the troops loaded and requested permission to close the ramp. As the ramp closed, the aircraft began to taxi to the active runway for takeoff. Forty minutes later the pilot called the loadmaster and gave him a 10-minute warning. The jumpmaster gave team one the 10-minute warning as the loadmaster opened the door. At the 5-minute warning the jumpmaster started his final series of commands. The final command was signaled by the green light over the door. The jumpmaster hit the man in the door on the back and gave the final command. "Go!"

Each member in turn was hit on the back and given the go command. The six team members exited the aircraft in less than 5 seconds. Once outside the aircraft and free falling at 170-feet per second, the sound of the aircraft soon faded away and the team was engulfed in total silence. The six free falling parachutists had approximately two minutes and thirty seconds to join up before reaching the 2500-foot parachute-opening altitude indicated over the LZ. Each member of the team had a strip of high intensity glow tape taped to the top of his helmet. The tape was activated just before jumping by an ultraviolet light in the aircraft and glowed for about 2 minutes after exiting. The glowing tape provided the only means of join-up during night jumps. The Captain gave the command to join up as he extended his arms and legs as far as possible for maximum drag. Lt. Deluca, the last man out, was tucked up tight and accelerating. He had to make up the four-second lead of the Captain. As the team joined up, each member took his place in the circle. They watched their altimeters as the Captain called out a countdown. At the command to 'pull' as planned, the circle first scattered to avoid mid-air entanglements, then each man deployed his main chute. The Captain delayed his opening slightly to ensure being first on the LZ. He observed his men as their chutes opened. On the lake in one of the three retriever boats the LZ officer was observing the drop with a starlight scope.

"I can see them now," he said. "One, two, three...four, five, and there is number six; the join-up is complete."

The LZ officer continued to observe the drop as he ordered the radio operator to notify the aircraft to continue on schedule and to alert the boats for pick up.

"The circle is dispersing, got one open, two open three, four, and five open - no wait! Four has a roman candle* and six has not...okay, six is open. Pull your reserve four! Pull your reserve!"

As jumper four streaked toward the ground, the troops in the pick-up boats used bullhorns to try to get him to deploy his reserve chute. Seventy feet over the lake, on the swampy East end, four's chute filled with air and broke his impact as he slammed into 3-feet of water. The Captain, having followed the jumper down until his own chute opened automatically, landed beside the injured jumper at the same instant the retriever boat arrived. The LZ officer grabbed the radio hand set from the radioman and took direct command of the emergency.

"Air Force 5-7-3-2 abort second drop! 5-7-3-2 abort second drop, return to base. Army MEDVAC 3-0-0-5 stand-by for a mission. Stand-by but do not start engine until all jumpers are on the LZ! MEDVAC 3-0-0-5, I say again, do not start engine until all jumpers are on the LZ!"

"Retriever three, what is the condition of the jumper?"

"LZ command, this is retriever three, the jumper is alive but unconscious - over."

"Retriever three - command, who is it?

"It's Lovejoy, Sir!" boat three answered.

"Retriever two, this is LZ command, how many jumpers do you have on board now?"

"LZ command, this is retriever two, we have three jumpers on board -over."

"Retriever three - command, how many jumpers do you have?"

"LZ command, this is retriever three, we have three jumpers on board and are on our way to the north shore - over."

"MEDVAC 0-0-5, this is LZ command, have you been monitoring? Over."

"LZ command, this is 0-0-5, we have been monitoring and will rendezvous with boat three on the north shore - over."

"Red Dog* operations, this is LZ command."

"LZ command, this is Red Dog - go ahead."

"Red Dog - LZ command, call Udorn operations on HF and have them notify the hospital of our emergency. Has anyone notified RED Dog 6, over?"

"LZ command - Red Dog, Red Dog 6 is being notified - over."

"Red Dog - LZ command, roger -out."

The night air was cool and calm causing a slight mist to form over the lake. The coxswain of boat three killed the engine and let the boat glide silently into shore. As the bow of the boat ran aground, Captain Coxe and the boat radioman jumped into knee-deep water and pulled the boat up onto the grassy shore. Lovejoy was gently removed from the boat and placed on the grass to await the helicopter. The Captain picked out a landing area for the helicopter and set out a strobe light. At the first sound of the approaching helicopter, Captain Coxe made radio contact and informed the pilot that he would be acting as ground control for the landing.

"MEDVAC 3005, this is ground control, can you see my strobe? Over."

"Roger - ground control, I have your strobe. What is the best heading for my approach? Over."

"005 - make your approach on a heading of 350 degrees. There is no wind. Over."

"Ground control - 005, are there any obstacles in the approach path of landing area? Over."

"005 - ground control, a heading of 350 degrees will bring you in over the longest part of the lake so a normal approach to the strobe from 500 AGL[41] feet will keep you clear of the trees. Your point of touchdown is in a grassy area that is 50 meters deep and 200 meters wide. The area is bounded on the south by the lake and on the north, east, and west by 100-foot trees. There are no wires - over."

"Roger ground control, I'm on my way in."

---

[41] Above Ground Level

Operation Minerva

The Captain stood behind the strobe light and observed the helicopter's approach over the lake, as the aircraft got closer, its landing and searchlights flooded the area with illumination. Immediately upon touchdown two medics carrying a litter and medical bag jumped from the ship and ran over to Lovejoy. After a short examination, Lovejoy was carefully placed on a stretcher and loaded aboard the waiting helicopter. Captain Coxe gave the pilot an all-clear signal as the helicopter came to a hover. The pilot made a hovering turn to 170 degrees and took off over the lake, within seconds the helicopter disappeared into the night. With the helicopter out of sight the members of team one slowly began to move around collecting equipment and loading it on a pick-up. Later, Sergeant Cook, in the operations jeep, pulled up beside the truck and offered the Captain, Deluca and Dawson a ride up to camp. Before the Captain had a chance to answer, Sergeant Applewhite told him to go on, that he and Tamashiro would finish up. After the jeep pulled away, Tamashiro threw the last chute onto the truck and Applewhite placed the three PRC-25 radios on top.

"Applewhite," Tamashiro asked, "why do you take care of the Captain like he was your own kid? I've never seen an NCO[42] take care of an officer like you take care of him." Applewhite dug down under the wet parachutes to an ice chest and pulled out two beers. He threw Tamashiro one and then laid back on the grass.

---

[42] Non-Commissioned Officer

"Do you know who the Captain's daddy was?" Applewhite asked.

"I know he was a general, that's all."

"Well," Applewhite continued, "his daddy was General Vincent Chase Coxe, a personal friend and confidant of the Kennedys. I was on the General's staff for six years; he was a soldier's general. He would have made the top slot if he had lived a little longer. The General died almost five years ago from a heart attack."

"I first saw the Captain when he was still at West Point. I drove the General to the Point to visit the Captain during his last year there. He didn't see me because I stayed in the car. However, two years later when the Captain took his first command, the General asked me to go along to keep him out of trouble. I've been following him around ever since. I think he'll be a hell-of-a-good general someday, just like his daddy. And we need some good generals, Oh, God, do we need some good generals! I thought we would see some improvement in Vietnam since last June when they replaced Westmoreland with Abrams, but nothing has changed."

"So why were you so dedicated to the general? What the hell did he ever do for you?"

"The general took care of me and my family, especially my brother, like we were his own relatives. He was also there when we needed him when my Father died."

After a long silence, Tamashiro asked, "Do you think Lovejoy will be okay, Sarge?"

"Yeah!" Applewhite said, "he's too mean to die. He's going to be sore as hell for a few weeks, through."

Sergeant Cook dropped the Captain and Deluca at operations then continued to the officers quarters with

Operation Minerva

Dawson. Dawson entered the building and started down the dimly lit hallway to his room. About half way down the hall he saw Lieutenant Francis standing by her open door waiting for him. She was dressed in powder-blue pajamas with the legs and sleeves cut off short. Dawson stopped and looked at her for several seconds without saying a word. The sight of her made him forget that he was tired, wet, and cold. She motioned for him to come closer. As he approached she put her fingers over his mouth to warn him to be quiet then led him into her room. Inside the room with the door closed, she whispered to him.

"My God, Jack, I thought it was you. I was so afraid that it was you. All I could find out was that a chute had failed to open and that a jumper on the first team may have been killed. I know you are on the first team."

Genie put her arms tight around him and started to cry. Her deep concern and display of affection took Dawson by surprise. He stood motionless for a moment not knowing really how to respond. Still crying, she started to unbutton his fatigue shirt.

"You're so cold and wet, let me dry you off and get you a drink to warm you up.

She removed his fatigue shirt and while he took off his T-shirt, she got a towel and a drink. Genie dried Dawson as he sat on the edge of her bed sipping his drink. After he was dry, she sat behind him, legs crossed, and scratched his back with her long fingernails. Dawson finished his drink and gave the glass to Genie; she walked over to her locker put the glass down then bolted the safety latch on the door. She held out her arms to him. She dug her fingernails into his back as they kissed.

Operation Minerva

"Are you warmed up now?" she asked.

"Honey, I'm just about as hot now as I've ever been."

She responded with a soft inviting giggle as she pulled him to her.

He ran his hands down her back and into her pajama bottoms.

"Oh, your hands are cold!" she said, as he pressed her body closer to his.

"I've had a hard time keeping my mind on training. Every time I stop what I'm doing and there's a break in my concentration, I think of you. You have no idea how many times I think of you every day. You have no idea how many times I've tried to picture you nude. In my dreams you dance for me, nude, then we make love."

Once again, she responded with a soft inviting giggle. However, this time she unbuckled his belt, unbuttoned his fatigue pants and put her hand inside.

"I've been wondering, too," she said, "wondering if you are the same tiger in bed as you are on the battlefield."

His fatigue pants fell to the top of his jump boots. He sat down on the edge of the bed to undress while she stood directly in front of him and pulled off her pajama top. She was not wearing a bra and the sight of her full, firm breasts made him think of his favorite verse from the Song of Soloman, 'Thy two breasts are like two young roes that are twins.' She removed her pajama bottoms and pink panties; then slowly turned around holding her arms up over her head giving him an unobstructed view of her beauty.

"There's the first part of your dream," she said, "now let's work on the second part."

Operation Minerva

He stood and picked her up in his arms and kissed her then placed her on the bed. He stood and looked at her for a moment as she lay on the bed nude. She was the most perfectly built, beautiful and intelligent young woman that he had ever known.

What the hell are you doing here with me? He thought.

"God, you are beautiful!" he said as he sat on the edge of the bed.

He leaned over and tenderly kissed each of her beasts. Slowly he moved his tongue around each nipple and continued to trace the curvature of her soft warm body with his tongue down to her navel. He moved one hand down between her thighs, she responded instantly to his moves anticipating his advance. His tongue moved slowly down from her navel, down between her legs; his tongue searched through the hair until he found her clitoris. She has the texture of canned peaches, he thought, with the taste and smell of strawberries. He put a rolled blanket under her hips as she pulled her knees up to her breasts.

"Are you comfortable?"

"Yes," she answered.

He made long slow traces with his tongue; he could feel and see the muscles in her stomach and thighs pulsing and pulling as he explored her body. Her sexual tension was building. Her lungs released a sigh, then as she took a deep breath, she squeezed his head between her legs; she grabbed him by the shoulders and sank her fingernails into him. Her body trembled for a few seconds, then she relaxed.

"Christ, baby," he said, "when you have a climax you really have a climax!"

"Come here," she said, pulling him up onto her. "I want you inside me."

He moved up, kissed her breasts, her neck, then sank deep into her vagina. He got an overpowering feeling of being consumed. He wished he could thrust his entire body deep inside her, to become a part of her.

After both were exhausted, he told her, "I've had another... not dream, but fantasy about you."

"Oh, tell me!" she insisted eagerly.

"Well, I have this fantasy where my tongue is a banister and you slide down on it, nude."

She squealed with delight as she crossed her legs and drew her knees up to her breasts.

"That sounds fantastic!"

She sat up and started to rub his chest and stomach.

"I love for a man to have hair on his chest." After a few moments of silence she added, "You know, everyone knows you carry three knives; but, I know something they don't know. You also have a magic sword." She leaned over, gave it a kiss, and said, "I dub thee Excalibur."

She laughed and dropped back with her arm across his chest. They talked for a while before falling asleep.

The next morning the team received word that Sergeant Lovejoy had survived his fall with only a broken ankle and some pulled ligaments. Now, the Captain was faced with the problem of choosing Lovejoy's replacement from team two.

"Well, who are the candidates to replace Lovejoy?" the Captain asked.

"Either Webb or House," replied Lieutenant Deluca.

"Who do you like?"

Operation Minerva

"They both look good to me, Sir," said Deluca.

"How about you, Dawson?"

"I like Sergeant Webb."

"Why Webb?"

"He has good training background and three years of experience in Southeast Asia."

"So does House," replied the Captain.

"Yes," said Dawson, "but Webb doesn't brag about it all of the time!"

"I get your point. Lieutenant, have Sergeant Webb report to me at 1300 hours today and report the change to SOG headquarters."

At 1300 hours Sergeant Webb reported to team one operations. He was greeted by Sergeant Cook and informed that the Captain was out with the team and would be delayed.

"Do you know the other enlisted men on the team very well?" Webb asked.

"Yes, I have served with both of them before. The senior NCO is SFC Applewhite; he's the biggest black man I have ever seen in my life. Chief Dawson is always kidding him about being such a big target and tells him that when the shooting starts he's going to hide behind him."

"How the hell did a warrant officer ever get assigned to a mission like this?"

"Well, that's a long story that I will have to tell you sometime."

"How about the other guy?"

"That's SFC Tamashiro. He and Applewhite are like Mutt and Jeff. Tamashiro is only five-foot-five and one-hundred-ten pounds, he's Oriental-American. The

168

Operation Minerva

Captain calls him the Tasmanian Devil because of the way he fights."

"Sounds like a real good crew."

At that instant the operations door opened and the team came in. As they stacked their weapons and unloaded their gear the Captain told Webb, "Give me about five minutes to get my office straight and then come on in."

"Yes, Sir!" he answered.

After the Captain closed the door to his office Sergeant Cook introduced Webb to the other members of the team. In exactly five minutes Sergeant Webb knocked twice on the Captain's door and entered.

"Sergeant Cook," asked Lieutenant Deluca, "will you tell the Captain that Sergeant Applewhite and I have gone to the comm center?"

"Yes, Sir!" replied Sergeant Cook.

The room was quiet for a few minutes then Dawson asked Sergeant Cook if he would mind taking a walk for a few minutes.

"I want to talk with Sergeant Tamashiro," he explained.

"Yes, Sir!" replied Cook. "I need to go over to supply any way."

Sergeant Cook quickly departed and Dawson and Tamashiro were alone.

"You didn't act like you were really interested in the training session this morning Sergeant. Is something wrong?"

"No, Sir, nothing's wrong."

Tamashiro paused for a few moments, walked around with his fists closed and his thumbs into his belt, then added, "Sir, we've done them same maneuvers over and over and over, I'm gettin' sick of 'em!"

"Tamashiro, I know you have heard all of this before, but I'm going to give it to you one more time. The main difference between a live Green Beret and a dead Green Beret, when he meets his enemy in the jungle, is training. You can roll your pants legs up some if you want to because I'm going to tell you a real 'no-shit war story' about the Captain and me. We were in an E and E[43] situation about two years ago with a helicopter crew. The helicopter crew had never been on the ground before, so I took the point and the Captain took the drag. We were jumped by some Viet Cong troops that must have thought we were easy pickings. Well, we killed some, and some ran off. If the Captain ever tells you this story he will tell you that I killed three of the Viet Cong. So, big deal! What does that have to do with training? Well, roll up your pants legs some more because I only remember killing one of them - the last one. I killed the first two while in some automatic emergency mental mode that took place without having to think about it. The third one, the only one I remember, I killed hand-to-hand with my K-bar."

Dawson walked over to the chalkboard and picked up some chalk.

"Let me try to relate our escape and survival possibilities with training. For training to be effective, our kind of training, it must be repeated until the action becomes instinctive. The most superior fighter you will ever see is one whose actions are involuntary reflex replies to any mode of attack."

---

[43] Escape and Evasion

He drew a star on the board and then three small squares 120 degrees apart around the star.

"I have always been fascinated with knives. When I was a boy I'd bet my Dad beat my ass a thousand times for sticking knives into trees, barn doors and anything else that was within range. Well, I never did stop throwing knives, but I did stop throwing them at things that I knew would piss-off dad. I took three 6-foot long two-by-ten boards and stick them into the ground in a thirty-foot diameter circle. I would stand inside the circle and practice sticking knives into the three boards as I turned around. After awhile, I got so good that I replaced the two-by-ten boards with two-by-fours. I continued to do it over and over and over. My Father accused me of being obsessed with knives. I think it came from being a Tarzan fan when I was little and thinking it was so neat when Tarzan would throw his knife and save Jane or Boy from harm. Well, I have been doing it for 20 years and I still continue to practice."

He put the chalk down and walked over to Tamashiro.

"Do you understand now why I don't even remember killing those two Viet Cong?" It was an instinctive reaction. I didn't have to think about it."

"The Captain told us the story," Tamashiro said, "the day you reported in."

The Captain opened the door of his office and asked for Lieutenant Deluca or Sergeant Cook. Dawson told him that the Lieutenant had gone to commo and that he had sent Cook away so he and Tamashiro could talk.

"Are you finished?" asked the Captain.

"Yes, Sir!" Dawson answered.

"Well then why don't we go get some late chow?"

Operation Minerva

"Hey, Spoon!" the Captain shouted as they entered the mess hall, "how about some chow?"

Dawson, Tamashiro and Webb sat down at a table while the Captain walked back into the kitchen. A moment later the Captain came out and said they would have some chow in a few minutes. In less than 2 minutes, the cook and a KP came out of the kitchen with a big platter of sandwiches and pitchers of cold milk and iced tea.

Just at that moment, Sergeant Cook ran into the mess hall.

"Captain!" he said. "I just got a message from the comm center that Bangkok has a helicopter on its way here to pick you up." The Sergeant looked at his watch then added, "It should be here in about fifteen minutes."

"Christ!" he said, "What now?"

The Captain left with Sergeant Cook and the others started to eat.

"Red Dog," the pilot said into the microphone. "This is Air Force triple nickel four."

A reply came back immediately: "Air Force triple nickel four this is Red Dog - go ahead."

"Red Dog, triple nickel four requests landing instructions - over."

"Triple nickel four - our helipad is between the camp and the lake, there will be grape smoke."

"Red Dog - is our passenger ready to go?"

"Triple nickel four - your passenger is on the pad."

"Thank you Red Dog and would you pass the word that I have a package for Highpockets[44] - over."

---

[44] Lieutenant Francis' code neme.

"Yes, Sir, I'll pass the word."

Later in the operations trailer Lieutenant Francis was showing Lieutenant Deluca and Dawson the aerial photos she had just received.

"These were taken yesterday," she said, "and they show some new activity."

"Looks like they're building something in that big field south of the school," Dawson said.

"Can you tell what it is, Genie?"

"It looks like a speaker's platform to me," she replied.

"Well, hell!" said Dawson, "maybe they're going to have a parade."

"That would sure give us an opportunity to collect more significant intelligence. If we can be there during the parade," added Lieutenant Deluca.

"Yes," said Dawson, "but if they are going to all of this trouble for a parade..."

Dawson paused for a moment then added, "Who is going to be the guest speaker? A big-brass speaker could mean a security problem for us. I'll bet that's why the Captain is on his way to Bangkok."

"I guess we'll find out tomorrow after the Captain gets back," said Deluca as he walked out the door.

CHAPTER 10
The Rifle

Lieutenant Deluca, Mister Dawson and Sergeant Cook were at the helipad when the Captain's helicopter came in from Bangkok. The Captain looked tired as he got off the aircraft and approached them. He had been up all night and had not had the time to eat breakfast or to shave. A military intelligence officer also got off the aircraft and walked over to the jeep with the Captain. The helicopter was departing immediately so they waited until the noise and wind died down to speak.

"Good morning, Sir!" Lieutenant Deluca said as he saluted the Captain. "How did it go?"

"Just fine, Lieutenant," he said. "just fine."

He did not return the salute but put his arm around Lieutenant Deluca and said, "Captain Jamison, this is Lieutenant Deluca my second in command".

"Lieutenant," Captain Jamison mumbled, as he reluctantly extended his hand.

"This is Chief Dawson," the Captain continued, "the warrant officer on our team."

"Well, how do you do, Chief? I've heard quite a bit about you," he said, as he shook Dawson's hand.

"And this is Sergeant Cook, our operations Sergeant."

Operation Minerva

"How are you doing, Sergeant?" he said, returning the Sergeant's salute.

"Captain Jamison will be spending the night with us and returning to Bangkok in the morning. Sergeant Cook, will you take the Captain up to the BOQ and fix him up?"

"Yes, Sir!" the Sergeant replied. "Right away."

They all rode in the jeep as far as operations then Sergeant Cook continued to the BOQ with Captain Jamison. Once inside operations the Captain did not volunteer any information about his trip to Bangkok and no one asked. He had a rifle in a carrying case and Dawson did ask him about that. "What did you do, get a new rifle?"

"Come into my office and I'll show you." The Captain laid the rifle case on his desk and opened it.

"Wow," Dawson said, as he held his hand out for the rifle.

"Do you know what kind it is?" the Captain asked.

"Yes, Sir," replied Dawson. "This is the Dragunov (SVD) the newest Soviet 7.62mm semiautomatic sniper rifle," he said. "And I'll bet you could break a dinner plate with it at 1500 meters. Isn't this the most beautiful thing you've ever seen?"

Dawson asked, as he handed the weapon to Lieutenant Deluca.

"I'm afraid I'm not as much of a gun nut as you are," Deluca said.

The weapon was replete with match ammo, PSO-1 telescopic sight and IR[45] detection scope. The Captain

---

[45] InfraRed

said a Mr. Smith at the embassy had the rifle and thought it just might come in handy on the mission. Mr. Dawson did not seem to place too much significance on the event. However, Lieutenant Deluca did not like the portentous feeling that ran through him as he held this new addition to the equipment list.

"I have a meeting with Captain Jamison just as soon as he gets back from the BOQ," the Captain said, "but, after chow let's go down to the lake and bust a few caps[46]."

Dawson was anxious to fire the new weapon and Lieutenant Deluca agreed to go along. Lieutenant Deluca felt that the Captain's enthusiastic attitude had in some way been altered by his trip to Bangkok. He displayed his usual surface enthusiasm, but deep down where the fire burns that inspires men to follow... , Lieutenant Deluca detected a cooling. Dawson's intense interest in the new weapon, Deluca thought, blinded him to the change in the Captain's feelings. After lunch the Captain, Dawson and Deluca went down to the lake to test fire and zero the rifle. The lake was the only place they could get a clear shot for 1000 meters. They took one of the boats and set up three targets on the far side of the lake. They had a spotting scope to check hits but the sun was not in a good position. Each officer fired three rounds then they crossed the lake to check the targets - all shots were on paper. The Captain adjusted the weapons sight according to his shot group. Dawson and Deluca mentally adjusted their impact points against his. They fired three more rounds each and again checked their targets. This time all

---

[46] Shooters jargon for firing rounds of ammunition.

three had killing hits on the silhouette targets. The Captain and Dawson wanted to practice more so Deluca left them and walked up the hill to camp alone. He couldn't figure out what was going on. Surely the Captain was not called to Bangkok just be given a rifle; but, why hasn't he told us anything? Well, he thought, the Captain will tell us when the time comes. Deluca hoped they would not stay down at the lake too long, they had a lot of work to do. Captain Jamison was in operations when Deluca returned.

"Good afternoon, Captain," he said. "May I help you?"

"No," he said, "just looking around. Where is the Captain?"

"He's down at the lake with Mr. Dawson shooting his new rifle."

"I think I'll walk down to the lake, maybe he'll let me try it out."

Captain Jamison walked out of operations. Who the hell is he? Deluca thought, and what is his function in this mission? Deluca asked Lieutenant Francis about him.

"He didn't say a word to me, he just looked around. However, he did seem interested in the newest aerial photographs we have. The one showing the construction," she replied.

Thirty minutes later the Captain, Captain Jamison, and Dawson walked into operations,

"Mr. Dawson, will you clean this weapon for me?"

"Yes, Sir, love to."

The Captain and Captain Jamison walked into the Captain's office and were not seen again until breakfast the next day.

Operation Minerva

"Good morning, Captain Jamison," Lieutenant Deluca said, as they met in the chow line. "How are you this morning? Was your room okay?"

"Yes," he answered. "Everything was just fine."

No one did much talking during breakfast and after breakfast the Captain and Captain Jamison once again disappeared into the Captain's office. At 1030 hours, Captain Jamison's flight to Bangkok was due.

Lieutenant Deluca knocked on the door to remind them of the time.

"Sir," he said. "Captain Jamison's helicopter will be here in twenty minutes."

"Thank you, Lieutenant," was the reply from behind to closed door.

They could hear the helicopter passing over the camp when the Captain Jamison emerged from the office.

"Sergeant Cook," Lieutenant Deluca ordered, "run the Captain down to the helipad in the jeep."

"Yes, Sir," replied Sergeant Cook as he stood up and headed for the door.

Captain Jamison followed him out. The Captain did not come out of his office until it was time for chow. Again, during lunch, there was little or no talking at the table. Lieutenant Deluca knew by now that Dawson was also aware of the Captain's burden. Dawson tried unsuccessfully several times to get the Captain's mind off his problems. This was the last work day before the mission. The Captain had declared the next day a day of rest. Tomorrow evening they would leave for North Vietnam.

CHAPTER 11
Until The Daybreak,
And The Shadows Flee Away . . .

Lieutenant Francis and Dawson were alone in the operations trailer late in the afternoon. She was giving him a lesson in aerial photo interpretation. She was showing him how to analyze an area by comparing infrared photographs with regular black and white photographs. She had been tracing footpaths and trails in white ink on the photographs the team had selected to carry on the mission. She asked Dawson something about the mission that had been bothering her:

"Why are all of you using Soviet-made AK-47 weapons?"

He answered her question with a question.

"If someone outside were to fire an M-16 or an AK-47 right now could you tell the difference?"

Genie thought for a while, then answered, "Yes, I think I could!"

"So can the enemy, honey," he replied. "If we started shooting M-16s in North Vietnam we might just as well wave American flags and have a band with us."

"I get the idea," she said, nodding her head.

"Tonight's our last night together," she said as she put her hand on his, "let's not go to the club tonight. After supper this evening come to my room."

Operation Minerva

She pressed her body close to him and whispered into his ear, "I want you to spend all night with me."

"Honey, if we both disappear tonight, everyone will know for sure what they have only suspected up to now, that something is going between us. We have been very discreet up to this point, why chance ruining your reputation just to save two or three hours?

You don't want any stories to follow you back to Saigon."

"I don't give a damn," she insisted. "This is our last night and I want it to be something special."

He took her into his arms and told her softly that he would do his best to make this last night as special as he could.

"I have something for you," she whispered. "A going-away present that I hope will inspire you to come back to me."

She walked over to her purse and took out a gold chain and small locket.

"A Buddha box?" Dawson asked.

"It's a Buddha box, but I've taken the Buddha out and put something else in his place."

She handed the locket to him .

"Open it up!" she said.

Dawson took the little box, slid the lid open and removed a small piece of pink silk that was cut in the shape of a heart.

"Smell it!" she said.

"I can already smell it," he said. "Tabu."

He held the little heart up and told her, "I've seen this little pink heart somewhere before."

"She giggled and answered, "Yes."

"The pink panties you had on the first night we. . ."

Dawson stopped talking and looked at her. Tears filled her eyes as she looked at him and said,

"Please come back to me, please. I have never felt this way about any man before in my entire life; I think I could really truly love you for the rest of my life."

Dawson held her close. Now, for the first time in his career, he wished that he did not have to go away. He had discovered a feeling deep within himself that he had never before experienced. He loved Genie and could not stand the thought of leaving her and possibly never seeing her again.

"You will have to keep this and give it to me just before I get on the aircraft tomorrow evening. We will be checked to ensure that no personal belongings are taken on the mission."

Genie put the locket back into her purse then she and Dawson left operations for the mess hall.

Later that evening, after a shower and fresh uniform, Dawson knocked quietly on Genie's door.

"Genie," he whispered softly as he knocked, "it's me."

She opened the door just a few inches and, hiding behind it, peeked out. "Jack," she whispered. "Close your eyes and come in".

She told him that he must keep his eyes closed until she told him to open them. He closed his eyes and she led him into the room. As he entered he could smell the scent of Tabu, his favorite perfume now, and the only kind Genie ever used. She positioned him and then stood back and told him to open his eyes. She turned around slowly showing him the poncho type shorty nightgown she had made from the silk of an old parachute. Dawson could see the dark nipples of her breasts through the thin material. He thought that of her one-hundred-seven pounds, that the last seven pounds must be titties. Her short black hair was fluffed-up just the way he liked it and she had on all the make-up that he had ever seen her wear - lipstick and bright red fingernail polish. He loved her fingernails and the way she used them.

"My God," he said. "You're so beautiful."

"How do you like the top?" she asked, turning around again.

"I think it's lovely."

"How do you like my bottoms?" she asks, as she coyly elevated the hem of her gown.

She raised it just enough to tantalize him; she had no panties on.

"You have the most fantastic bottom I have ever seen. Are you trying to give me a heart attack, honey? You know, at the rate my heart is going right now, if we do anything else I could have a cardiac arrest and die right here."

She quietly giggled and moved over to him.

"I want you to stand right there and let me undress you," she insisted. "You must behave yourself and not touch me until I give you permission."

She giggled again as she unbuttoned his shirt and removed it. He stood still; he was not wearing a T-shirt; she didn't like them.

"Sit down," she said, "so I can remove your boots."

He sat down and Genie knelt at his feet.

After his boots were off, Genie stood up and held out her hands to him; he stood up and grabbed her.

"No, no!" she said. "You're supposed to behave yourself, remember?"

He dropped his arms.

"That's better," she said, as she unbuckled his belt and unbuttoned his pants.

Then she put her hands inside his fatigues pushing his shorts and pants down together until she was kneeling on the floor in front of him. She motioned for him to step out of his clothes. He was standing before her wearing only his dog tags, every muscle in his lean, hard body, tense and ready.

"I love to run my nose and lips through the hair on your chest and stomach," she murmured as she moved down on him, fondling, kissing and gently biting.

She looked up at him and said, "You didn't know I was a sword swallower, did you?"

Dawson's heart was pounding so hard that he could hardly speak as Genie stood up in front of him.

"Is it my turn now?" he asked.

"Okay," she said.

Dawson pulled the tie string and her silk gown fell to the floor. He picked her up and placed her on the bed and lowered himself slowly over her, resting his weight on his elbows, his head even with her beautiful twin breasts. Suddenly Genie threw her legs around his chest and locked her ankles.

"Do you know what I dreamed last night?" She didn't wait for an answer. "I had the wildest dream about your fantasy; only, I must say that I made some improvements. I dreamed that I was nude and sliding down this long tongue, my arms and legs wrapped around it, only in my dream the big tongue has a thousand little tongues protruding from it. Each little tongue was charged with the electricity of an orgasm. As I slid over each of them I could feel the electricity going through my breasts, my thighs, my stomach, and even my toes. I don't know how long the dream lasted but I woke up covered with sweat and was exhausted."

"Well," he said. "I don't know if I can follow that act or not."

"Honey, you are the act. Every time I rub my nipples through the hair on your chest I get the same feeling in my breast that I had all over my body in the dream."

"If you'll let me go, honey, I'll see what I can do for you." Genie dropped her legs and Dawson moved down on her. "Ah, lovely," he said. "No douche. Strawberries are okay but I like your natural smell."

She relaxed with a contented little sigh as he buried himself between her thighs.

Across the camp from the BOQ, a private party was being held in the operations trailer of team one. Captain Coxe and his team, Captain Kenny and his team, and the Air Liaison Officer, Lieutenant Blair, were sitting around a long table. Lieutenant Simon, the executive officer of team two, stood and proposed a toast:

"To the President of the United States."

Everyone stood and, as they raised their glasses, all repeated the toast. Then Lieutenant Blair proposed a toast:

"To the United States Army."

Lieutenant Blair's toast was followed by a toast, proposed by Captain Coxe, to the United States Air Force.

Finally, Captain Kenny proposed a toast, "A toast to team one and to a successful mission."

All of team two repeated the toast, Lieutenant Deluca added an epigram, "The mission cui bone[47]," he said in a lowered voice.

Captain Coxe, standing beside Lieutenant Deluca, shook his head slowly and told him, "Lieutenant, if you are going to get philosophical and afflict us with your education, I'm going to have to throw your ass out of here."

Everyone laughed as they were seated, including Deluca.

"I don't think Lieutenant Francis and Mister Dawson are going to make it tonight, do you?" Lieutenant Deluca asked the Captain.

"No, I think they are having a private farewell party of their own. They seem to have become quite attached to one another," the Captain replied.

"Yeah!" said Sergeant Tamashiro, "I'll bet they're attached to each other right now."

A lusty laughter filled the room for a few seconds before Captain Coxe interrupted.

"Okay, you knot-heads, knock-it-off! Did we come here to gossip or to get drunk?"

The Captain stood, raised his glass and made a final toast, "Here's to women all around the world, God bless them."

Every man in the room noisily rallied to the toast, then the Captain continued,

"Now, let's get down to some serious drinking."

Laughter again filled the room as everyone sat down.

---

[47] Latin – For what use?

Operation Minerva

Sergeant Tamashiro pulled Sergeant Webb off into a corner to talk:

"O.K. what do you want to talk about?" Webb asked.

"Mister Dawson," replied Tamashiro. "What do you think about him?"

"You're going to have to be a lot more specific," said Webb. "You must have something in particular on your mind."

"Well, no," Tamashiro said. "I just can't figure him out. He don't laugh, he don't get drunk, he don't smoke. Hell if it weren't for his love affair with Genie, I'd swear he was queer for the Army. All he ever talks about is training, training, training - Christ, you'd think he would get tired of it sometime. Have you ever talked with him?"

"Yes, we had a rap session just a few days ago, I don't think any of it was about the Army or training. We talked about home and when we were kids."

"Well, what's his problem then?" asks Tamashiro.

"I don't think he has a problem. You know you were goofing off last week when he chewed you out for not really trying during that training problem."

"Yes, I know," he answered, "but that's not what's buggin' me. Why is he so damned serious?"

"I can only tell you why I think he is so serious, but it's just my opinion."

"Let's hear it," Tamashiro said. "If you have an opinion, that's more than I have.

"First," Webb continued, "and maybe most important, he is ten years older than we are. He's even older than the Captain. We all consider ourselves professional soldiers; however, you and I have a tendency to approach, and accept, all of this as a sort of a game. To Mister Dawson this is all a very serious and deadly business and he knows that only the best survive. He wants us to live through this and . . . "

"I want us to live through this too," Tamashiro interrupted.

"Yes," Webb said, "but it's different with us. You don't want to die from cancer do you?"

"No," Tomashiro said.

"Well then why don't you quit smoking?" Tamashiro did not answer so Webb continued, "I'll tell you why, your'e not really serious about your health, you think it can't happen to you. You're not willing to go through the discomfort of quitting even under the threat of cancer and death. It's the same thing with training. You're not willing to go through the discomfort of repetitious training, even under the threat of death. Mister Dawson is serious about his life and health, that's why he don't get drunk, smoke, or even over eat.

"I think I can see what you are getting at," Tamashiro said.

"He is also," Webb said, "I think, somewhat introverted. I know he don't like crowds. He prefers a small group of close personal friends as opposed to a large group of people at parties. And lastly, he has a drive to be the best at whatever he chooses to do."

"You two must have had a hell of a rap session," Tamashiro said, "how did you get that close to him?"

"I didn't really have anything to do with it," Webb said. "He picked me for this mission you know, it was a toss-up between House and me. I thanked him for his recommendation and he told me that it was my attitude that had made the difference, then, we just started talking."

Across the room, Captain Coxe, Lieutenant Deluca and Sergeant Applewhite were talking.

"Sergeant Applewhite," the Captain said, "Lieutenant Deluca informs me that your brother has arrived in Saigon. I'm sorry that you won't have time to visit him before we go on this mission."

"That's okay, Sir," said Applewhite. "I'll see him when we get back."

"What does your brother do?" asked Deluca.

"My little brother is a Captain in Military Intelligence."

"A Captain," exclaimed Lieutenant Deluca. "Why haven't you ever told us about him?

Does he give big brother a hard time?" Deluca said, laughing.

"Oh, he tried once. I told him to knock-it-off or I was going to spank him."

"I have four brothers in the Army; Jim is the only officer - we call him the 'black sheep' of the family."

This comment drew a hearty laugh from both Captain Coxe and Lieutenant Deluca.

"Are any of your brothers in Special Forces?" Deluca asked.

"No," he said, "they're all a bunch'a legs[48]. Dad was airborne during the Second World War with the 101st."

"I didn't know we had any black airborne troops then, wasn't that before the Army was integrated?" Deluca asked.

---

[48] Not airborne.

Operation Minerva

"I really don't know if we had any black airborne troops then or not. You see, my Father was half-white. My Grandmother was white. Dad was very light skinned and passed for white when he enlisted."

"Where is your Father now?" Deluca asked.

"He died a few years ago from a heart attack."

"Your Mother must really be proud of her sons.

"Yes, Sir, that's all she ever talks about according to the neighbors."

Lieutenant Blair walked over to the Captain's party and asked, "How can you all be so damn calm? If I knew that tomorrow night I was going to have to jump with you guys, I would be a nervous wreck. I'm nervous about it now and I'm not even going!"

"I think," said the Captain, "the first major step in becoming a good Green Beret is learning to control pre-mission jitters. We all have it, we all control it. In our own individual way."

The evening passed and everyone accomplished the goal established earlier by the Captain - to get drunk.

Across the camp, Dawson and Genie were sitting on her bed enjoying a cup of hot chocolate and a mellow afterglow.

"Jack", Genie asked, "where did you learn to make love to a woman the way you do?"

He was quiet for a while, thinking about what he should tell her. Should he tell her the truth or should he lie to her and tell her that it just comes natural to him. He decided to tell her the truth.

"Well," he started, "when I was a young boy... I think about fourteen years old, I had a wonderful and gentle woman who spent the summer teaching me to be the lover that she wanted but could never have."

"Fourteen," she blurted, "a woman! Just how old was this woman?"

"Well, let me start at the beginning and tell you the whole story. That summer was the year that our neighbor's wife died and he was committed to an old people's home. The house they had lived in was 60 years old, was never painted, the back porch was sinking into the ground and ... well; you get the idea. It was run down, a dump! All the neighbors had hoped that someone would buy the house and fix it up. It was an eyesore even to a neighborhood as poor as ours. However, it was not long before an old railroad man and his daughter, Mary Jo, rented the house. I felt so sorry for her. She had only old tattered clothing, no shoes to talk about, and everyone avoided her. Everyone, that is, except my Mother. My Mother came from a poor family in West Virginia so she knew what it was like not to have anything. My Mother gave her clothing, shoes, soap, and helped her fix herself up. After Mother had finished with her she turned out to be very good looking. Her Father would go away for weeks at a time with the railroad and she would be at home alone. He was an old and dirty looking man. Even when he was washed, he looked dirty and had a bad smell about him. He was a nice man though, he was always good to me and thanked my Mother for helping Mary Jo. Mary Jo did not like leaving the house because the neighbors would turn their backs to her and not speak. I could never figure out why anyone would act like that so I asked Mom about it. She said I would understand when I got older. That explanation did nothing for me because

Operation Minerva

Mother always said that to me. Since Mary Jo did not like to go out, she would stop me as I walked by and ask me to go to the store for her. I was always happy to do it because she would always sit on the back porch and talk to me when I got back and sometimes she would give me a Coke. It wasn't long before I knew her life story. She always talked about the boy she left back home. Sometimes when I looked at her she looked like she should still be in high school. One day I asked her if she had graduated. She told me she almost did. So, I asked her why she quit. She said that she had quit school two years earlier just before she and Sam left Tennessee and that she just never did go back.

One warm evening while I was on my way uptown to the movies, she called me inside. I had never been inside the house before except to deliver the groceries to the kitchen table. This time she invited me into the living room. Well, I thought it was the living room. As it turned out, they didn't have a living room. What should have been a living room turned out to be her bedroom. The room had only a single dim light bulb hanging from the middle of the ceiling. The walls of the room had holes in the plaster and there were no curtains on the windows. The room had a stale damp smell. The sheet on the bed was too small and didn't cover all of the mattress. The pillow didn't have a cover at all. I thought it was a strange bedroom for a woman, not anything like my Mother's room. But, I didn't have much time to think about it before she took my mind off the room and onto her. She told me to sit down in the only chair in the room and then started talking and acting very strange. First, she started to complain about the lack of an evening breeze, then

191

turned the complaint to the humidity. As she walked around the room fanning herself with a paper, she asked me if I minded if she took off her house coat. Well, I had no reason to object so, I said it was ok with me. When she dropped it to the floor I could see that she had nothing on except the top layer of a nightgown that my Mother had given her. She was not the first woman that I had seen with almost no clothing on, I had seen my Mother's younger sisters at various times with little to nothing on. Mary Jo, however, was in a whole new category. She had long black hair, her eyes were so dark they looked black and her skin was absolutely white. She was a tall girl, much taller than I was at fourteen, and had, I noticed then for the first time, a magnificent set of titties. I was struck speechless by the sight of her standing in front of me. Her dark pubic hair and nipples were visible even in the dim light of the room. My heart was pounding and I became short of breath as she walked to me and started to run her fingers over the top of my head. She asked me what was the matter and then pulled my head to her breast. The smell of her perfume and having my face against her breasts generated feelings within me that I had never felt before. My heavy breathing made me feel dizzy and my sight became blurred. I thought I was going to pass out right there in her arms. She talked to me for a long time. She told me how lonely she was and that she needed someone to keep her company. She told me that she really liked me and wanted me to be her special friend. After a while my breathing and my heart slowed to the point that I figured I wasn't going to pass out. Then she took my hands and put them on her breasts and told me that it was ok for me to feel them. Once again my breathing and heart took off to the point that I felt faint. Again she talked to me and calmed me down, telling me the whole time that she liked me and that it was ok. Somehow, I think she knew I was reaching my physical limit in adjusting to this new situation. So, she asked me if I would like a drink. I said yes. As we walked into the kitchen, she put her housecoat back on. After having a glass of milk, and talking about other things, she asked me if I liked her and wanted to come back to see her again. I had no words to express to her the passion and excitement that I felt when she touched me. I could not open my mouth and tell her how much I wanted to see her and touch her again. So, I only stammered, and told her that I would like to see her again. Just before she let me out the back door, she kissed me ever so gently and rubbed my penis with her hand. She asked me if I liked that and I managed to get one word, "Yes". Then she instructed me on how to kiss her as she took my hand and placed it between her legs. I had never had my hand between a woman's legs before and I was amazed by the amount of heat that was there. As I was kissing her and running my hand between her legs I became crazy with passion. I pulled up her nightgown and started to rub her again. Soon, I had my fingers up inside her. When that happened, she stopped me and said "later".

That night, I went to sleep smelling the scent of Mary Jo on my hand. We became intimate lovers that summer. I would go to her house three or four times a week and there were many times when we would make love twice in one afternoon. She instructed me in great detail about what a woman liked and what a woman wanted in a lover. She introduced me to the pleasures of oral sex and took me to a level of pleasure that I never dreamed existed. Then she instructed me in how to give oral sex to a woman and taught me how to enjoy giving it as much as I enjoyed receiving it. By the end of the summer, when they moved away, she had not only told me about what she liked and the parts of her body that responded to a man's touch, she had also conveyed to me all the intimate details that other women had secretly revealed to her. Intimate details about what they liked, what parts of their bodies responded to a man's fingers, a man's tongue, a gentle rubbing, a kiss or just a gentle caress. Years later, when I was home visiting Mom and Dad, I asked Mom if she remembered Mary Jo, the woman that had lived in the old house. What she told me came as a complete surprise and almost brought tears to my eyes. Mary Jo was the wife of the old railroad man, not his daughter. Mother told me that the old man had actually bought Mary Jo from her parents in Tennessee. Her Father, Mother told me, made her work as a prostitute to help support the family. After I talked to Mother I walked over to the old house; it was empty now, and uninhabitable. I walked through the house and stopped in Mary Jo's bedroom. Visions of her and our times together in that room ran through my mind like they had been recorded on video tape inside my head. I could see her standing by the bed, I could smell her perfume, I could feel her breasts in my hands. A warm feeling came over me as I remembered seeing her laugh for the very first time. She was a magnificent woman for an eighteen year old, and I wish I knew where she was so I could thank her for the education."

"Well, that is a sad and interesting story. I would like to thank her too," Genie said.

CHAPTER 12
The Picnic

Early in the morning, before the camp had called reveille,
Genie opened her eyes and looked at Dawson. He was
sound asleep beside her. God, let this be my man, she
thought. Please let this be the one. He is everything I've
been looking for. The one Mother always said would
show up 'just at the right time.' First light was just
filtering through the camp as Genie reached over her
head to turn out her night-light. She could hear the hum
of the camp loud speakers as its antique public address
system amplifier was warmed up. She could hear, and
visualize, the fumbling of the sleepy Thai soldier trying
to place the phonograph needle in the grooves of the old
record. She could hear the stylus running in a groove
where no sound had ever been recorded and then the
scratchy bugle call to reveille. Dawson opened his eyes
and saw Genie, wide-awake, smiling and looking at him.
He stretched his arms over his head and growled, then sat
up on the edge of the bed. He put his hands around his
neck and moved his head around, first in one direction
and then the other. The joints of his neck and back
cracked loudly as he flexed his muscles. He stood,
stretched and growled again as he walked over to Genie's
dresser and picked up her mouthwash; then, after taking a

mouthful and swishing it around several times he walked over and spat the mouthwash through the screen to the ground.

Genie started laughing at him as he walked back to the bed to sit down. He turned and looked at her through half-open, tortured eyes. She shook her head and told him, "You act like an old grizzly bear that has just come out of hibernation. You know, I've heard you make these strange sounds every morning that we have been here and I've always wondered what the hell you were doing."

She moved up behind him and started to massage his neck. "You act like you hurt all over," she said.

"I do," he answered quietly. "I do."

She continued to work on his back and neck until most of the stiffness was gone. She dropped her arms to her side as he turned around to look at her. He reached out and touched her forehead with the index finger of his right hand. Then he slowly moved his finger down the length of her nose, across her lips, chin and neck. He stopped when his finger came to rest on her bare chest. With a sign, he dropped his arm.

"What the hell are you doing here with me?" he asked shaking his head.

"I'm not here with you," she replied in a pseudo sarcastic tone. "This is my room and you are here with me."

Dawson looked at her, his eyes still not fully open, and said, "Okay, Miss Snooty, what am I doing here with you?"

"Well," she replied, maintaining her sarcastic tone. "Last night we were screwing. Today, however, all we have managed to do is talk."

"I'm not going to get a serious word out of you, am I?" he asked.

"Not if you're going to lay that old man bullshit on me," she said laughing.

She sat nude on the bed, legs crossed, hands on hips, back straight and a defiant look in her eye. Both were quiet for a few moments, then Genie said, "Let's make today a day that we will remember for the rest of our lives. Just like last night was, for me anyway," she whispered.

He took her left breast in his right hand and nibbled gently on the nipple. Genie held his head in place with one arm while slowly easing herself to her pillow with the other. As her head sank into the pillow she dropped her arm from Dawson's head, stretched out and relaxed with a sigh.

Captain Coxe was just leaving the mess hall as Genie and Dawson arrived. They met outside and talked for a few minutes. The Captain said he had missed them at the party. Genie spoke up to defend Dawson saying that is was her desire not to attend the party that had kept Dawson away. The Captain said that he understood. Dawson asked the Captain what he was going to do to keep him self busy for the day. The Captain thought for a few moments, then answered, "I think I am going to listen to Mozart, write letters and finish off the French chocolate Mother gave me."

The Captain reached out to Genie and took her hand in his. Her hand looked so small and pale resting in his powerful sun-browned hand. Then, like a scene from an Errol Flynn movie, the Captain, with grace and charm, kissed Genie's hand.

Operation Minerva

"Enjoy yourselves today," he said. "I'll see you tonight at supper."

"I think that little sundress you have on rather captivated the Captain," said Dawson.

"He looked so lonely," Genie said, taking Dawson's hand. "I wish my girlfriend Sue could be here. I think they would get along beautifully together. I must introduce him to Sue when you get back; she works in Saigon with me."

Dawson and Genie had a long leisurely breakfast. The hot sun was shining through the window onto her bright yellow dress as they finished their last cup of coffee.

"Let's have a picnic today!" she said, barely restraining her enthusiasm for the sudden idea. "Where could I get the food?" she said, her enthusiasm dropping.

"Honey," Dawson said. "If you walk back into the kitchen in that dress and talk sweet to the mess sergeant, I'm sure that you can get anything you want."

"Do you think so?"

"Trust me!" Dawson said, laughing.

Genie got up and quickly disappeared into the kitchen. She had only been gone about five minutes when she emerged from the kitchen, her face beaming with success. "I'll have everything ready in an hour," she said.

"Can you get a jeep?"

"I think so," he replied.

"Can we go down to the lake?"

"Yes."

"Is it safe?"

"It will be okay."

Dawson left Genie at the mess hall and walked to operations to get a jeep. Across camp, Sergeants Webb and Tamashiro were making plans for the day.

"Sergeant DeVito said there are four or five good-looking young Thai girls at this place. It was just an abandoned hut until they started their business." Tamashiro said, "It really looks good now. Come on! I want to get laid before we go on this mission."

"It's not near the village, is it?" Webb asked.

"No, it's about three clicks out of the village and not on a main trail," Tamashiro answered. After a few moments of thought Webb replied, "Well, what the hell!" I don't want to die horny! Let's go."

In the team operations trailer, Lieutenant Deluca was writing a letter to his girlfrend and Sergeant Applewhite was on the telephone to Saigon.

"Saigon? No! I want Saigon, operator. Yes, give me MAC-Vee[49] headquarters. MAC-Vee? Yes, I want to talk to Captain Jim Applewhite in G2."

"Hello, Captain Applewhite speaking, may I help you, Sir?"

"Don't give me that Captain-and-Sir shit! This is your big brother."

"Hey, man, where are you?"

"I'm in Bangkok on R and R[50]"

"Well, big brother, that tells me that you have either just returned or are about to go out on a mission. Which one is it?" the Captain asked.

---

[49] Military Assistance Command Viet Nam
[50] Rest and Relaxation

Operation Minerva

"Man, we ain't doing shit here, just sitting around watching the trees grow."

"Do you mean to tell me that you haven't been out chasing Viet Cong through the jungle and blowing up bridges and all the other neat stuff you Green Beret killers do?"

"Jim, what the hell have you been doing, reading recruiting posters?"

"Sorry-bot-that, big brother, just thought I would pull your leg a little."

"How was Mom when you left home last week?"

"Mom is okay. She worries about you twenty-four hours a day. You know that next to God and Dad, Mom thinks you are Number One."

"Does that bother you, little brother?"

"No, not really because next to God, Dad and Mom, you are Number One with me too. I'll tell you something though, big brother, you are a tough act to follow."

"Well, relax, how would you like to be me and have to follow Dad."

"I see what you mean."

"In six months, you will be eligible for some R and R, we'll get together and have a long talk."

"That sounds good to me."

"Well, don't get caught in Saigon after curfew and always know the location of the nearest bunker. That's all the big brother advice I have for you, okay?"

"Thanks for calling, take care of yourself."

"Goodbye, Jim."

"Goodbye, big brother."

Dawson walked into the operations trailer just as Sergeant Applewhite was hanging up the telephone.

"Sergeant Cook, may I use the jeep for about three hours, maybe four?"

"Lieutenant Deluca, do you mind if Mister Dawson uses the jeep?" the Sergeant asked.

The Lieutenant looked up and answered, "No, I don't care. If we need a jeep we can get one from the camp."

"It's all yours, Mister Dawson," the Sergeant said.

"Thank you Sergeant," Dawson said as he walked out.

Lieutenant Deluca looked down at his letter and began to read what he had written:

Dear Jennie, If you are reading this letter, then you have received my personal effects from the Army and know that I have, as they say in the song, met my fate. I knew when I volunteered for this mission that it was a high-risk job. However, I feel that the benefits that can be gained, by a successful mission, outweigh the risk. I feel honored to be a member of this elite team of Green Berets. I know that if we can't do the job - the job can't be done. A member of our team will visit you within the next few months and answer your questions. He can't tell you everything, but he will tell you enough. Do not be too bereaved honey, as least I did not die a stupid, useless death in an auto accident like Pete, or in a drunken barroom fight like cousin Eddie. Years from now, when you are asked about me you will not have to be ashamed of your answer. I do feel that I am the least qualified man on this team. All the others are combat experienced, highly trained, professional soldiers - true Green Berets. Sometimes, when we are out working on field problems, I get such a proud feeling in my chest that I feel like I'm going to explode. To serve with these men, on this mission, is an honor. I would rather be counted as

*one of these men for a few weeks, than live a hundred
years in blank safety among lesser men.*

He leaned back in the chair for a moment and thought
about home:

"Patrick! Patrick! Your Father is home."

*Pat walked out of the woods and waved to his Mother as
he started down the hill to the house. The temperature
was dropping fast, as it always does in late October in
Ohio just after sun down, and Pat could see his breath so
he pretended to be smoking as he walked. The evening
air was clean, clear, and crisp; this was his favorite time
of year. The blowing leaves swirled around him as he
walked along with his .22 caliber rifle over his shoulder
and the two squirrels he had bagged that afternoon
proudly displayed on his belt. As he got closer to the
house, he could hear a man with a very deep, loud, and
angry voice talking on the back porch.*

"Patrick, come here son," his Father said.

*"I see you got two squirrels. How far back into the woods
did you have to go?"*

"I got them up by the flint pile."

*"Then you did not go over the top of the hill this after
noon?"*

"No, sir," he replied.

*"How many rounds did you take with you?" his Father
asked.*

"Five, sir."

*"How many shots did it take you to get the two
squirrels?"*

"Two, sir."

"Did you target practice any son?"

"No, sir."

Operation Minerva

"Show me the remaining rounds."

Pat pulled his glove off, put his hand into his jacket pocket and pulled out three .22 caliber rim-fire cartridges. His Father smiled and patted him on the head.

"Patrick," his Father said. "I want you to load a round into your rifle and shoot one of Mother's clothes pins off the clothes line."

"Yes, sir."

He turned around to face the backyard. The clothesline was thirty feet away and ran parallel to the back porch. There were socks and dungarees on the line. He inserted a cartridge into his single-shot rifle and took aim. The sharp crack of the rifle was followed instantly by an exploding clothespin and a white sock drifting to the ground.

"Why did you pick that clothes pin?"

"So the bullet, after going through the clothes pin, would hit in that pile of dirt by the drainage ditch."

"Good job, son. Go pick up the sock then go into the house and get washed up for supper."

"Yes, sir."

Once in the house he placed his rifle beside his Father's rifle in the rack and handed the sock and squirrels to his Mother. She could see in his expression the questions he wanted to ask.

"Go to your room and clean up, son."

"Your Father will tell you what this is all about later."

"Well, Mister Ramsey, do you still think my son shot your goat?"

"No, I don't believe so. Thank you for putting up with my ranting and raving without throwing me out on my ear."

Operation Minerva

At the bottom of the walk, Mister Ramsey turned and looked back at Patrick's Father on the porch. "You've got a good kid there Mr. Deluca," he said.

"Yes, I know," he answered. "I'm proud of him."

The Thai guard at the gate could not keep his eyes off Genie. He nearly dropped his rifle as he saluted Dawson and waved the jeep through. Dawson turned the jeep down the hill to the lake. He and Genie laughed as they bounced along the rough road. They laughed at the Thai guard and they laughed just because it was so good to be alive and be able to laugh.

"Do you see a spot you like?"

Dawson asked, stopping the jeep at a point where Genie could see most of the north and west shore of the lake. She stood up and looked around the lake. Dawson looked at her as she stood with her left hand on her hip, her right hand, finger extended and ready to point to her selection, was close to her face like a small girl trying to make a difficult decision at a candy counter.

"There!" she said, pointing. "There, under that big tree."

She was pointing to an area on the northwest shore of the lake where one long tree was standing just a few feet from the lake. She would pick that spot, Dawson thought as he put the jeep in gear. Dawson would have preferred an area situated in full view of the camp. Genie had selected one of the few places that was hidden. However, the fifty-meter clearing between the lake and the tree line gave Dawson a certain amount of solace. He parked the jeep just east of the tree and close to the lake, a point where it would least obstruct his field of view, then unloaded the food that she had packed. Genie spread a nylon camouflaged blanket on the grass and began setting

Operation Minerva

out the food. Dawson took off his equipment harness and positioned it carefully beside his M-16 rifle. Then he removed his .45 caliber automatic from his belt holster and placed it in front of him as he relaxed on the blanket. Genie was crawling around on her hands and knees carefully placing each container of food within easy reach for Dawson. After the last item had been set out she sat back on her heels and shook her head to get her hair out of her eyes.

"Do you see anything that you want to eat right now?" she asked.

She saw a sly smirk develop very slowly on Dawson's face. She smiled at him and replied with a giggle, "That's for dessert."

It was cool under the tree and the air was sweet with the smell of flowers from across the lake. The only sound to break their quiet communion was the occasional trill of a bird. Genie sat with her legs crossed as they picked at the food and talked. Dawson searched Genie's body with his eyes, trying to record every detail for the time he knew was coming when he could only have his memory of her to enjoy.

"What are you thinking about?" she asked, noticing his loss of attention to the conversation.

"I'm trying to burn the vision of your body into my memory so I'll never forget how lovely you are."

She smiled at him and asked, "Would you like a better picture?"

"Now, just what do you mean by that?" he asked.

She stared into his eyes. The impish little smile on her face told him that she was about to pull one of her seductive tricks on him. Their eyes remained locked

206

together in an unblinking stare as Genie slowly pulled the hem of her dress tight across her knees. Dawson's eyes finally broke away and looked down as Genie exposed her thighs. He continued to look as she continued to pull her hem towards her waist. Dawson could feel his body responding to the sight of her thighs; his heart started pounding and his mouth was getting dry. He groaned and fell back, as if in misery, as Genie exposed the fact that she was not wearing any panties.

"Oh! My God," he said. "You are better at torturing a man than the Viet Cong. I saw you put skivvies on this morning; what happened to them?"

Genie laughed as she crawled over on top of Dawson.

"I took them off and put them in my purse while you were unloading the jeep. I thought they might get in the way later on in the program."

Genie lay on top of Dawson for a few moments, kissing, wiggling, and laughing.

"Honey," he said. "We can't do this out here."

"Why?" she asked.

"Because too many people are looking at us, that's why."

She sat up and asked, "Who's looking at us?"

"Honey, this damned jungle is full of eyes. I would be willing to bet that at least ten people are watching us right this minute."

"Ten of whose people?" she demanded, getting off him and fixing her dress.

Dawson sat up and looked at her.

"Don't worry about who it is," he said.

They were quiet for a few minutes as she pouted and pretended to pick at the food. All the while she was secretly peaking up to see if she could spot anyone.

Operation Minerva

"I don't see anyone. Do you see anyone?" she asked.

"Not now," he answered. "But I have seen some movement on the southwest corner of the lake, just inside the wood line."

Genie took a long breath and exhaled in a short loud sigh.

"This sure throws cold water on our picnic," she said.

"Do you like poetry?" he asked.

"Yes, I do," she replied. "Why?"

He reached down into the leg-pocket of his tiger-striped fatigues and pulled out some folded papers.

"I have allowed very few people to see my poetry," he said. "Mainly, I think, because I see it as inconsistent with what I do for a living. Would you like to read it?" he asked.

"Yes, I would," she replied softly, looking somewhat surprised.

Operation Minerva

Mother's Kitchen

Mother's kitchen is Happiness and Life
Where love protects you from pursuing strife;
A forum where the day's problems are solved,
A sanctuary where peach can be found;
Love fills Mother's kitchen when she's around.
Mother's kitchen - the crossroads of my world,
No matter through how much space I'm whirled, A point
which I seem always to return;
Oh, so many dark valleys I may roam,
But end up in Mother's kitchen - at home.

Genie looked up at Dawson. "Has your Mother seen this?" she asked.
"Yes, I mailed her a copy the day that it was written."
"What did she say about it?" Genie asked.
"I received a letter telling me that my poem was to become a permanent part of the kitchen. Dad framed it, and Mother placed it by the door where everyone would see it." Genie smiled and returned to the poems.

Operation Minerva

Quiet Village

Quiet ... empty - but you can't tell;
Over there! By the village well,
The square comes alive with sharp sound
As the soldier slumps to the ground;
His black pajamas turn deep red
As I check to see if he's dead.
Listen! Do you hear that faint cry?
Watch it Jack! The VC are sly;
It's coming from that bamboo hut;
First I see a little brown mutt,
Then her, inside, out of the heat;
She's so small sitting at my feet.
A tear runs down her dusty face,
A trail of clean skin marks its trace;
In blood-stained white cotton she's dressed,
And tied close to her soiled breast
By string, a treasured piece of lace;
So lost she looks out of place.
Little girl with slanting brown eyes,
Kneeling and fighting away flies;
Soothing one younger, drying tears,
What a task for one of eight years;
Holding sister in her arms ... cries,
For she lives and her sister ... dies.

Tears filled Genie's eyes as she finished the second poem.
She removed a small lace handkerchief from her pocket,
dried her eyes, and continued.

Operation Minerva

Battlefields And Children

She makes mud pies near a black stagnant pool,
He pretends to Captain a wooden ship –
Stern wheeler made from old discarded spool;
They must be giving their teachers the slip,
No, there is no schooling for them to skip.
Thunder sounds across a cloudless blue sky,
They hasten not to shelter - there's no rain;
She makes mud pies, ask me not how or why;
His wooden ship has now become a train,
Oh, how can they play and ignore the pain?
How can he Captain with only one leg?
How can she patty-cake with only one hand?
How can they live out life - except to beg?
 Justify raping this people, this land.
They laugh and play! I'll never understand.

Genie dropped the papers to her side and dried her eyes again.
"Are these true?" she asked.
"Yes, they are." He replied. "I don't think I'm very imaginative. I can only write about things that I've seen or things that I feel."
She looked at him for a moment, then very quietly said,
"Let's go back to my room."

Operation Minerva

"It's a boy, boy! ... poochai."
The Thai Mother said to Webb and Tamashiro as she pulled the diaper off her three-month old baby and proudly displayed the baby's penis to them. Webb backed off a few steps as she thrust her naked baby at him. Tamashiro laughed and patted the baby saying it was beautiful boy.
"Thai Mothers are super proud when they have a boy," Tamshiro said to Webb.
"Every Thai woman I have talked to wants all boys. I don't think they have ever stopped and thought about what would happen if everyone had only boys."
The Mother squatted down to re-diaper her baby and Webb and Tamashiro continued down the trail.
"I think most primitive societies are like that," Webb said.
"The United States was like that not too many years ago. People were producing workers and males were workers."
Webb and Tamashiro could hear American music and the giggling of young girls as they approached the house. The barking of a young frisky pup alerted the girls to the arrival of the customers. Activity around the house exploded as they were identified as Americans. There were ten young girls at the house ranging from age twelve to seventeen. The seventeen-year-old was considered, by the younger girls, to be the madam of the establishment. Tamashiro's father was Japanese and his mother was a very beautiful Malaysian. This combination of oriental genes gave Tamashiro a uniquely well-proportioned body and a handsome oriental face. He was always an instant success with the girls and these young Thai girls were no exception, each tried to win his attention before giving up and turning to Webb. However, it made no difference to

212

him because the sound of the young girls laughing sent his thoughts to another time and another place:

The doorbell rang and Monique called to her Mother, "Will you get the door, Mom? I'm not ready yet!"
"Yes, dear," she answered, "I'll get it."
Monique's Mother was anxious to see this new boy that was causing such a pitch of excitement in her daughter. Monique was only six weeks away from graduation and in all her high school dating she had never before displayed total infatuation. Up until now she had always dated tall boys at school. So, when her Mother opened the door and found a short, oriental looking, young man, neatly dressed in a military uniform she was more than a little surprised.
"May I help you?" she asked, not being sure this was him.
"Is Monique ready?" he asked.
"Please come in. She will be ready in just a moment."
He took off his cap and stepped inside.
"I'll go see if she is ready yet," Monique's Mother said, walking toward the back of the house.
"Monique," she said, in an impatient whisper. "He's short, he's in uniform and he's... he's oriental!"
Monique turned slowly and looked at her Mother. "So?" she said.
"So!" her Mother answered.
"Father told me not to go with Blacks, Jews, Mexicans, or Puerto Ricans. He did not say anything about Orientals," she said, very matter-of-factly.

"Oh, my God. Can you really be that naive. Don't you know that your Father is prejudiced against anyone that's not white and Protestant?"

"Tommie's a Protestant," Monique said, her face lighting up with hope.

"Oh, God," her Mother sighed again as she walked back to the front of the house.

She found the boy standing at parade rest exactly where she had left him by the door. Oh, my God, she said to herself, I forgot to ask him to sit down.

"Please sit down. Monique will be out soon."

The next few minutes were very strained as the two sat quietly looking at each other across the coffee table. Monique's Mother broke the silence,

"What is your name?" she asked.

"Thomas Lee Tamashiro," he replied.

"What nationality is that?" she asked.

"My Father is Japanese and my Mother is from Singapore, she's Maylaysian. I was born in San Francisco."

"How long have you been in the Army?" she asked.

"Not long." he answered. I just got home from basic training."

"Do your parents live here in Lubbock now?"

"Yes, we moved to Texas when I was five years old."

Monique's mother looked at the clock on the wall and then at her wristwatch. Monique's Father would be home at eight o'clock; she had 10-minutes to get these two kids out of the house. She walked to the back of the house again trying to get Monique to move faster.

Operation Minerva

"Monique, your Father will be home in ten minutes.   If you two are not gone all hell is going to break loose."

"I'm ready, Mother. I'm ready."

"Monique's Mother walked out onto the front porch with them.   The evening air was warm and sweet with the smell of flowers.

"I think I'll sit out here on the swing and wait for your Father.   This is such a beautiful evening."

"I'll be home before midnight Mom, okay?"

Monique's Mother did not answer but just waved to them as they walked out to the car.   As they walked around the car to the passenger side, an old truck slid recklessly to a stop beside them.   A thick cloud of dust from the truck's over-sized tires engulfed the two teen-agers.   A big red-faced angry man stepped out of the truck.

"Daddy," Monique shouted. *"You got my new dress all dusty! It's ruined!"*

Monique started to cry as she tried to brush off the heavy brown dust.   Monique's Mother had bolted from the porch at first sight of the truck and was between her husband and the boy. Monique's Father was paid every two weeks and every payday from five o'clock until eight o'clock you could always find him at the Silver Spur Inn. The boys at the Silver Spur knew about Monique's date.   They also were fully aware of the extent of her Father's prejudices. For more than 2-hours he was the butt of muffled laughter and obvious side-looking glances, glances that were followed by whispers and a turned shoulder, glances that were pointed and sure to irritate. Finally, angered to the point that he could no longer hold himself back, he grabbed one of the offenders and slammed him into the wall. The Father of one of Monique's girlfriends had

215

learned of the eight o'clock date by overhearing his daughter talk about it on the telephone. He quickly spread the news around the Silver Spur and waited for the results. Monique's Father released the man and looked at his wristwatch, it was seven-forty-five. Monique's Mother stood firmly in place between young Thomas and her husband.

"What the hell is going on here?" he bellowed, shaking his fist at his wife.

"The children are going to a movie, that's all," she said.

"My daughter ain't goin' to no damn movie with no god-damn chink. You got that?"

He turned his attention to Monique and commanded, "You get your little-white-ass in the house right now girl. I'll deal with you later."

Monique began to cry again and ran for the house. Monique's Father made a move toward young Thomas but was blocked by his wife.

"The boy is going home now," she said, as she motioned for Tom to get into his car. "Go inside the house and sit down, relax. It's all over."

"Don't tell me what to do, god damn it!" he said, as he grabbed her by the hair and threw her to the ground. "It's not over until I say it's over."

Young Thomas was bending over, helping Monique's Mother to her feet, when a fist came crashing down behind his left ear. Thomas crumbled unconscious on top of Monique's mother.

Tamashiro was more-or-less selected by one of the dominant Thai girls of the house and taken to her room where they spent the remainder of the day. Webb had already disappeared into one of the adjoining rooms.

"Tamashiro," Webb called, "let's go." I don't want to miss chow, I'm hungry!"

Webb had spent the afternoon with one of the girls that he had found particularly attractive. They were sitting on a log in front of the little hut when Tamashiro, sporting a bare breasted girl on his arm, came to the door. "Have you ever seen such a magnificent pair of tits as this girl has?" Tamashiro asked Webb, motioning to the girl on his arm.

The young Thai girl was highly pleased with what nature had given her. She knew exactly how to show them too. Upon Tamashiro's insistence to display them, she took a deep breath, held her arms high over her head and turned around slowly.

"Oh, shit!" Webb said. "I was just getting settled down and you had to do that."

He stood up, took his girl by the hand and led her back into the hut. Tamashiro and his girl laughed at Webb's frustration, then returned to their room.

Genie looked at Dawson and shook her head in disbelief, "It's hard for me to comprehend that in just twelve hours you will be on the ground in North Vietnam,"

He raised his left arm up around Genie's neck and checked his wristwatch, it was four o'clock.

"You're right," he said, placing his hand back on her breast and drawing her close to him.   "Are you hungry?" she asked.

"Yes."

Operation Minerva

"Let's go get something at the mess hall."
Genie and Dawson walked into the mess hall at four-thirty. They were thirty minutes early for supper so Dawson went to get two cups of coffee from the kitchen while Genie sat down at the officer's table. Captain Coxe walked into the mess hall and sat down across from Genie.

"Sergeant Cook told me you and Dawson went on a picnic. How did it go?" he asked.
"It was very nice until he told me that people were watching us from the woods."
The Captain laughed at Genie as she slightly animated her comment.

Dawson walked up to the table and asked the Captain if he would like some coffee. The Captain said he would really like to have a glass of cold milk, so Dawson returned to the kitchen to get some.
"You will have to forgive Dawson for spoiling your picnic. He's a damn good soldier. One of the reasons that he is still alive is that he never allows himself to relax. A Viet Cong may step out from behind a tree someday and get the drop on him, but it will not be a surprise - he expects it."
"Here is your milk, Captain," Dawson said, setting the glass in front of the Captain.
"Thank you, Dawson," the Captain said.
Dawson walked around the long table and sat down beside Genie.
"I saw you two coming over here so I thought I would join you for awhile."

218

Operation Minerva

No one spoke for several minutes and Genie could feel tension building up in the silence. "Is everything ready for tonight, Captain?" she asked.

"Yes, everything is ready."

The squeaking sound of the screen door signaled the arrival of Lieutenant Deluca and Sergeant Applewhite.

"Well," Lieutenant Deluca said, laughing. "I don't think we are the first ones here after all."

Deluca and Applewhite crossed the room and sat down on both sides of the Captain.

"I was just saying to the Lieutenant," Applewhite commented, "that we were so early for chow that we should be first in line. I guess everyone had the same idea."

The mess cooks came out and began to set up the serving line under the watchful eye of the duty cook. After a few minutes, the cook called to the group at the table and said they could go through the line if they wanted to. Everyone stood and walked up to the serving line, each watching to ensure that the Captain arrived first. The Captain stopped as he reached the line and motioned to Genie. "Ladies first," he said, then added as he took Dawson's arm, "with her escort."

Genie and Dawson thanked the Captain and walked through the line. During the meal, casual conversation began only after each had settled back to enjoy a last cup of coffee. The mess hall was crowded now so the conversation was guarded. Each talked about what they had done during the day and Genie's description of the picnic received a round of laughter. The Captain looked at his watch, then said, "It's 17:45. Remember, we have to have our personal items ready for storage at 18:30 hours. Sergeant Cook will be in operations to take care of anything you need. The helicopter ETD[51] is 19:00 hours - see you at the pad."

Sergeants Webb and Tamashiro were just coming into the mess hall as the Captain was walking out. He reminded them of the schedule and then continued on his way. The topic of discussion at the table where Webb and Tamashiro sat down was hippies and beatniks. Tamashiro joined the group adding his condemnation. Webb, however, just smiled as he remembered a childhood friend and their last meeting in Savannah:

Mike Webb and Dan Bradford were best friends and always together. Their friendship was due, in part at least, to the fact that their backyards joined together without benefit of a fence. Webb had been adopted into the family when he tried to get work and a place to stay. He had run off from an orphanage and they did not want to send him back. He became the child that they were never able to have. The nature of the two boys could not have been more unalike. Webb got good grades in school, Dan failed frequently. Webb never got into any trouble and Dan was always in trouble. If the two boys had been walking down a country lane and a passing car splashed mud into the air - the mud would instinctively seek out Dan. Their friendship flourished until Webb joined the army after graduation. Dan tried to enlist but his juvenile record, long hair, and hippie attitude kept him out. During the first year that Webb spent in Vietnam fighting

---

[51] Estimated Time of Departure

the Viet Cong, Dan spent at home fighting the local police. He never got into any real trouble, just minor events that led to his being known, on a first name basis, by every police officer in town and nearly every deputy sheriff in the county. All the communication between the two young men was through their Mother's talking over a newly installed fence between the backyards:

"Mike is coming home Friday and he wants Dan to pick him up at the airport." Dan's Mother said that she would tell him.

"Maybe if Mike comes home for a spell he just might get Dan to straighten up a bit."

As Dan sat down in the waiting room at the airport, he noticed that the two women sitting on either side of him were studying him closely. Both ladies were in their forties and tastefully dressed in the latest fashions. Dan began scratching and pretending to find little vermin in his hair and beard. Each time he feigned a discovery he would carefully, and with great intensity, dramatize its execution between his thumbnails. The two women were unaware that they, along with Dan, had become the center of attention in the waiting room. With each execution, Dan would crack one of his knuckles, both women would grimace and flinch with each report. The woman on Dan's left was leaning away from him to the extent that the people across the aisle were leaning in sympathy. The woman on Dan's right was holding her hand up in a protective manner, to her hair.

While everyone was watching Dan's right hand search for another victim, his left hand found a bug-size pebble in his pants cuff. As he brought his hands together for the ceremonial execution, he placed the pebble on this thumb and flipped it toward the woman who was protecting her hair. All eyes were on the sandstone "bug" as it sailed into the air and plummeted into the woman's hair. The woman screamed as she jumped up and began slapping at her head violently. She ripped her hat off, then her scarf, then her jacket. She was pulling at her blouse when Dan noticed Mike coming through the arrival's door. A crowd was gathering around the woman now and Dan was forgotten.

"What's all the excitement about?" Webb asked as they clasped hands in greeting.

"Some crazy woman over there thinks she has a bug on her." Dan answered at they walked out.

"I'm so hungry," Webb said, "I could eat a damn door knob. Can we go someplace and eat?"

"We can if you have some money."

"I've got money! Let's eat."

Dan drove into Savannah and stopped at a better-than-average restaurant. Everyone looked at them as they entered. Webb was a clean, polished, crew-cut Green Beret; Dan was a grubby, shaggy, long-haired hippie. The headwaiter came to the table and refused to serve Dan, but he said Webb was welcome. Dan argued with him saying he could not refuse service and refused to leave. Webb talked him into leaving when he saw two big cooks coming to the waiter's aid. Outside, Dan took a raisin from a small box in his pocket and put it up his nose. Then he walked over to the big window of the dining room and looked inside. All the diners were watching him as he pulled the raisin out of his nose, smashed it on the window and streaked it across the window for about three feet and then wiped his finger on his pants. This caused quite a stir within the restaurant and, once again, the two cooks were called out to back up the waiter he chased Dan and Webb down the street.

"I see you haven't changed, Dan," Webb said, after they had out-distanced the waiter and cooks.

"Well, what the hell," Dan replied, "it keeps life interesting." They were both laughing as they turned the corner and walked into McDonald's.

"What do you think of hippies?" Tamashiro asked Webb.

"What do I think? I think they should catch everyone of them and give them a GI bath and a haircut!" he replied laughing.

Under his breath, he said, "Don't worry, Dan. I know you can run like hell."

Genie was sitting on Dawson's bed in the BOQ watching him pack.

"Well," he said, after he finished. "All I have to do now is deliver this to operations and I'll be ready to go."

"Not quite!" Genie said, leaning back on his bed. "You have one other job to take care of."

Dawson looked at his wristwatch and then at Genie.

"I guess I have time for one more job."

Chapter 13
The Flight

Sergeant Applewhite was drinking coffee and looking out the window as their plane pulled into formation with the two escort aircraft. He looked at his wrist watch; he knew that two hours from rendezvous was jump time. Right on schedule, he thought as he looked at the other team members. Dawson was talking to the jumpmaster, the Captain was going up to the flight deck, Lieutenant Deluca was asleep, and Webb, Tamashiro and the loadmaster were looking at a Playboy centerfold. Applewhite returned his gaze to the window and, as he finished off his coffee, thought of another flight years ago.

"Soldier," the stewardess said. "Would you like more coffee?"

"No, thank you," he said, handing her the empty cup.

He picked up a magazine, thumbed quickly through its pages and threw it down. He searched through his pockets and pulled out the tattered telegram. He knew his Father was dead before the telegram had arrived. He also knew Red Cross confirmation was necessary in order to get emergency leave. He read the message again:

Operation Minerva

FATHER DIED 10 PM FEB. 18th.
U.S. ARMY HOSIPIAL FORT BENNING, GA.
REQUEST COMMANDING OFFICER GRANT
EMERGENCY LEAVE.

"Samuel," his Mother said, "Jimmy's runnin' with some real bad boys. He's got no respect for nobody. Now he's talkin' about quitin' school. Will you talk to him? He's been such a burden on me, Daddy bein' sick and all."

"I'll talk to him, Mother," Applewhite said. "I think I can get his attention."

He walked down to the corner poolroom where he knew his little brother would be. Several young men were sitting on the curb in front of the building. They were passing around a bottle concealed in a brown bag. Some of them recognized Applewhite and offered him a drink. The glass front of the building had been broken so many times that it had finally been replaced with plywood and iron bars. The smoke inside was thick, visibility was limited to just a few feet. He found his brother in a small back room with no windows or ventilation and the only light in the room was over a gambling table.

"Jim, come outside." Applewhite said, "I want to talk to you."

"Hey, brother," one of the three men sitting at the table said," we're all together here, we ain't go no secrets. Do we Jim? Say what you gota' say."

Applewhite's brother and two other young boys were sitting up against the back wall. The three men at the table continued to play cards.

"Well," Applewhite said. "I guess I can say what I have to say right here. Jim, Mother has been worried about you. She has the idea that you got mixed up with a tough gang."

"Damn, that must be us," the man at the table said.

Applewhite ignored the comment and continued to talk, "I'll tell Mom she has nothing to worry about."

"That's right, man. We take care of our own," the man at the table said.

Applewhite continued to ignore his comments and continued to talk, "I'll tell her that all I saw down here was three pussies playing cards in the dark."

The room was instantly quiet as the man that had been doing all the talking got up from the table. As he approached Applewhite he pulled a switchblade knife from his pocket, flicked open the blade, and began to toss it from one hand to the other.

"Ok, man," he said, "We'll see who the pussy is around here."

The other two men got up and fell-in behind their leader.

Applewhite waited until the man with the knife was within range then told him to stop.

"I'm going to give you just one chance to walk out of here and let my brother and me alone. Think on it real serious now because the next step you take, whether it is toward that door or toward me, will determine if you wind up outside for some fresh air or on the table at the emergency room."

The man looked at Applewhite and began to laugh. He checked behind to see if his two friends were backing him up. Then, as he turned back to Applewhite, he made a lunge with the knife.

Applewhite intercepting the thrust in mid-flight and clamped a vice-like grip on the man's wrist and twisted the arm until the elbow was up. Then, a crushing blow from Applewhite's right fist broke the man's arm at the elbow. Before the first man had time to cry out in pain, Applewhite dropped each of the other two with sidekicks to the head. His brother and the other two boys were rendered almost catatonic by the speed and violence of the display. Their eyes were wide open with fear and their mouths hung open as if gasping for air. The confrontation was so short that pool players in the main room were unaware of any trouble as Applewhite and the three boys walked out.

"Sergeant," the loadmaster said, "do you want more coffee?"

"Yes," he said. "We won't be having any good coffee for awhile. I'd better fill up now."

"Did you get to talk to your brother today?" the Captain asked.

"Yes, sir. I called Saigon this afternoon. We had a good talk."

"Is everything ok at home?"

"Yes, thank you, sir. Jim said Mom asked about you the last time they talked. He said she wanted him to check to make sure that you were keeping me out of trouble. He also told me that my brother Bryan is coming over in September."

"Bryan is a sergeant in the engineers isn't he?"

"Yes sir," Applewhite answered," another leg." The Captain looked at his wristwatch. "One hour, better start getting ready."

"Do you feel OK Captain?" Applewhite asked. "You look pale."

"I have an upset stomach," he answered. "Too much booze last night, I think."

Applewhite put his hand on the Captain's forehead.

"You have a temperature, Alex. I don't think you should jump."

"I'll be OK Sam," he said taking Applewhite's hand," I'll be OK."

The action made Applewhite think of his girlfriend.

"Sam, when are you going to stop following that little white boy around like you were his daddy?"

"Paris," Applewhite said," *that white boy's Father gave my Father several extra years of life by becoming personally involved in his lawsuit with the army."*

"I know all that shit, Sam! But, are you going to follow him around for the rest of your life?" she asked.

"I promised his Father that I would look after him for as long as I could."

"You just got back from Vietnam less that a year ago. Why are you going back so soon?"

"Paris," he said, " I am a professional soldier. I like being a soldier."

"Can't you be a soldier here?" she asked. Applewhite looked at her for a few moments then said, "A good cook loves the kitchen, a good teacher loves the classroom, and a good Green Beret loves a fight."

"Sam, won't we never be married?"

"I've already tried that once. All my ex-wife did was bitch about the army and tell me that I had to make a choice between her and the army. You know the choice I made. So, why do you want to get into it with me?"

"Don't you ever intend to retire?"

Operation Minerva

"What the hell would I do if I retired? I don't like golf. I don't collect stamps. Fishing gives me a pain in the ass. What would I do?"

"I guess I'll just have to be satisfied with loving a vagabond soldier," she said," and continue to follow you around the country from camp to camp."

"Why do you wait on me? Why don't you get married again? I know your ex-husband has been trying to get you back." Paris put her arms around him and rested her head on his chest. "I'll wait for you, you big gentle teddy bear, because you are the only real man that I have ever known."

The lights inside the aircraft changed from white to red to give the jumpers time to adjust their night vision. The pilot gave a thirty-minute warning. Everyone was in place now and each was submerged in thought. Dawson was thinking of Thailand. A smile came over his face and he laughed quietly.

Dawson got up early that April 14th. He had been assigned the extra duty of helping the Thai's repair the antique phone system that served the post at Lop Buri. He selected his best fatigues and put an extra shine on his boots. As he put on his green beret, he inspected himself in the mirror. Seadang was washing dishes when he called good-bye to her and walked out. Outside, Dawson again checked his uniform and the blouse of his trousers. An old woman that he believed to be the wife of the night watchman was walking through the compound with a small bucket of water. The old woman was laughing as she approached Dawson and the closer she got the louder she laughed. At a distance of about three feet she threw the water on Dawson, laughed hysterically, and danced around 'in a circle. Dawson was dumbfounded. He thought the little old woman had gone mad. He looked at his wet uniform and then at the crazy old woman dancing around in front of him clapping her hands. Dawson had to laugh as he walked back toward the house. He stood quietly beside Seadang, waiting for her to notice.

"You wet," she said.

"No shit," he replied," that crazy old woman threw water on me!"

"This is water festival time."

"What is water festival?" he asked.

"Water festival is fun," she answered." All people go around throwing water and having fun. Tonight everyone will be in street eating, dancing, and drinking.

"And throwing water?" he added.

"No, no throw water after dark," she said, "just in daytime."

Dawson was almost thrown out of his seat as the aircraft went into an evasive maneuver. The aircraft was under fire and this was where the jump aircraft would break out of formation and make for LAOS.

"Fifteen minutes!" the jumpmaster shouted, "fifteen minutes."

Sergeants Webb and Tamashiro helped Dawson reposition his equipment as he tried to make himself comfortable again. Webb pushed himself back into the seat, took a deep breath and tried to relax. The aircraft had settled down and each returned to his thoughts.

Operation Minerva

Webb's thoughts were of Kansas, his sister, and the state operated farm where they were raised and separated.

"If you run away, Michael, I'll never see you again," his sister cried.

"I'll be back for you. I promise."

"Where are you going to go?" she asked.

"I've got my compass," he said showing it to her, *"I'm going west to California, Mary,"* he said. *"What color is my shirt?"*

"Red," she answered.

"What color are my shorts?"

"White" she said.

"What do I have in my sack?"

"Food," she said.

"Good, remember that," he said, *"I've got to go now. I'll be back for you."*

Michael Webb was 6 years old and had run away from the orphanage three times. Each time he found out a little bit more about how he was caught. This time he had a change of clothes in his sack, not food. This time he was going east, not west. This time he was sure he would escape. He made it all the way to Indiana before he was picked up and returned to the orphanage. Later that year his sister was adopted and taken away. Michael was not adopted because of his record of being a runaway. At the age of 12 he made his final escape from the orphanage. He returned to the orphanage after he turned eighteen to find his sister. The orphanage had been closed and no record of his sister's adoption could be found. He had returned every year since then, during his annual leave, to search for his sister.

"Mary," he said to himself. "Maybe I'll find you this year."

"Stand up!" the jumpmaster roared through the bullhorn.
As the team members struggled to their feet, Sergeants Webb and Tamashiro helped Dawson to his feet. The load master helped secure the seats in the up position to clear the aisle for the jumpers.

"Check equipment," the jumpmaster roared as he slapped his chest with right hand - the signal for check equipment.
Each jumper checked his own equipment and then the equipment of the jumper in front of him. The last jumper in the stick, Lieutenant Deluca, had to turn around and be inspected by the jumper in front of him, Sergeant Webb.

"Sound off for equipment check," was the next command.

"Six OK," Lieutenant Deluca answered.

"Five OK," from Sergeant Webb.

"Four OK," from Dawson.

"Three OK," from Sergeant Tamashero.

"Two OK," from Sergeant Applewhite.

"One OK," from Captain Coxe.

"Stand in the door," the jumpmaster ordered.
During the next few moments the aircraft became quiet, the engines whispered, and for the jumpers, and stood still.

Sergeant Applewhite's thought turned to his brother's graduation from military intelligence school at Fort Devans, Massachusetts.

Operation Minerva

"Second Lieutenant James Applewhite," the announcer said.

Jim walked up to the Colonel, saluted and was handed his gold second lieutenant's bars. He took one step back, saluted again, did an about face and walked away. On the parade ground, Jim handed his Mother the shiny new gold bars.

"Will you pin them on me, Mom?"

"I think Sam should have the honor, son. You wouldn't be here today without his help."   "Why don't we compromise," Sam said, "Mom, you pin one on and I'll pin one on. OK?"

After the bars were in place, Sam gave his little brother his first salute. And, in keeping with tradition, he collected one dollar for the service. Bryan was next in line to salute his brother; however, his salute was followed by a brotherly hug.

"Sam," Jim said. "I want to thank you for saving me that day in the pool hall.

The two men that were playing cards that day are in prison for murder. And, one kid that was with me that day has been in prison twice since then for dealing."

Sergeant Tamashiro was enjoying the cool fresh air that was blasting through the open door. The heat inside the aircraft had intensified familiar odors that were not normally offensive and made them sickening. Several times, before the door was opened and the cool air circulated around him, he thought he was going to vomit. He relaxed now, took deep breaths, and felt better.

"Oh! Thommy," Monique squealed," don't you just love a convertible."

Operation Minerva

Monique got up on her knees in the front seat and stuck her head into the wind. It was spring in Texas and the night air was fresh and warm.

"Let's not go to the movies," she said, "let's just drive around for a while and then find a nice place to park."

About thirty minutes later they pulled up along a dry creek bed under a railroad bridge. A full moon flooded the area with silver light. Monique and Tom leaned back in the seat and looked up at the stars.

"How long will you be gone?" she asked.

"My training should be over in about three months. Then I'll have two weeks leave before I go to Vietnam."

"Will you come to see me during your leave?"

"Yes, I'll be here." *Tom placed his hand on Monique's breast as they kissed.*

She responded by pulling him closer to her. *They fumbled around for a few moments trying to find a comfortable position.*

"Let's get in the back seat," he suggested.

"OK," she answered quietly.

Monique's blouse was made of white raw silk and buttoned up the front with very small pearl buttons. Once in the back seat Tom tried in vain to unbutton it. He was so excited and clumsy that she thought he was going to tear the Fabric.

"Wait!" she said," pushing his shaking hands away. "Let me do that."

Slowly, Monique released each button. Then, she reached inside and pushed the bra strap off her shoulder. Tom nervously put his hand inside her bra and exposed her breast.

Operation Minerva

"Oh, God," he said looking at her lovely full breast. Then he added without thinking, "They're real!"

Monique just laughed at his comment. She had heard the stories the other girls in school had spread about her, that she was half cotton. Tom had never touched a woman's breasts before and the sensation thrilled him, sending his heart racing.

"Your skin is so cool and smooth," he said, "it feels tight, not like mine at all."

Tom's fascination with Monique's breasts lasted for about half an hour, then his hand worked its way down between her legs.

"I've never gone all the way before", she whispered.

"I haven't either."

"Do you have a rubber?" she asked. "I don't want to get pregnant!"

"Yes," he answered. "I have one."

"Is it a good one?"

"I guess it is," he said, "it's new."

"You didn't poke any holes in it did you," she asked.

"What the hell would I poke a hole in it for?"

"Mom told me that boys like to get girls pregnant so they can brag about it. They tell the girl that they are going to use a rubber and then they trick them by using one that has a hole in it."

"Here, take it," he said, "check it. Make sure that I'm not trying to trick you."

"How do I know if it has a hole in it? I don't know how to check it."

"Your Mother told you everything else, why didn't she tell you how to check for a hole? What are you doing?"

"I'll blow it up."

235

"What?" he said laughing.

"I'm going to blow it up. If it holds air, then it doesn't have a hole in it."

"Jesus Christ," Tom said collapsing back in the seat, *"I can't believe this."*

Monique blew up the rubber until it was the size of a watermelon.

"Well," Tom said. *"What's the verdict?"*

"Well, I guess it doesn't have any holes in it."

"I guess it doesn't. Can we use it now?" he asked.

"Yes," she answered.

As she handed the inflated rubber to Tom she let go too soon and it jetted off into the night.

"Oh, shit, Monique!" Tom roared, "that's the only one I have."

Tom got out of the car and searched several minutes for the lost rubber.

"I can't find it," he said as he returned to the back seat and sat down.

Tom and Monique were sitting as far apart from each other as they could get. They sat quietly and looked up at the stars. After a few moments Monique began to laugh, then Tom began to laugh. Tom mimicked the sound of the rubber as it shot away from the car and made a sweeping gesture with his hand. Both roared with laughter as they rolled around in the back seat of the car.

"How do I know it doesn't have any holes in it?" Tom said trying to mimic Monique's voice. *Again the two young lovers roared with laughter.*

"Maybe it's better this way," he said.

Tom and Monique fell asleep as they held each other and looked at the stars.

Operation Minerva

"My God, Tom, "Monique said, "It's 2 a.m. Mom will kill us. We've got to go".

"Go!" the jumpmaster screamed.
Seconds later, falling through the dark night at 120 miles per hour the Captain called,
"Join up, join up!"

CHAPTER 14
The Captain's Log

First Day:
The HAELO[52] drop last night was literally a textbook operation. We were on target and had no injuries. By dawn today we had buried all jump equipment and concealed ourselves in a gorge just off a small dry tributary of the Song Da (Black River). The aerial photographs of the area were invaluable in selecting a suitable hideout for the first day. Highpocket's idea of tracing the paths and trails in white ink was a stroke of genius. By knowing exactly where the trails and footpaths were, picking an area where there was little or no traffic was a simple matter. We are in a gorge (aerial photo 2365 coordinates 537, 250). Sergeant Applewhite is guarding one end and Mr. Dawson the other. We have seen only light traffic on the river and no traffic in the surrounding terrain. We will move to our first OP[53] after dark. Everyone is resting and getting their gear ready for tonight's trek.

---

[52] High Altitude Exit Low Opening free fall parachute jump
[53] Observation Point

Operation Minerva

Day Two:
Last night during our movement to the OP we inadvertently ran across an old man in the woods. Before he could make a sound, Sergeant Applewhite killed him - broke his neck. I was worried about him being found and more worried about someone searching for him. Lieutenant Deluca had the idea of placing him on a path (so he would be easily found) and making it look like he had fallen and broken his neck. So, that is exactly what we did. Our OP is approximately two-thousand meters from the school and in an area devoid of trails. It provides good natural concealment - Aerial Photo 2366, coordinates 350, 575. We made our first observations of the school this morning. Activity at the school started at 0730 hours. Some personnel arrived by bicycle from the small village two-thousand meters to the west. However, the majority of school personnel are billeted in the school complex.

Mr. Dawson and Sergeant Webb are taking pictures. Lieutenant Deluca and Sergeant Tamashiro are on flank positions. Sergeant Applewhite and I are observing the objective with field glasses. The school has a small (six-man) guard force. They raised the flag this morning as. There are indigenous laborers (eight men and three women?) working on the parade grounds and stand. We have observed no motorized traffic in the area, only bicycles. At 1200 hours the school broke for lunch. We counted 28 students and 5 cadre. Two local ladies from the village set up shop outside the school and started cooking chow at approximately 1130 hours. Some of the students went to the mess hall and some patronized the local vendors in the front of the school. It made me think of my own school days at Fort Bragg; we also had a choice: the roach-coach[54] or the mess hall. I guess soldiers are the same around the world. During the lunch break (1200 to 1230 hours), Mr. Dawson and Sergeant Webb took several pictures. I recognized one of the men! He was even dressed in South Vietnamese tiger fatigues. His name is Van Linh; and, he is supposed to be one of our agents. I saw him in Nha Trang two weeks ago. His code name is Tiger Tim. It would appear that he is acting as a guest instructor because he is only associating with the instructors. Sergeant Applewhite is preparing a tape for the transmission of this information to team A4610 at Nan, our contract for this time period. All activity at the school today has been inside. Photographs were taken of all persons arriving or departing. The training day ended at 1700 hours. There has been no activity since the flag was taken down and there does not seem to be a guard posted. Mr. Dawson and Sergeant Tamashiro set up a directional antenna at 245 degrees for the transmission of our message to Nan. At 1400 hours ZULU we received (on our monitor frequency) the command signal to transmit. We transmitted the message on our primary frequency; the transmission time was 8 seconds. At 1430 hours ZULU we received confirmation of a 100% copy of our message.

I have posted the following sentry schedule for tonight:
2000 hours to 2400 hours Lt. Deluca and Sgt. Webb

---

[54] Lunch Truck

Operation Minerva

2400 hours to 0300 hours Cpt. Coxe and Sgt. Applewhite
0300 hours to 0700 hours Mr. Dawson and Sgt.
Tamashiro

At 0400, Dawson heard someone coming up the hill
toward the OP. He pulled his k-bar out. Whoever it is, he
thought, they certainly are making enough noise." As the
sound got closer, Dawson wiped the sweat from his hand
and took a new firm grip on his knife. Only a few more
steps now, he thought, Ok, ok, right...now! Dawson
grabbed the intruder by the throat, kicked his feet out
from under him and followed him to the ground ready for
the kill. He realized immediately that the small body
under him could not be a soldier. He held his knife to the
small throat as he searched for a weapon. He found
nothing. It was too dark to see anything except vague
forms. He felt the face and arms of the intruder. "It's a
little boy," he said softly. "What the fuck are you doing
running around out here this time of night?" He picked
the boy up and carried him to the OP. He knew the
scuffle had alerted the team so before walking into the
OP he gave the password.
"Mary," he whispered.
"Wanda," was the reply from the dark.
"What the hell happened?" the Captain asked.
"I caught this kid coming up the hill."
"Lieutenant," the Captain whispered, "Find out what that
kid is up to. Why is he wandering around out here at
night?"
Lieutenant Deluca interrogated the young prisoner for
several minutes then reported to the Captain.

"First," Deluca said. "She's not a boy. Her name is Lyn, she's 10 years old and she's a runaway orphan. She said she ran away from a work camp two days ago."

"Where was she trying to go?"

"She said she was trying to get to Hanoi. That's where she was when she was picked up and put in the camp."

As Lieutenant Deluca and the Captain talked, Dawson fed the little girl and put her in his sleeping bag. She was sound asleep in seconds. Dawson sat down against a tree and waited for daylight. Cold chills ran through him as he thought about how close he had come to killing the little girl.

Day Three:

Early this morning, Dawson captured a small girl wandering through our area. Lieutenant Deluca questioned her and she is apparently an orphan. She is tethered, by one ankle, to a tree. She has made no attempt to escape and she makes no noise. She just sits on her heels and looks at us in amazement. Team morale is high, everyone is busy with assigned duties, there is almost no talking - no need, each man is like a gear in a silent, smooth running, machine - each doing his part.

Activity at the school started at 0730 hours, the students were dressed in a different uniform. Tiger Tim did not show up this morning.

At 0800 hours the students assembled on the parade field and went through squad hand signals and immediate action drills - they looked good!

Operation Minerva

At 1000 hours two military trucks (approximately 5-ton) pulled up in front of the school, all the students were loaded on the trucks and taken away.

At 1130 hours a medical truck arrived and was positioned in front of the school. Judging from the preparations, I think they are going to have a parachute drop on the parade field.

"Captain," Dawson said, "take a look at this!"

"What is it?" the captain asked, reaching for the binoculars.

"A new U.S. Army jeep just pulled up in front of the administration hooch."

The captain took the binoculars and watched as the passenger, an old NVA officer, got out of the jeep and walked into the office. The driver walked around to the side of the building for a smoke.

"How the hell did they get a new jeep up here? We couldn't even get a new jeep at SOG headquarters and we had a full bird working on the problem!"

Moments later the passenger, three young officers and two enlisted men came out and inspected the jeep. The five men were like children who had just awakened on Christmas day and found the toy of their dreams under the tree. Two of the young officers struggled to get into the driver's seat at the same time. As the quickest one sat down behind the wheel, he spoke to the older officer and made a circular gesture with his arm. The older office nodded his approval and the young officer went flying around the parade ground kicking up clouds of dust.

The new jeep caused just about as much excitement on the hill as it did on the parade ground. The captain was furious. He thought about all the times he couldn't get military items from supply while at the same time he could walk downtown and buy the needed items on the black market or even from street vendors selling US military items in the open. He wanted to know how the NVA[55] got a new jeep inside North Viet Nam when it proved impossible to get one at SOG[56]. The captain wanted the serial number off that jeep. With the telescope they could tell the jeep had never been assigned to a unit, or even had a serial number painted on it. They could also see that it still had the registration plate on the dashboard. The captain vowed that if that jeep spent the night there, he would get the serial number and report it to SOG. He thought the serial number of that new jeep might prove to be the information that would allow the CID[57] and MI[58] to identify the people involved in diverting military equipment to the black market. He believed that it would not be that difficult to trace a brand new jeep from the factory to Vietnam and identify where the paper trail ended and who signed for it.

At sundown the jeep was still parked in front of the administration hooch. All they had to worry about was the guard who walked around the area during the night.

---

[55] North Vietnamese Army
[56] Special Operations Group
[57] Criminal Investigation Division
[58] Military Intelligence

Operation Minerva

They had come to know the guards and their habits during the past few nights of observing them. If they were lucky, they would get the sleeper (he always found a good place to sleep for the night) or the path guard (he never got off the path around the compound).

The captain selected lieutenant Deluca for the job. He thought Deluca was best for the assignment because he understood Vietnamese and because he was very quick and resourceful in tight situations.

At 02:00 lieutenant Deluca started down the hill to get the serial number of the jeep. The Captain and Dawson took turns watched him through the starlight scope. He had to go 800 meters to the east in order to keep from going through the clearing they used as a parade ground. Once across the road and into the brush he moved quickly to the administrative hooch. He watched the guard and felt lucky that the path guard was on duty. He timed him as he dutifully followed the well warn path around the parameter of the camp. He knew this guard never left the path or changed directions during his watch.

As the guard passed the jeep, Deluca crawled up to the passenger's side, pulled out a small flashlight, checked the serial number and wrote it down in his notepad. This thing is so new, he thought, it smells like it just came out of the box. This is not a reconditioned jeep; this is a new jeep. Just then he could here the distant sound of big guns and bombs going off over Hanoi. At first he did not get too excited about the noise. However, seconds later a fast moving, low flying jet screamed across the camp and climbed out of sight. Deluca covered the five meters from the jeep to the porch in seconds. He disappeared under the porch just as everyone in the camp ran outside to see what was going on. He didn't know if the jet was one of ours or one of theirs and he didn't care. Either way it almost cost him his life. Most of the men went back to bed right away, however a few stood around talking and smoking.

Deluca listened to two solders talk about their mothers, their families and their girlfriends. Deluca marveled at how much they sounded like any other two young men around the world having the same conversation. If people around the world would just stop and think about how much we are all alike instead of thinking about how much we are different, we would all stop fighting. Under other conditions, these two young men could be my friends. As he lay there in the dust, his mind started racing from one thought to another.

He started to get worried after nearly an hour had gone buy. He had to get out of there before it started to get daylight. The thought of being captured brought back memories of his POW[59] training in Panama. The memory caused a flood of fear to fill his mind and a sickening knot to form in his belly. He had to fight to compose himself and regain his confidence. The porch was too high and too open to provide a safe place to hide during

---

[59] Prisoner of War

daylight. He kept talking to himself. Trying to convince himself that the situation was not that bad. Except for the occasional rat passing through and the dust that was being kicked up by the wind, there was nothing for him to worry about, except how to get out. The North Vietnamese have no idea what a service they do for us by killing and eating all of the dogs, he thought.

Finally, the remaining men returned to their quarters and, as he watched the guard disappear around the corner of the building, he started to crawl out of camp. It was 04:30 when he crossed the road and started up the hill to the OP and first light when he walked into camp.

Dawson tapped the Captain on the shoulder and directed his attention to an aircraft approaching from the east.
"Looks like an old Dakota," Dawson whispered.
"Yes," the Captain replied, "but it sure don't sound like an old Dakota; they must have mounted new engines on it."
Dawson was observing the aircraft through the telescope lens on his camera. "The jump door is open," Dawson said to the Captain.
"Jesus Christ, they're going to jump! There goes the streamer[60] now."
The streamer was drifting to the south of the aircraft's east-to-west track. It was heading right for the OP.
"Oh my god!" the Captain groaned. "That god-damned thing is going to land right on top of us! Dawson!" the Captain ordered. "Get that streamer down the hill at least

---

[60] A long ribbon that indicates wind direction and speed

a hundred meters. A soldier is already on his way up here to get it."

Dawson scrambled around the area gathering up the 30-meter long streamer.

"Spread it out so he can't miss it," the Captain ordered, as Dawson started down the hill.

Dawson picked a clear area where he could create a reasonably acceptable fake landing for the streamer and make it highly visible for the soldier.

"It's all set," Dawson reported back to the Captain.

"Now all we can do is watch and wait." The Captain, Lieutenant Deluca and Dawson watched the soldier's progress up the hill.

"He's drifting off course to the west," the Captain said.

"The dumb shit is going to miss it."

"Maybe I can help him," Deluca said.

The Lieutenant picked up a golf ball size rock and heaved it up over the trees toward the area of the streamer. Everyone was silent. All eyes were on the soldier as he stopped and looked to his left. He stood motionless for a few moments then moved toward the streamer.

"Jesus!" Dawson said. "That was close, too close."

"Where the hell did you learn to throw like that Lieutenant?" the Captain asked.

"That just comes from being a farm boy, Captain," the Lieutenant said softly.

"We have about five minutes before the first jumper comes out of that aircraft. Hide everything and conceal yourselves. If one of those jumpers lands directly on this OP, I don't want him to see anything or suspect anything."

"Lieutenant."

"Yes, Sir."

"Keep the kid with you."

"Yes, Sir."

By the time the first jumper exited the aircraft, the OP was secured. The drop on the first pass was right down the center of the parade ground. The Captain had predicted it would take two passes to get all the jumpers out because the drop zone was so short. On the second pass the first jumper out of the door had a steerable chute and began drifting south.

"Christ," Dawson said, "Look at that idiot. The only fucking jumper with a steerable chute and he's going to be the only son-of-a-bitch to miss the damn DZ[61]."

"It looks like he is going to land right on top of us," the Captain said quietly.

The jumper did not appear to be fighting his chute or attempting to change course. From the moment his chute opened he drifted due south. Within seconds, the jumper was directly over the OP and still drifting south.

"He must have landed in the clearing just to the south of us," the Captain whispered.

Two minutes after the jumper passed over the OP, the team could hear him fighting his way down the hill toward them. He was carrying his chute as he walked directly into the center of the OP and stopped. After standing quietly for a few seconds, the jumper dropped his chute and walked over to the tree that Sergeant Tamashiro had used to support his equipment. Dawson was close to the jumper and immediately saw what had

---

[61] Drop Zone

attracted his attention. Hanging on one of the limbs of the tree was a four-foot long nylon cord, gently waving in the breeze. The jumper reached out and took the cord, studied it for a few moments, then looked around. Dawson slowly pulled his knife from its sheath as he watched the jumper for any sign of alarm. Lieutenant Deluca was only five-feet from the jumper and could see his expressions. The jumper was smiling. Not a happy smile Deluca thought, but a smile of cunning deceit that he remembered seeing in old war movies about the Japanese. He also notices that this jumper was a lieutenant colonel. The jumper place the nylon cord back on the tree, picked up his chute, and continued down the hill to the DZ.

"What was that all about?" the Captain asked.

"That was not one of your run-of-the-mill students," Deluca said. "He's a Lieutenant Colonel."

"Dawson, keep an eye on him while we prepare to evacuate this area," the Captain ordered.

After all preparations for evacuation were made, the team gathered around the Captain to discuss the situation.

"What is our jumper doing Dawson?" the Captain asked.

"Not a damn thing," Dawson replied. "He threw his chute in the pile and walked off by himself for a smoke. He hasn't spoken a word to anyone."

"Do any of you have any ideas?" the Captain asked. "I can't figure out what's going on."

"I didn't like the look I saw on his face," Lieutenant Deluca said. "It was almost as if he knew something, like he knew we were here."

"Dawson, what do you think?" the Captain asked.

"Well," Dawson said, "let's look at the total picture. If they knew we were here, why haven't they done something? Why did the only jumper with a steerable chute drift off the DZ and land here? Why did he hang that cord back on the tree? Why not keep it? Why not throw it down? Why did he make it so obvious, when he returned to the DZ, that he did not report anything to anyone? He's still standing by himself, smoking."

"Good questions," the Captain said, "what are the answers?"

"I don't think they know we're here, not all of them anyway."

"What do you mean, not all of them?" Sergeant Webb asked.

"I think he knows," Dawson said.

"The question is, who is he? Is he working for Saigon or Hanoi or both?"

Everyone was quiet for several minutes while the Captain thought over the situation.

"Let's move one-thousand meters to the west and wait," the Captain ordered.

"I'll stay here and keep an eye on the Colonel," Dawson said, "so we don't lose track of him."

"Good idea," the Captain said.

Dawson watched as all the parachutes were loaded into the medical truck and taken away. All of the jumpers, except the Colonel, entered the school building. Dawson could see the Colonel checking his wristwatch and then looking east. Then Dawson saw what the Colonel was waiting on, a helicopter. The helicopter circled the area and then landed in front of the reviewing stand. The Colonel greeted two civilians from the helicopter and the three of them inspected the parade grounds and reviewing stand. After the inspection, the three men stood and talked for several minutes. As Dawson observed them through field glasses he got the feeling that the Colonel was having an argument with one of the civilians. At one point the Colonel made a wild gesture toward the reviewing stand, then turned his back on the civilians and walked away. He stopped several meters away and lit a cigarette. As he smoked, he tapped his foot on the ground nervously and looked directly at Dawson's position. Moments later he returned and they continued their conversation. After the helicopter left, the Colonel entered what Dawson believed to be the officer's quarters.

Day Four:
We are at a new OP 1000 meters to the west of our first OP, established because our presence may have been compromised. We have observed the school for four hours this morning and have noticed no unusual activity. I have decided that we will stay and complete our mission. At 1500 hours a gray staff car picked up the colonel that walked through our OP yesterday. I am sick with fever, headache and diarrhea. Sergeant Tamashiro has given me a shot and some pills. I have been ill for three days. However, it became unbearable during our move to the new OP.

"Captain," Dawson said, handing him the field glasses. "Check out the activity down there now."
"What do you think they're doing?" the Captain asked.

"I'm not sure. They are in field dress and holding a late formation for something."

"Oh, shit!" the Captain said. "They're going to run a night compass course."

"Well," Deluca sighed, "this should be an interesting night."

"Secure the OP," the Captain ordered. "Everyone find a comfortable place to spend the night. Lieutenant Deluca, keep the kid with you."

The team positioned themselves in a 7-meter circle. During the evening several students from the school wondered close enough to the team's position to cause alarm. However, at 0200 hours the school cadre began to look for a lost student. The team prepared for the worst. At 0230 hours the lost, tired, and frightened young soldier stumbled into the circle and fell down right in front of Dawson. Dawson was sitting with his back to a small tree; when the soldier looked up, he was looking Dawson right in the eyes. Dawson grabbed the soldier by the hair, jerked his head to the side and buried his knife between the shoulder blade and collarbone. He withdrew the knife with a slashing motion cutting the soldier's subclavian artery - he was dead in seconds. The cadres were getting closer and closer to the circle. Every member of the team feared what would happen if they had to kill any of the school cadre. The lost soldier may never be searched for in earnest and his loss never officially questioned. However, the disappearance of two highly trained, professional cadres would sound an alarm. At 0245 hours two cadres stopped just outside the circle, one leaned against a tree, smoked a cigarette, and listened while the second talked. After a few minutes the two cadres laughed about something and returned to the school. whis

"Jesus, that was close," the Captain said.

"Captain," Lieutenant Deluca pered. "Could you make out what they were saying?"

"No," he answered.

"They think he's a deserter. They said he's probably in some whore house in Hanoi by now. That's why they were laughing when they left."

"Oh, thank God for that." Dawson said. "They won't be looking for him then."

Day Five:
Most of the activity at the school today has been outside. A large sand table was set up early this morning in front of the bleachers. The students have been working out tactical problems on it most of the day. Lieutenant Deluca says one class was on "Viet Cong Tactical Doctrine." He could read the main points listed on a chalkboard:

Fast Advance,

Fast Assault,

Fast Clearance of Battlefield

Fast Withdrawal

All based on SLOW Preparation.

Sounds like good solid guerilla tactics to me. Two hours of today's class time was devoted to political indoctrination. No effort has been made to find the missing soldier that Dawson killed last night. The school cadre must truly think he deserted. I believe I am too ill to continue in command. The secondary mission that I alone am charged with must be passed to either

Operation Minerva

Lieutenant Deluca or Mr. Dawson. The parade is tomorrow afternoon and I am pressed to make my decision. Both Lieutenant Deluca and Mr. Dawson have the training and experience to survive the requirements of the secondary mission; however, Mr. Dawson is more psychologically suited for the job. The men always refer to Lieutenant Deluca as 'the Fox', and the nickname is well deserved. I have had few soldiers under me who could disappear as quickly and effectively as he can once into the woods. However, Dawson is older, he also has that fox-like ability to disappear into the woods; plus, he has the proven ability to hunt and kill like a wolf. I talked to him about my secret mission and he was not surprised. I think he suspected something, as Deluca did, the day I received the rifle. He accepted my mission without question. He told me that if I had accepted the necessity of the job, that was good enough for him. So, tomorrow, at 1400 hours, Mr. Dawson will assassinate the Defense Minister of North Vietnam - the guest speaker at the parade. The only request that Mr. Dawson made was that we evacuate the OP tonight so he alone will have to escape tomorrow. His request convinced me that I had made a good choice. I had also planned on giving the team a head start for the PZ[62].

I have passed command to Lieutenant Deluca and charged him with the evacuation. Mr. Dawson has left the OP to scout his own daylight escape route to be used tomorrow. We are all at odds over what to do with our

---

[62] Pickup Zone

little captive. Mr. Dawson has said he will just set her free tomorrow after the job is finished. She and Dawson can't talk to each other but there seems to be a bond between them. He gave her his sleeping bag the first night she spent with us. All preparations for the evacuation of the OP are completed; we will move out after dark. My condition is deteriorating. I know that is one reason Mr. Dawson wants us to leave tonight, he knows that I would not be able to keep up. I told Lieutenant Deluca that I thought I had failed my men as commander. Then he asked me: "If you knew this sickness had to strike one member of our team, which one would you have picked?" He did not let me answer, but answered him: "If you had the choice," he said, "you would have taken this sickness yourself to save us. I know you! You are the best commander I have ever served under." If he told me that just to make me feel better..., it did.

CHAPTER 15
The Lieutenant's Log 1

Day Six:
It has been 14 hours since we left the OP. I have halted the team for a few hours of sleep. Captain Coxe is extremely ill, he has all the symptoms of amoebic dysentery except it developed too slowly for that. We are nearly out of water and the Captain's loss of body fluids is becoming critical. Late yesterday afternoon, the Captain asked me to assume command of the team. We left the OP yesterday at sundown and have not made very good time. We started out to the south and were immediately held up. For nearly an hour, we sat along the side of Highway Six, east of Moc Chau and watched a bicycle convoy headed for Laos. The convoy was manned by men and women, young and old. They passed by so quietly with no expression on their faces, no joy, no pain - nothing. It was like a horror show I saw when I was a kid that showed an endless chain of mindless zombies walking through the woods, each driven by some evil mystical force. The sight sent a cold chill up my back. It was like having a glimpse into Dante's hell. This sobering spectacle momentarily changed the character of the team, for some time after the crossing we were each locked within our own thoughts. I felt it was

my first true insight into the concept of communism. The enemy here is not the Vietnamese people; our enemy is an idea, a philosophy that would take away my right to be unique in action and thought, a philosophy that would force me into that ant-like existence. I felt pity for those poor souls as they pushed those heavily loaded bicycles through the night.

At 2400 hours last night we ran across a road construction camp. We could see two camp fires burning as we circumnavigated the area. Only one person was up and walking around, possibly attending the fires. As we were about half-way around the camp a dog started to bark. Fortunately for us, the dog's alert was not taken too seriously - the fire attendant hit the animal with a stick to shut him up. Within minutes, we were out of the area. We crossed Highway Six, south of Moc Chau, and headed due west for the Laos - it was almost daylight. For the last two hours of travel, Sergeant Applewhite carried the Captain. I thought we were going to have to leave him behind when he passed out. We have given him the last of the medicine that we had for him. Sergeant Applewhite, however, would not have any part of leaving the Captain behind.

"We ain't leavin' anyone behind that's still breathing," He picked up the Captain like a rag doll and threw him over his shoulder, then he said, "Let's go Lieutenant."

Day Seven:
We are resting for the day in an area about 10 to 15 kilometers from the primary PZ. The Captain seems to be improving somewhat and is resting quietly now. We

are standing guard in pairs until we move out. Everyone is suffering from exhaustion, and to some degree, dehydration - we have all given most of our water to the Captain.

"Lieutenant," Sergeant Applewhite whispered. "I'm going to get some water for the Captain."I'll be back before dark." The Lieutenant knew he should tell Applewhite to stay with the team but he could not bring himself to give the order; and he doubted if Applewhite would have followed it anyway. Sergeant Applewhite headed for an area he had found on the aerial photographs that looked like a source of water. The lieutenant leaned back against a tree and removed a letter from his boot top. Folded inside the letter was a picture of Jennie holding a baby.

"Your Mother and I have named your son Patrick Arthur, after you and your Father. I hope you approve. The doctor said he was two weeks early. He is such a beautiful baby. Your Mother says he looks just like you, she got pictures out and showed them to me. Your Mother has been an angel to me ever since you told her I was going to have your baby. Since I quit my job in February and moved into your old room, she has been closer to me than my own Mother ever was. I hope..."

"Lieutenant," Sergeant Tamashiro said. "Come here."

"What is it?"

"The Captain is unconscious. I can't wake him up."

Sergeant Applewhite came across three men that looked like they were part of a Civilian Defense Force. They were not expecting any trouble. Their weapons were several feet away and they were playing some kind of

Operation Minerva

game. Applewhite could see that each had a canteen of water. He made his way to within 6 feet of them before they became alarmed. Two quick steps and a side kick disabled the first man, a karate chop to the neck disabled the second; the third man was trying to chamber a cartridge in his rifle when Applewhite grabbed him by the hair and chin and broke his neck. The second man was on his feet and armed with a knife as Applewhite turned around. He made two wild thrusts with the knife before Applewhite found an opening. On the third thrust Applewhite grabbed the man's knife hand, twisted his arms around to his back and forced him to drop the knife. Then he picked the man up and broke him over his knee like a piece of firewood. The first man down was now up and trying to get away. A crushing blow to the back of the man's neck as he tried to run killed him instantly. He collected the canteens and headed back to the team.

CHAPTER 16
A Time To Kill . . .

With the exception of the little girl, Jack Dawson was alone at the OP on the morning of the sixth day. The increased activity at the school reflected their anticipation of the afternoon's event - the expected event. As he observed the innocuous bustling of the men on the parade field, only Dawson knew the true climax of the day's activities. During the school's lunch break, Dawson started disposing of all excess equipment. At 1300 hours he took the little girl and moved to a new OP, 100 meters closer to his target. He then had 40 minutes to lay and wait for the parade to start.

I am ready, he thought, I have my vantage point and I am prepared to assassinate Trinh.

As he lay on the small hill approximately 1000 meters from the parade ground and made his final calculations, His mind became frenzied with questions. Had he planned his escape route carefully enough? Yes, yes! He said to himself. He had spent the previous day exploring his exact route of escape. Had the team put enough distance between themselves and him? Can they avoid discovery when the searching starts? Yes! He answered himself again, they have had nearly 18 hours head-start. They have to be clear. Dawson's thoughts continued to ramble and more questions flooded his mind: Had he sterilized the area well enough? Will they know they are searching for Americans? Once again, he assured himself that he had taken care of everything. He had buried all of the equipment and sprayed the area with ZBX, an odorless chemical that anesthetizes a dog's sense of smell. The only clue they will have to reflect upon will be the 7.62mm Soviet (SVD) sniper rifle that he would leave for them to find. He thought about who would be searching for him as soon as the confusion died down and someone took charge. The only really well trained troops in the area are the NVA regulars and there are only about 30 of them, they will be armed with the new AKM assault rifle. The Cong An (secret police) pose a small threat - too few of them. The largest group will be the Civilian Village Defense Force, poorly trained, equipped with old bolt action carbines and either too old or too young to be a great threat. Dawson believed what he was told during operations briefings about the local citizen soldiers not getting too far off the main trails. Conscripted troops are never overly zealous. So, keeping this point in mind, he had selected, for the first 30 to 40 minutes of travel, the cleanest, fastest route out of the area. For the second part of his escape route, he picked the roughest most inaccessible terrain he could find. Looking through the telescope at the bustle of activity below reminded Dawson of observing bacteria under a microscope - and then the thought of ants scurrying around and around; suddenly, in that moment, he was back home in Ohio observing the chaos generated by dropping a small pebble into an anthill. He remembered it was always several minutes before some ant took charge and got the stone removed. He was hoping for the same chaotic effect here, it was his only hope for escape. They are placing a chair for Trin, Good! he thought, he will be sitting still for me and not moving around. Everyone on the field was ready. After a short wait, a gray Citron pulled up to the reviewing stand, Trinh had arrived. He walked to the platform and talked for a short period, then sat down to observe a squad movement demonstration by members of the school. Dawson took aim at Trinh 6 inches below the chin. Right through the sternum, he thought. He started to squeeze the trigger..., something stopped him and panic flashed through his mind.

I can't! I can't do it! Dawson's heart was pounding so hard now that it made breathing difficult, he thought he was going to pass out. He rolled over on his back and took several long deep breaths. He was so aggravated that he started talking out-loud to himself.
"What the hell is the matter with me? Am I afraid to do it? Oh! Hell no! I'm not afraid to kill him. I've killed seven men eyeball-to-eyeball."
He lay there on his back arguing with himself, trying to get his heart to slow down.
"I must do it, I must. How can I go back to the Captain and tell him that I froze-up on the trigger. Christ, he would never believe that, I can't believe it."
He turned over and once again looked through the scope.
"Shit! He's gone, he's not in the chair. Now you've done it, jackass, you've lost him."
He searched the area with the scope and finally found Trihn inspecting troops in a corner of the formation.

"Can't get a shot at him now. I'll just have to wait for another clean shot."

After a few minutes, Trihn returned to his seat. By this time, Dawson's heart was settling down and he took aim one more time. The sun had gone behind some clouds and the heat mirage between Trinh and Dawson had decreased considerably. He adjusted for the new conditions. He was now determined to complete his mission and had decided to fire one shot and wait for effect - it would take about one second for the projectile to make the trip to its target. He took a deep breath and slowly released half, locked onto the target and slowly squeezed off the first round between heartbeats. Dawson saw the dust kick up just over Trinh's left shoulder and immediately corrected his point of aim. Down 6-inches and right 6-inches, he thought. He could tell by the expression on Trinh's face that he had heard the first shot go by his head and had heard the impact of the projectile hitting the dirt behind him. Dawson did not give Trinh time to react to the attack. He fired two rounds in rapid succession. As the first round hit Trinh in the chest his arms were thrown up across his face and his chair tilted back. The second round slammed into his abdomen lifting his knees and pulling his feet off the platform. He fell backwards off the platform. Trinh was dead. Dawson dropped the rifle, put on his pack, sprayed the area with ZBX, released the little girl, and started to run. The girl followed him! He knew his only hope of escape depended on his first 30 to 40 minutes of running. It would take at least that long to get a helicopter into the area. He was also hoping for a delay of at least 10 minutes due to the chaos on the parade ground. It would take at least several minutes for them to determine what direction the shot had come from. Finally, since they did not have any tactical vehicles, they would have to come by foot. That should add another five or ten minutes. It would be easier for them to catch a rabbit running through a briar patch, he thought.

After about thirty minutes of running, he came to a point in his escape route where he had to cross a ten-meter clearing, a project to convert a footpath into a road. He saw no workmen around, just some smoldering fires in the distance. He waited a few seconds to catch his breath and to ensure that the area was clear. As he stood quietly observing and listening he could hear the little girl catching up with him. For a skinny little kid, he thought, she sure is one hell of a runner. She sat down at his feet and looked up at him with her big almond eyes, she was not sweating a drop, but she was breathing so hard that she could not drink from his canteen. I wonder if Genie likes Oriental children, he thought. Well, I guess we're going to find out because I think this one has adopted me. Soon her respiration slowed and she drank from his canteen. After the short rest, he checked the area again and started across. As he was about half way across the clearing an old man quickly moved out from behind a tree and shouted some thing in Vietnamese. He was aiming an old bolt-action carbine, with the bayonet fixed, at Dawson. He was about eight meters from Dawson and 45 degrees to his left. Dawson dropped his AK to the ground and they stood looking at each other, then he saw the old man's eyes move away from him as he noticed the little girl. The old man talked with her for several seconds and Dawson could see he was becoming more and more agitated. What was she telling him? He started screaming violently at her and making pointing motions with his rifle. Dawson heard the girl shout something and then heard her start to run away into the woods. The old man shouldered his rifle. Dawson thought sure as hell he was dead. The old man's shot went past Dawson! He was shooting at the little girl! Instinctively, he took advantage of the foolish move the old man had made. He had taken his attention off Dawson and fired his old, slow, bolt-action rifle needlessly. With a look of great surprise the old man dropped his rifle and looked down at the handle of Dawson's knife protruding from his stomach. He took hold of the handle with both hands, sank to his knees and fell over on his side. Dawson ran to the little girl. She was dead. The old man's shot hit her at the base of the neck and her head was almost torn off. Dawson could not believe what had happened. Why did she run? Why did the old man kill her? Why? The old man was moaning as Dawson walked over to his side and knelt down beside him. Dawson was in a rage. He cursed the old man for shooting the young girl. Then he pulled his knife out of the old man's stomach and then drove it deep into the man's chest. The moaning stopped. Dawson threw the body into the woods away from the clearing, picked up his weapon and continued to run. His mind was in turmoil. Had anyone heard the shot? He continued to run until he reached the point on his escape route where he had planned to enter more difficult terrain. He stopped and checked his position. He had marked his map with Xs to indicate areas of activity he had found on the aerial photos. Areas where troops might be located and could possibly be alerted by radio of the assassination. He would have to pass between two such areas during the night. He moved into the dense under growth and continued.

At 2000 hours, He came upon a long cut in the woods. He remembered seeing it on the photos, he also remembered that this long cut connected two Xs on his map. The moon was bright, so he stayed in the shadow of the tree line as he checked for signs of life in the clearing. He felt uneasy, he could smell smoke in the air and smoke meant people. He decided to crawl across the clearing. He was only about 5 meters into the clearing when bullets started zipping around him. He rolled over and over until he was back in the shadow of the tree line, then he jumped to his feet and ran back into the woods. A few meters inside he stopped and waited. Two soldiers followed, each poking around with fixed bayonet. The soldier giving all the orders was closest to Dawson. Each time the moon came out from behind a cloud, shafts of blue light shot down through the trees and enabled Dawson to track the progress of the soldiers. Dawson was anxious to get moving; he knew the shots would bring more soldiers. As he knelt behind a tree, his knife in his right hand, the soldier with the loud mouth came past. Dawson drove the knife blade up under the soldier's ribcage and into his heart. He guided the dead soldier to the ground with very little noise. The silence, however, alerted and panicked the other soldier. Dawson had seen soldiers panic, and he knew this one was well on his way. The remaining soldier's breathing was heavy and irregular, when he tried to speak his voice broke and he sounded very young. He was working his way toward Dawson as another cloud covered the moon. Dawson could hear his steps and knew he was only a few feet away. The moon came out and covered the soldier's head and chest with a soft blue light. It was a young woman hardly more than a girl. Dawson had always wondered what he would do if this situation came up, now he would have to make the decision, and he would have to make it fast. He put his knife back in its sheath and stood up behind the tree. The woman found her comrade and as she leaned over to check him, Dawson hit her with a sharp karate chop behind the right ear. She was down and out instantly. Within seconds Dawson was across the clearing and out of the area.

At 0200 hours Dawson sat down to rest and drank the last of his water. He had eaten his last LRRP[63] ration at midnight while still on the move. Not having any more food did not bother him; however, the water was different. He knew that he could become weak and disabled in a matter of hours at the rate he was sweating. He started out again at a slower pace.

---

[63] Long Range Recon Patrol

Operation Minerva

CHAPTER 17
The Lieutenant's Log 2

Day Eight:
Activity in the area is increasing. Late yesterday afternoon, we heard a helicopter searching the area to the north of our position. I know they are looking for us. If Dawson's mission yesterday was a success, they are searching for an assassin, or a team of assassins. We delayed our departure yesterday until late afternoon to give the Captain more time to rest. And, considering the increased enemy activity, I thought it best to use the extra rest time to ensure our alertness. All night we moved slowly and deliberately, trying our best to avoid contact.

At 2100 hours, we approached a road and could hear girls laughing. I sent Sergeant Tamashiro ahead to investigate while the remainder of the team rested. Tamashiro reported two young girls with rifles sitting along the road, undoubtedly members of the Civilian Village Defense Force (CVDF). He said the two were laughing and talking. We did not try moving up or down the road to find another crossing. I thought this was the best point. We knew where these guards were and could keep our eyes on them. We moved up to the roadside 15 meters from the two laughing girls. I crossed first, then Sergeant Webb followed by Sergeant Applewhite. Sergeant

Operation Minerva

Tamashiro had not crossed yet when we heard someone coming. Two CVDF men walked between us and approached the girls. One of the two men proved to be the Officer-of-the-Guard. Upon reaching the two girls, he exploded into a merciless tirade about their decadent attitude and vowed to report them to comrade...someone? When the Officer-of-the-Guard left he replaced one of the girls with the soldier with him. I thought we were going to be in for a tough time now getting Tamashiro across the road. However, the soldier began deriding his young comrade so intensely that Tamashiro had no trouble crossing. With a feeling of great relief, we departed the area.

At 2300 hours, in spite of all our efforts to avoid contact, a three-man NVA scout team blundered into us. I suspect now, that they are only looking for one man, otherwise they would have used bigger search teams. We could hear them coming through the woods, stopping periodically to fire a flare - we hid quietly. They walked right into our position and touched off a flare. As the flare drifted down the soldiers walked around searching the area. Sergeant Applewhite had been carrying the Captain and was hidden close to him. One of the soldiers was passing within a few feet of their position when the Captain moaned. Turning to investigate the noise, the startled soldier shouted an alert. He was too late and too slow. Sergeant Applewhite kicked the soldier's feet out from under him and he came crashing down into Applewhite's arms. There was a muffled cry and the sound of bones breaking. Sergeant Applewhite had broken the soldier's neck. The flare went out and the two remaining soldiers started firing wildly into the night. We returned the fire and immediately killed both of them. Now we had to get out of this area as fast as we could. We had no idea who may have heard the brief firefight. Sergeant Applewhite picked the Captain up and we moved out quickly. Sergeant Tamashiro took the point. Later it started raining, the rain allowed us to move faster - it was refreshing and it covered up the noise we were making.

"Lieutenant," Sergeant Applewhite whispered. "The Captain's temperature is going up again, he's delirious."
"Okay," the Lieutenant replied. "We will stay here a few minutes longer."
Applewhite crawled back to the Captain, poured some water from his canteen onto a bandage and wiped the sweat from the Captain's face. He poured some of the water over the Captain's short blond hair and again wiped his face. The Captain said something but Applewhite could not understand. He got closer to the Captain and asked him, "What are you saying, Captain?" What do you want." Applewhite moved his ear close to the Captain's mouth as the Captain again struggled to talk.
"Oh, shit,"
Applewhite said out loud as he took the Captain into his arms and hugged him, rocking back and forth.
"What did he say?" the Lieutenant asked.
"Snow, he said snow. Doesn't the snow look beautiful?"
Tears came to Applewhite's eyes as he rocked the Captain.

"Snow, Mother. Look at the snow"

Operation Minerva

"Yes, yes, I know," she said. "It's been snowing all night."

"May I go out, Mother? May I go out, please?"

"Yes, you may, but you must dress properly," she added as he ran up the stairs.

Moments later Alex pushed the big heavy door open that led to the east play yard. The wind pushed the door closed again as he jumped through. Today was Alex's tenth birthday and this was all he had asked for, snow. He checked the window to see if his Mother was watching; she was. He waved to her and she returned his wave with a smile. He threw his arms up over his head and fell back into the deep snow to make a snow angel. Alex, covered with snow, jumped up and checked the window again for his Mother; she was still there watching him. Snow always made Alex happy. And he was happy now, running around in circles, kicking the snow into the air and his Mother watching his antics. He scooped up a big hand full of snow and ate some of it; then looked at his Mother. He knew she would disapprove and make a face at him.

"Come out, Mother, let's make a snowman. Please," he pleaded.

Within a few minutes his Mother was at his side helping. As the snowman started to take shape, Alex ran to the basement to get all the necessary trappings that a respectable snowman required. His Mother called to Franklin, the butler, to take a picture of them. It was Franklin who had helped Alex build his very first snowman, so, his Mother also took a picture of Franklin and Alex by this new snowman.

Sargent Applewhite wet the bandage again and wiped the sweat from the Captain's face and neck. The Captain was quiet now. He had not made a move in several minutes. Applewhite laid him down and leaned back against a tree. He looked up and could see the stars in the sky through occasional holes in the clouds. He thought about the first time he and the Captain served together.

"Captain, Coxe, I'm Sergeant Applewhite."

"Hello, Sergeant," the Captain said vigorously as he returned the salute and then extended his hand to Applewhite. I'm glad to have a man with your background and experience on my team."

"Thank you Captain," Applewhite said, shaking the Captain's hand.

"I'm sure we will have a successful mission."

Applewhite smiled as he looked at the Captain, asleep now, and thought about that first introduction.

"I knew that was your first command," Applewhite said to the Captain in a whisper.

"The General asked me to go along and keep you out of trouble."

"You were so young looking, and so full of piss and vinegar. After a few days with you I knew that somewhere buried under all that brass and spit-and-polish there was a damn good officer trying to get out. Do you remember the time those six cowboys[64] jumped us in Saigon as we were leaving that bar? We had one hell-of-a-fight that night, didn't we?"

---

[64] Saigon hoods

"Move out, move out," the Lieutenant said as he crawled past each member of the team.

Applewhite took the Lieutenant by the arm as he came past.

"I don't have to carry the Captain any more," Applewhite said. "He's dead."

We stopped and established a perimeter in an area we calculate to be about twenty minutes from the primary PZ. Through a rain scattered morning sky we could hear a helicopter approaching from the east, it came directly over us and landed somewhere up the mountain. The helicopter made three trips, we all knew what that meant - they were inserting troops on our primary PZ. We figured they must be carrying between seven and ten troops each trip, so we had twenty-one to thirty NVA troops to contend with. As daylight started to find its way through the trees, we could hear them moving down the mountain. One of the flank troops moved right through our area and broke our perimeter. The undergrowth was heavy but the soldier spotted Sergeant Webb on his right just an instant before Sergeant Tamashiro (on his left) seized him and drove a knife into the soldier's right kidney. The encounter was brief and quiet, the only trouble was...how soon will they miss their man? Within seconds of the first encounter, and even before we had time to hide the first body, a second and third soldier walked into our area. These soldiers were close and in view of others they flanked. This skirmish was not as brief or as quiet. No shots were fired, but the noise of hand-to-hand struggle in the dense undergrowth alerted the other troops. Sergeants Webb and Tamashiro fought for several seconds with the two NVA soldiers before the NVA were killed. Sergeant Webb received a slight cut on his left arm. The other soldiers were not able to see exactly what was going on through the thick undergrowth, so they retreated and called for an assembly of troops. We quietly moved to an area bout one hundred meters to the west and established a tight perimeter. Our last encounter was about an hour ago. It is full daylight now and the rain has stopped. An attack on our position can't be more that a few minute away.

CHAPTER 18
A Time To Die ...

On the seventh day, Dawson approached the area of the primary PZ[65]. To that point, he had not seen any signs of the team. He was exhausted and every inch of his skin was on fire from insect bites, scratches, and sweat, he had been out of water for the past six hours and was thirsty as hell. He fell down and rolled over on his back. With his eyes closed he pulled out the Buddha box Genie gave him and opened it just enough to smell her Tabu. He thought of their last night together, her gown, her giggle, then he fell asleep. He was awakened late in the evening by the sound of Vietnamese voices. He lay motionless and listened. Suddenly, a flare lit up the area. Dawson closed his eyes to save his night vision.

"Come out!" a Vietnamese voice commanded in English, "I see you."

You dumb-ass, Dawson thought, that was already an old trick when Hannibal was kicking Rome's ass 200 years before Christ was born. The flare went out and Dawson opened his eyes. He could hear three soldiers talking and poking around in the bushes. They were getting closer. There was an old log lying parallel to Dawson that had

---

[65] Pickup Zone

about a foot of clearance between it and the ground. He had to get under that log! They can't talk and listen for me at the same time, he thought. As soon as they start talking again, I'll slide under. Dawson had just gotten himself under the log when another flare went off directly over him.

"Come out!" the same voice commanded, "I see you."

Christ, Dawson thought, he doesn't give up does he? Dawson felt the pressure on his chest as one of the soldiers climbed over the log. Another flare lit. One of the soldiers walked up and stood beside the log. He stood there talking, shifting his weight from one foot to the other. All the while he was standing on Dawson's hand. They continued to move and within several minutes they were out of the area. Dawson continued to lay under the log while he evaluated the situation. They know they are after Americans, he thought, and they know we are in this area. He didn't think they were after him specifically. The team must have made contact in this area, he thought, maybe they were scattered. Should I go to the secondary PZ? He asked himself. I don't have the radio; he said to himself, so I can't order the aircraft to the secondary PZ. Dawson decided to stay where he was and make the primary PZ the next day.

A morning rain woke Dawson the eighth day. He remained motionless and listened but could not hear anything over the noise of the rain. During his sleep, Dawson had moved out from under the log. It had been thirty hours since he drank his last water. As he laid on his back looking up into the rain he opened his mouth. He could feel his energy returning with each drop of rain that cooled him and eased his thirst. He sat up and positioned his poncho to catch more of the rainwater. Then he dug through his rucksack and pulled out a small bottle of Tobasco sauce, a small bag of salt, and his last Slim Jim. He leaned back against the log and slowly ate and drank water. He rested for a few minutes to allow the food, salt, and water to get into his blood. He filled his canteen with water from his poncho, secured his gear and stood up slowly to examine the area. After checking his position on the map he started up the hill to the PZ. About 30 minutes later, just after the rain stopped, he saw movement several meters ahead of him. He froze in position, not breathing, not blinking an eye. There were NVA troops just ahead of him. They were going the same direction he was, up the hill. He could tell from their quiet advances that they must have an idea of the team's location. He wondered if there were any NVA stragglers. Perhaps a soldier, or maybe two, that were out-of-shape and unable to keep up with the squad. He listened quietly. Very soon he heard a noise. A straggler was breathing hard and not being too quiet. Dawson waited for him behind a tree. As he walked past, Dawson grabbed him and drove his knife deep into the soldiers kidney. Dawson held the soldier momentarily until he stopped struggling then laid him down quietly and started up the hill again. Further up the hill, he could see another soldier starting to lag behind. The soldier stopped and leaned against a tree to rest. Dawson continued up the hill, keeping the trees between him and the soldier. Dawson was about 5 meters from the tree when the soldier spotted him. The soldier started to raise his rifle at the same instant Dawson's knife left his hand. The knife ripped through the soldiers hand, pinning it to the rifle stock. The soldier screamed out in pain before Dawson's second knife buried itself deep in his chest. The soldier's knees collapsed and he went crashing down the hill. A voice called from up the hill and Dawson could hear someone coming. He hit the ground. The two soldiers soon found their dead comrade. Before they could decide upon a plan of action, shooting started up the hill. Well, what the hell, Dawson thought, the cat's out of the bag now. He opened fire on the two soldiers killing them both. After he retrieved his knives, Dawson once again started up the hill. This time he circumnavigated the NVA troops and the firefight. He wanted to get on the other side of the team's position. Through a break in the trees he could see the NVA pulling back down the hill. He could tell from the shooting just about where the team was. He worked his way in as close as possible. He did not want to be killed by one of his own men so he remained under cover as much as he could.

"Martha Raye," he shouted.

"Shit stomper," was the reply.

Dawson entered the team's perimeter. "Any casualties Sergeant?" he asked.

"No, Sir!" Applewhite answered, "Webb got grazed on the arm is all."

Dawson crawled around checking the positions.

"Where's the Captain?"

"He died last night from...,"

The Lieutenant's voice broke and he choked on the words,

"from whatever it was he had. We left him where he died. Covered him with some brush."

Operation Minerva

Dawson was stunned by the news. He hadn't known the Captain was that ill. Inside, Dawson was crying. However, the outside continued to operate as trained.

"I think those bastards went for help," he said, "and I think we should change our position before they get back. I've seen them and they are not too swift. If we run for it, I think we could reach the PZ and hold them off there."

"I'm not running any more," Applewhite said with a sigh as he fell back against a tree. "Well, then, we had better find a good position, and get ready for a fight," Dawson urged. The Lieutenant agreed with Dawson's suggestion so the Team moved to a new position and set up a perimeter.

"We were a little surprised by their attack," Deluca said. "We thought the full attack was coming from up the hill where the helicopter landed. They also attacked from down the hill."

"How long until the Jolly Green Giant picks us up?" Dawson asked.

"Three hours," the Lieutenant answered. Sergeant Tamashiro crawled over to Webb and started to bandage his arm.

"Do you really think I'm going to live long enough to die from that fucking little scratch?" Webb said, sarcastically.

"I think it would be one hell-of-a waste to survive this mission and then die from an infection," Tamashiro replied.

"Tamashiro," Webb said. "You'll make some lucky woman a good husband someday."

"Yeah, sure," he answered, leaning back against a tree for a rest.

Webb's comment made Tamashiro think about Monique and his first contact with her family, then about the second contact two years later:

"Mother, you remember Tom."

"Yes, I do. How has the army been treating you, Tom?"

"I can't complain, I guess."

"Did Monique tell you that her Father and I are divorced now?"

"Yes, she did. I'm sorry it didn't work out. I hope it had nothing to do with me."

"No, son, you had nothing to do with it. I find that I am much happier this way and I think Monique is too."

"We must hurry, Mother. The movie starts in twenty minutes."

"Okay, dear. Have a good time."

At the theater, they discovered that the advertised times were wrong. The movie they wanted to see would not start for another 45 minutes. They decided to walk over to an old high school hangout and get a Coke.

"Are you going back to Vietnam again after this leave?"

"Yes," he answered, "that's where the war is."

"You sound as if you like the war."

"Not really," he answered. "It's just a question of activity. Do I want to stay here in a perpetual state of training and brass polishing, or go to Vietnam and do what I have been trained to do? Training situations are not high points in my life. I know I must be trained, but I like to get it over with as soon as possible and get on with the real world."

Operation Minerva

As Monique and Tom turned the corner onto the main street they came face-to-face with her Father. A chill ran through Tom as he remembered how terrified he had been of this big red-faced man during their first encounter. Now, however, it was different. Tom had, during his first combat tour in Vietnam, experienced the change that takes place in a man's character when he faces and overcomes fear. It happened to Tom when he killed three men in hand-to-hand combat. This kind of experience dulls the cutting edge of surprise and reduces the possibility of becoming excited by something less. Monique's Father was surprised by the encounter and, upon recognizing Tom, became highly agitated.

"You Chinks must be as damn dumb and hard-headed as niggers," her Father bellowed, "Didn't I knock the shit out'a you a couple a years ago for bein' with my kid?"

Tom examined his emotions while listening to this wild man. He discovered that he had no emotions at all for him, except maybe disgust. Tom took Monique's hand and started to walk away, back toward the theater. With one sweep of her Father's big hairy arm, Monique was knocked across the sidewalk and into a parked car. Tom turned to face him, ducking a wild roundhouse right. Monique's Father charged at Tom and tried to hit him with another wild roundhouse, Tom moved out of his way again. He cursed at Tom, roaring that he knew how to handle fast and slick little pretty boys like Tom. As he pulled his belt off, Tom could see that it was made with pockets and Tom knew the pockets were full of lead shot. "This will slow your little chink ass down, sonny," Monique's Father laughed. By this time, a crowd was gathering around trying to see what all the excitement was about. Monique's Father rushed at Tom swinging the belt frantically around his head. Tom backed up against a parking meter and waited. When the belt came into contact with the parking meter, Tom was gone and the result was two or three ruptured pockets in the belt. The sidewalk was now littered with lead shot and people were starting to fall down. Monique's Father had worked himself into a mad rage. Despite all his efforts he had not touched Tom. A police officer arrived and tried to calm him down but was attacked and knocked out. The crowd started running in panic as he took the unconscious officer's gun and aimed it at Tom.

"Okay, you little smart ass," he said, "let's see how fast you are now."

Tom stood perfectly still and looked directly into his eyes.

"Well, chink," he said, "aren't you goin' to run? I thought you people were good at running."

Tom noticed the police officer regaining consciousness and reaching for Monique's Father's leg. At the instant Monique's Father looked down at the officer, Tom hit him with a flying sidekick to the face. He went over the hood of a parked car to the street.

"Lieutenant," Webb whispered, "I can hear movement down the hill."

The Lieutenant motioned to Webb that he had also picked up the activity. Then, about one-hour after the first attack had broken off, mortar rounds started pounding their old position. The enemy dropped twenty rounds into the area, then initiated their attack. As Dawson watched this gross tactical error unfold, he told

Operation Minerva

Webb, "The officer in charge of that goat roping contest must have been an OCS drop out."
The attack frenzy died quickly as the NVA troops overran the deserted position. The woods became incredibly silent when the attackers discovered the gross error they had made. Now, they did not know where the Americans were.

"They will regroup now," Dawson said.
"Yes, I would hope so," Deluca said.
"What do you think they will do now?" Dawson asked Deluca.
"Well, they will have to scout around to find out where we are. And, if we are lucky, may be we can kill a few more of them if they are careless in their search.
During the next few minutes two NVA troops were killed after they stumbled across the team.
"Everyone knows where we are now!" Deluca said. "I think we can get ready for an attack from at least two directions. First over there," he said, pointing to the Northeast. "And then, from over there," he said pointing to the South. "I think they will attack us from the South with a larger group since that direction provides better cover for them."
"Sounds good to me," Dawson said.
Sergeant Webb, Sergeant Tamashiro and Dawson took positions one meter apart on the South perimeter, the suspected direction of the larger attack. Lieutenant Deluca and Sergeant Applewhite guarded the Northeast. For ten minutes there was not a sound of any kind in the woods. No wind, no birds, it was as though the forest itself was reverently hushed to observe the final act of

this conflict. Suddenly, there they were, about twenty meters away, screaming like fiends from hell and coming as fast as they could run from the Northeast. At first, Lieutenant Deluca and Sergeant Applewhite were taking them down as fast as they were advancing. Then the attack from the South hit their position. Weapons were soon emptied on the charging, screaming NVA troops. Then they were in the pit with the team. The pit was full of men, back-to-back and shoulder-to-shoulder fighting and dying. Dawson was locked in battle with one NVA soldier; they were face-to-face, when the NVA soldier's face was blown away. At that same instant Dawson felt something hit him in the back like a hammer then a huge weight fell on him. As he tried to free himself, he could hear voices, shots, explosions, and then quiet. He felt like a tree had fallen on him. Finally, when he got free, he saw that the tree was Sergeant Applewhite, dead. Dawson reached over his left shoulder with his right hand to examine himself. He could feel a lump just below the skin. Immediately, he suspected what had happened; the shot that had killed Sergeant Applewhite had passed through the sergeant and hit him. The thought came to Dawson about all the times he had teased Applewhite about hiding behind him when the shooting started. Now Applewhite had, on purpose or accident, saved his life. The pit was full of dead NVA soldiers. A quick count told Dawson that a few had survived and pulled back. He wondered why as he looked around. Sergeant Webb was up and on the perimeter. Lieutenant Deluca was covered with blood, but also up and on guard. Sergeant Tamashiro, lying beside Dawson, was dead. Dawson took his place on the perimeter.

Operation Minerva

"How much time do we have before pick-up?" Dawson asked.

"Thirty minutes," the Lieutenant answered.

"It's got to take us 20 minutes just to get to the PZ," Dawson said "Hadn't we better get our asses out of here?"

Dawson and Webb were about to make a litter for the Lieutenant, but found they would not be able to move him. His left leg was almost gone at the knee and his stomach was ripped opened. He told them that he didn't hurt as long as he didn't move and that he had no intention of moving. Then he put his hand into his fatigue shirt and pulled out a small notebook,

"The Captain's Log," he said, giving the book to him.

"Dawson," the Lieutenant said.

"Yes, Lieutenant."

"Take this too. I don't want them to find it."

The Lieutenant pulled a folded paper from his right boot and gave it to Dawson.

"Go see her. Tell her what happened and that I love her."

"I'll see her," Dawson promised, placing the paper into a hidden pocket on his knife scabbard.

Dawson and Webb gave the Lieutenant their last two hand-grenades. He pulled the pins and holding the levers down, placed them under his right leg. After loading all the weapons they could find in the area and placing them beside the Lieutenant, they said good-bye to him and started out slowly.

Lieutenant Deluca waved to Dawson and Webb as they disappeared. He leaned back and looked up at the sky through the trees. The rain had passed and the sun was shining now. The loss of blood was making him sleepy and he was having delusions. He thought he was home on the back porch and playing soldier and the bad guys were coming up the hill. He began talking to himself and giving his imaginary soldiers orders on how to protect the fort. He knew how to protect this fort; he had done it many times.

"Ok, is everyone ready?"

All of his imaginary troops gave him a thumbs-up.

"We're ready and we have the advantage of position, general."

He drifted off for a few moments; then the sound of a bird woke him. The sun was shining on him now and the heat felt good to him. He looked over at Tamashiro and Applewhite:

"This is going to be a beautiful day," he said.

But neither Tamashiro nor Applewhite answered.

CHAPTER 19
And Only I Escape Alone To Tell

Sergeant Webb looked Dawson over, trying to determine where and how badly he was wounded.

"You have so damn much blood on you that I can't tell where it's coming from. Jesus, you have cuts all over you."

"I think I have a slug in my back."

"Where at?"

"Left shoulder."

"I can feel it," Webb said. "Don't look too bad. Can you use your arm?"

"Yes, it hurts like hell but I can use it. I think most of the blood on me belongs to Sergeant Applewhite."

Dawson and Sergeant Webb started up the hill, trying to be as quiet as possible. They were both worn out and their climb was slowed by thick undergrowth that exhausted them even more. They stopped for a brief rest when they heard gunfire and the explosion of hand-grenades down the hill - Lieutenant Deluca's last battle. They knew that, after a body count in the pit was taken, the NVA would be after them. With new energy they started up the hill again, wrestling with the undergrowth.

"He must've put up a hell-of-a fight!" Dawson mumbled.

"What did you say?" Webb asked.

288

Operation Minerva

"I said the Lieutenant must have put up a hell-of-a fight, considering the amount of gunfire that went on."

"Yes," Webb said. "He bought us some time."

Finally after 20 minutes of hard climbing they were at the edge of the PZ. A clearing they had picked out from one of the aerial photographs. It wasn't long before they heard the NVA troops coming up the hill. Now, they were not being quiet; they were shouting commands and screaming to each other. Dawson and Webb found a good defendable position and waited for them to show themselves. They saw two groups of five soldiers each almost running up the hill. Dawson took one group and Webb took the other. Their opening shots dropped the first two soldiers in each group. The remaining soldiers scattered and returned fire.

Dawson could hear the helicopter approaching. He took out a red smoke grenade. The red smoke would both tell the pilot the direction of the wind, and also warn him that there were enemy troops in the area. Sergeant Webb made radio contact with the helicopter. He told the pilot to look for red smoke and the location of the hostel fire. He also told the pilot there were only two to be picked up and that they would be close to the smoke. At first a small puff of crimson rose in the still air and hung close to the ground. Then, a slight wind caught and swirled the small deep red puff into a huge bright red cloud. Dawson and Webb moved into the clearing close to the smoke. They tried to conceal themselves in the tall grass and red smoke. They could hear the NVA at the edge of the clearing. Sergeant Webb radioed the new position of the NVA troops to the pilot. As the helicopter touched down in the center of the area, the rotor-wash whipped up the smoke filling the bowl-like clearing. Eight Air Force combat troops in blue berets jumped out and established a perimeter around the helicopter. A .50 caliber machine gun, firing from a side port, gave covering fire for Dawson and Webb as they ran for the safety of the helicopter. Just as they were a few meters from the aircraft they could hear enemy fire hitting the aircraft. Two Air Force air-crewman helped them aboard. Dawson could hear rounds hitting the ship as the perimeter troops boarded. The 50 caliber continued to deliver covering fire as the helicopter lifted off. Dawson and Webb were lying on the deck face down. The helicopter was climbing out so fast and steep that Dawson thought he would slide out the open tailgate. After the aircraft leveled out Dawson raised himself up on one elbow and slapped Webb on the back.

"God dam, we made it, Sergeant!" Dawson yelled over the noise of the aircraft.

Sergeant Webb did not move - he was dead. He had been killed in the final seconds of the escape. Tears filled Dawson's eyes as he put his arm around Webb and rested his head on his shoulder. Suddenly, Dawson was overcome by a terrible feeling of loneliness and despair.

"Why me, God?" he cried, "Why me?"

The chopper was shaking and jerking as Dawson began to lose consciousness. He could hear voices around him and feel someone pulling and poking at him. He could hear noise but it sounded like it was off in the distance. Everything looked red to him. He blinked his eyes but everything was a dull red blur. He felt as if the chopper were spinning around and around. His hands found two

Operation Minerva

tie-down rings on the deck He held on tight as he started
to fall into a red whirlpool. He was spinning and falling.

Five days later
Air Force hospital in Thailand

"Well, good morning," a soft feminine voice said to
Dawson. "Welcome to the world."
Dawson was conscious and struggling to move but
couldn't get his eyes open. He felt like he was drunk, the
world was in slow motion and someone was gently
washing his face with cold water.
"Wake up, honey," the voice said. "Wake up."
Dawson finally got control of his eyes and managed to
get them open. At first all he could see was a blurry white
figure hovering over him, talking to him, washing and
massaging him. As his vision cleared, he could see that
the white angel hovering over him was an Air Force
nurse, a Major. Everything around him was white; the
ceiling, walls, door, curtains, and even his bed. The only
color in the room was the tan face, blue eyes and golden
blonde hair of the nurse.
"Don't say anything!" she said. "I don't know anything
and I'm not supposed to know anything. I have strict
orders to notify Colonel Johnson when you wake up."
"Just who the hell is Colonel Johnson?" Dawson asked
"And what the hell an I doing here and where is here?"
"Colonel Johnson is your doctor, honey," she said as she
turned to leave. "And he will have to answer any
questions you have."
She walked out of the room and locked the door from the
out side. Why is she locking my door? I'm locked in!

291

Am I a prisoner? Wild thoughts ran through his mind as he tried to remember how he had arrived in this room. Seconds later the door was unlocked and a white haired Colonel Johnson stepped into the room.

"I'm Colonel Johnson. How do you feel?" he asked.

"Hungry," Dawson replied.

"That's good. I'll have Bianca bring you something to eat."

"Bianca?"

"Your nurse, Major Lanturi," the Colonel answered. "You are lucky to have her taking care of you. She is a senior nurse who thinks her sole purpose in life is to provide loving care for sick or wounded military men. He then turned and left the room without further comment.

Again the door was locked from the outside. Dawson could not figure out what was going on. Why was he here in this room? His head felt so thick. He felt like he was trying to make his way through a big jar of honey. Dawson knew he was at or near an airfield, he could hear aircraft taking off, but which airfield, in what country and why? What had happened? Had he been in an accident or was he wounded in combat? Combat where and how long ago?" The questions seemed never ending. Later, the nurse brought a tray in.

"Bianca," Dawson said, "why..."

"Well!" she said with great surprise. "You can say my name right."

"Bianca," he persisted. "Why am I locked up in this room? And what Air Base is this?"   "Honey," she said, "you are not locked in, everyone else is locked out! I don't know who you are or what your rank is, if you even have a rank, and only Colonel Johnson and I know

you are here. I can't tell you where you are, I've been
ordered not to. We have also been ordered to keep no
records on you."

"Can you tell me how long I've been here?"

"Five days," she answered. "I was beginning to wonder if
you would ever wake up."

Dawson ate everything he could from the tray and fell
asleep again.

"Sir, wakeup, please! Wake up, you have someone here
to see you."

Bianca was rubbing Dawson's face with a cool, damp,
washcloth trying to wake him. Dawson opened his eyes
and saw a tall, lean civilian dressed in tailored,
camouflage jungle fatigues. He asked Bianca to leave
and only after she had gone out of the room he
announced that his name was Mr. Smith, and that he was
with the American Embassy in Saigon.

"We have an Air America 'Black Eagle' flight to Saigon
in two hours. Can you make it?" he asked.

"Yes, Sir!" Dawson said. "Can you tell me why I'm
going to Saigon? Why I'm here? Was I injured in an
accident?"

"Later," Mr. Smith said, "later."

Then he pointed to a set of fatigues and a pair of boots on
a nearby chair and said, "I'll see you in about an hour and
a half."

Bianca came in as soon as he left.

"I'm supposed to help you get dressed," she said.

Dawson didn't think he needed any help until he started
to get out of bed. Every part of his body ached as he tried
to move.

"Watch your stitches!" she ordered as she grabbed his arm.

"What stitches?" he asked, sitting on the edge of the bed.

"Honey," she said, "we have you sewn together like a rag doll. You have eight stitches in your back, over your left shoulder blade, four stitches in your chin, seven in the lower right side of your back, ten in your right wrist and five in your right knee. You must have been in one hell-of-a brawl," she said.

Then he remembered. For the first time since he woke up in that room, he remembered.

"Yes," he said, "I guess you could say that I was in one hell-of-a brawl. If you really want to do something for me," Dawson said. "Get me something more to eat."

"I'll try," she said. "But I can't promise anything. Put your arms around my neck first and let me help you over to the chair."

As Bianca bent over and put her arms around him, her hair brushed his face and Dawson filled his lungs with the sweet smell of her perfume.

"God, you smell good," he said as he sat down in the chair and leaned back.

He took another deep breath and closed his eyes. Instantly his mind was flooded with visions of Genie. He could see her so clearly. He could even smell her Tabu. He knew she was in Saigon and that he would be seeing her soon. Bianca came in later with a tray and they talked as he ate.

"Did I have a gold chain and locket on when I came in here, Bianca?"

"Honey, when they brought you in here you didn't even have dog tags on!"

Operation Minerva

"Will you please ask the Colonel if he can find any of my equipment, especially a gold locket and chain?" It's very important to me and someone must have it."
"I'll try," she said as she left the room.
In just a few minutes she was back with Dawson's harness and knives and said all of his other things had been burned. He noticed that his harness had been washed and his knives cleaned.
"The Colonel said he was there when they undressed you and he didn't see any locket."
"I must have lost it then," Dawson mumbled.
Mr. Smith came back and rushed Dawson out of the hospital and into an Air Force station wagon. It was dark outside and Dawson could see almost nothing. He didn't know how long the flight to Saigon was, but every minute of it was sheer torture. His entire body hurt and he couldn't get comfortable no matter what position he tried. During the flight, Mr. Smith sat directly across from Dawson. As they sat in silence looking at each other - Dawson remembered that it was a 'Mr. Smith from the embassy' that had given the sniper rifle to the Captain. Why, Dawson thought, had Smith not asked about the Captain, the team, or the mission? He knew how many men had gone on the mission, and he knew that only I returned alive. It annoyed Dawson that Smith could sit there so calm and disinterested. Dawson's thoughts of the Captain and the team depressed him so he tried to concentrate on Genie. As soon as he closed his eyes he was at the lake, their last day together and the picnic. He was lying on the blanket with his head on her lap. The fresh clean scent of her yellow sundress, flavored with a trace of body powder, filled his entire being. His senses

recalled with amazing detail and clarity the sensation of slowly and gently running his hand up her leg and fondling her. Dawson fell asleep with his senses full of warm sunshine, a yellow sundress, fresh breezes and the smell of Genie. He was awakened by the loadmaster with the warning that they were on final approach for Tan Son Nhut and that he must fasten his seatbelt. He struggled upright, fastened his seatbelt and then looked out the window. Saigon, at night, after curfew, was always a paradox. To an observer in an aircraft, the conditions of the paradox were not consciously registered until the total was realized. Saigon, at night, from several miles away, lit up a large segment of the horizon. The lights gave the impression of a city alive with activity; however, as the distance decreased, and buildings came into view, it became obvious that every building was dark. The final, chilling, disturbing fact was the realization that there was no traffic and no people on the well-lit streets. To Dawson, it was always like looking into some unreal, frightening 'Twilight Zone'. It was a place where Nature's laws had been voided. Flying away from the city and looking back, the sight wedged in his brain, he saw the buildings, standing tall and black, like megalithic gravestones, each mourning its lost legions of dead.

After touchdown, the aircraft was taxied to a remote parking area and shut down. Outside was another familiar, blue Air Force station wagon. Mr. Smith and Dawson got in and were once again whisked away into the night. The debriefing building was a standard two-story, gray and blue, Air Force barracks converted for the Agency's use. Only after entering the building and penetrating the bleak reception room, could a visitor truly appreciate the effectiveness of the building's disguise. Inside was a second reception room, this one with sea foam-green carpeting, mint-green walls, stateside office furniture and an Agency guard. The Agency seal hung on the wall behind the guard and a closed circuit TV camera, on the opposing wall, monitored the activities of the room. Since Dawson was without identity papers or his military I.D. card, not even Mr. Smith could positively identify him.

Dawson wondered, as he stood there, just how they were going to work this problem out. At that moment, the thick, and obviously assault-proof door to the rear of the guard, buzzed and was pushed open. It was Sergeant Cook. Dawson was so happy to see a friendly and familiar face that he felt like hugging him. Sergeant Cook had a large brown envelope that contained Dawson's personal effects, collected the evening they left on the mission. Dawson dumped the contents of the envelope on the guard's desk and began stuffing his pockets. Along with his wallet, keys, loose change, and a C-ration can opener; he found an earring and a letter. The earring was Genie's; she had taken it off during the picnic. The letter was also Genie's, she had given it to Sergeant Cook after Dawson had gone. He put the letter in his shirt pocket, gave his ID card to the guard, signed a receipt for a red visitor's pass, and was escorted into the inner-sanctum of the Agency's Saigon office.

CHAPTER 20
All the rivers run into the sea...

Upstairs, in the north end of the Agency's Saigon office, Colonel Sims and Major James Edwards were watching Dawson on the security closed circuit TV monitor as he arrived in the reception room downstairs. The Colonel had given orders that Dawson was to be isolated in his room and that only Sergeant Cook could see him.

"He looks terrible," Colonel Sims said, looking at Dawson, "Are you sure he is ready for this?"

"The doctor said he was ready."

"Who has been assigned to debrief him?"

"Frank and John, I think."

"Have you talked to them?"

"Yes, Sir." the major replied, "We had supper together this evening at the officers club."

"Will they be on the level with us?"

"They told me that we could monitor the debriefing from beginning to end through the CCTV."

"Good," the Colonel said, then added, "Has that shrink reported in yet from Japan?"

"No, Sir. Not yet."

"Make sure he doesn't see Dawson until after we're through with him."

"Yes, Sir."

Operation Minerva

"What information has MI passed to us about Sergeant Vine?" the Colonel asked."

"Sir, the boys at MI must have really put the fear of God into Vine. As you read this transcript you get the idea that he really poured his guts out to them."

"How did Vine and Major Quan get together?"

"Major Quan had an effective, if not unique, method of recruiting. He would buy gambling debts of soldiers that were in position to help him. Then he would get them involved in something just slightly illegal to pay their debt. He would follow this up with a plan to ensure that they would get into debt again, usually by seeing to it that they were granted extended credit by gambling houses. When they were in really deep trouble he would save them again, if they would help him. His second request was normally for information that was classified confidential. He would carefully select information that the victim would rationalize to be harmless. Once a security breach was accomplished and the victim was in debt again, the Major could get anything he wanted."

"How did Major Quan know to ask about Operation Minerva?"

"He didn't. Sergeant Vine had worked himself into debt so deeply that he would regularly sell Major Quan items he thought might be of interest."

"Any news about Major Quan?" the Colonel asked.

"None, Sir!" the Major replied, "Vietnamese security took him into custody at his apartment and there has been no word of him since."

"Well, Major, I imagine they had him secreted away somewhere deep in the bowels of city prison, probably crushing his fingers one joint at a time, one finger at a time, with a hammer and an anvil. They will squeeze every drop of information from his head, and when they are satisfied that they have all that he knows they will crush his testicles and smash both his knees. Then, after he has suffered for six or eight hours, he will be shot in the head and thrown into the Saigon city dump."

The room was quiet for several seconds after the Colonel's comments about how the Vietnamese treated spies.

"Sergeant Vine is god damn lucky he's not Vietnamese," the Major reflected.

The telephone rang and Colonel Sims answered, it was Mr. Smith and he was on his way to the Colonel's office. The Colonel told Major Edwards to dig up more information on Major Quan, and then motioned for him to leave. As the major left, the Colonel told him to leave the door open. Moments later Mr. Smith walked into the Colonel's office.

"Jerry," the Colonel said, walking across the room and shaking hands with Smith, "How was the flight?"

"Dan, you know I hate that Black Bird flight with a passion. Do you have to ask?"

"Sorry about that Jerry," the Colonel chuckled.

"Do you have any coffee? Fresh coffee!" Smith asked.

"Major Edwards," the Colonel said, pushing his intercom but ton down, "Get some fresh coffee in here please."

"Yes, Sir. Right away."

"Do you think Dawson is in good enough shape for this debriefing?" the Colonel asked.

"Yes," Smith answered, "he's weak as a kitten and sore as hell but if he's not pressed too hard or worked too long he'll be ok." Smith threw the Captain's notebook onto the Colonel's desk.

"Dawson had that on him when he was picked up. It's very interesting reading. It's a log the Captain and Lieutenant kept of the mission. It's strictly against procedures, but as it turns out, quite informative."

The Colonel picked up the notebook and began reading. Major Edwards delivered the coffee with some fresh doughnuts and returned to his office. After a few minutes the Colonel placed the notebook down in front of Mr. Smith.

"Those poor bastards. They made such a valiant effort. And all the time they never had a prayer. So, Dawson was the one who fired the shot. We will have to tell him the truth. He will find out sooner or later anyhow."

"I think it will go down better if we tell him," Mr. Smith said.

"This is your room, Sir," Sergeant Cook said, opening the door for Dawson.

"You will find the refrigerator stocked with ice cream and soda. I told them you were not a drinker. I'll bring all of your meals to you. The officer's club delivers them to the back door. You can order whatever you want from the menu on the desk. The TV is on about 18 hours a day, but it repeats the same programs every 8 hours or so."

As Sergeat Cook showed Dawson the room he held his fingers to his mouth to warn Dawson to be quiet. Then he pointed to a tiny microphone in the lamp and another bug in the wall by the bed. He continued to talk as he wrote a note on a small pad, *What happened to the Captain?*

Dawson took the pad and pen and wrote his answer, *All dead!*

Operation Minerva

Sergeant Cook was shaken by the news. He quickly turned and walked toward the door, but not before Dawson saw tears run down his cheek.

Dawson got a cold Coke and sat down to read Genie's letter.

My Dearest Jack:

If you are reading this letter you are back in Saigon and we will be together soon. For now, you have only been gone for an hour and already I miss you so much. This past week has been the happiest time of my life. I don't think I could ever be happy with another man after knowing you. You are a soft gentle lover, a man without hate, and a soldier with the heart of a tiger. I have only truly loved two men in my life, my Father and you. If you want me my darling, as much as I want you, we can spend the rest of our lives together.

I love you,

Genie

Dawson could smell Genie's Tabu on the letter. The scent filled his body with desire and his heart began to pound. He knew she was there and he wanted to call her but the thing his room did not have was a telephone. The shot the doctor gave Dawson before he left the hospital was wearing off and sharp pains were beginning to accompany each move he made. He carefully made his way to the bed and tried to undress. The effort was too much, he rolled over onto the bed and went to sleep with his cloths on. His sleep was neither sound nor restful. He was having a nightmare that would plague him for the rest of his life. In the dream, he is on the aircraft with the team. The yellow warning light is on and it's just one minute until jump time. The Captain is standing in the door waiting for the green light. He could see Sergeants Applewhite, Webb, and Tamashiro and Lieutenant Deluca. He could not figure out why he was just looking at them and not in line himself. He looked at the Captain and noticed that he was not wearing his parachutes. The Captain had a harness on but no chute. Then he noticed that Sergeant Applewhite also had no chute. He tried to get to them but something was holding him back. He tried to scream but no sound came out. The closer he tried to get to them the further away they became. Then he could see that Sergeants Webb and Tamashiro and Lieutenant Deluca were holding static lines that were cut, they were not attached to their backpacks. Dawson thought that maybe he could throw his own reserve parachute to one of them. Then he realized that he also had no parachute, just a harness. The green light came on and the Captain disappeared, then Applewhite. Dawson struggled to get to the door to go with the team. Sergeant Tamashiro jumped through the black hole followed by Lieutenant Deluca. Dawson got to the door just in time to grab Sergeant Webb by the arm but he too disappeared into the darkness. Dawson tried to pull Webb back into the airplane. When he pulled his hand in from the black hole he only had Webb's arm. Dawson screamed and tried to jump through the door but he could not get through. Dawson woke up screaming as Sergeant Cook ran into the room.

"Sir, are you okay?" Dawson looked around the room, then at Sergeant Cook.

"Can you get me something for this pain?"

"Yes, Sir. I'll be right back."

Operation Minerva

Within minutes Sergeant Cook was back with medication. He dropped two pills into Dawson's hand.

"The red one," he said, "will ease the pain. The gray one will put you to sleep until noon tomorrow. When you wake up I'll have lunch here for you."

"Thanks, Sergeant."

Dawson took the red pill but saved the gray one until later. He was not in a hurry to go back to sleep. He opened a Coke, turned the TV on and relaxed on the couch. He watched two episodes of his favorite TV show *Star Trek* and was half way through the evening news when the base came under attack. He walked over to the window and watched the fire fight taking place at the air field. He could see 50 caliber tracers and the explosions of what he believed to be rockets hitting the airfield. After several minutes of fighting a Cobra gunship showed up and delivered some devastating fire along the perimeter of the airfield. As he stood in the window watching the show a stray projectile penetrated the window and went through the far wall of his room. Dawson did not flinch of move; he looked out of the window until the show was over then returned to the couch. The TV station had gone off the air so he decided to take the gray pill.

The debriefing lasted five days, and during those five days Dawson did not leave the building. Sergeant Cook performed the duties of room service without a sign of complaint. Sergeant Webb and Dawson had taken twenty rolls of pictures. Dawson had to look at, and explain, every frame. During the debriefing the mystery of the parachuting NVA Colonel who walked through their OP was solved. Dawson was shown a picture of the Colonel and told that he was an NVA military intelligence officer. He also found out that the Colonel did know they were there. He was told about Major Quan and Sergeant Vine.

"NVA intelligence," Colonel Sims told Dawson, "allowed us to continue the mission, or to think we were, while they manipulated us, and the situation, to eliminate two of their undesirables. The man you shot was not the defense minister. He was a powerful political opponent of the policies established by the NVA intelligence community. Tiger Tim's success as a double agent had gone to his head, and his pocketbook. His heavy dealings with the Saigon black market got him labeled as a decadent and dangerous money grabber. Our Special Operations Group Commander, upon receiving your information, had Tiger Tim killed and his body thrown into the bay. Then, some damn leg-sergeant's conscience started to bother him and he spilled his guts out to the press. The results, the Group Commander was relieved of command and forced to retire."

Dawson asked Colonel Sims what they were going to do if they were successful in identifying any more agents.

"I guess we will just have to slap their wrists," he answered. "Unless we want to shake up the press and the folks back home."

Dawson told Colonel Sims that he wanted to stay in Saigon for a few days to visit his girlfriend before returning to Lop Buri.

"Sergeant Cook," the Colonel ordered. "Fix Mr. Dawson up with some classified courier orders to cover the next 10 days. That should give you some priority when you get ready to hitch a ride back to Thailand. You won't have to sign in when you return to Fort Nari, just turn in your courier orders to the commander. According to the records, you were signed back into the 46th on the day you left for North Vietnam."

There was a long pause before the Colonel said anything further, then he put his hand out to Dawson.

"I think you and the team performed in the highest tradition of the United States Army and Special Forces."

Dawson stood for a moment, thinking about what a disaster the mission had been. Now, he was to accept this 'atta' boy' and go back to his company like nothing had ever happened.

"All the rivers run into the sea and yet the sea is not full...," he mumbled to himself.

"Did you say something?" the Colonel asked.

"No, Sir, it's nothing," he said as he saluted, did a snappy about-face and walked out of the Colonel's office.

Operation Minerva

CHAPTER 21
A Time To Say Goodbye

Dawson collected his gear from the guard in the reception room, turned in his pass and walked out of the Agency's building. He stood for a moment in the warm sun trying to figure out where he was because nothing looked familiar. An Air Force jeep was passing by so Dawson waved him down.

"Can you tell me where the officers club is?"

"Sir, you're on the wrong side of the base for that. Jump in and I'll take you there."

"Thank you, Sergeant."

They drove for several minutes. Dawson had no idea that Tan Son Nhut air base was so big. Once in front of the officers club, Genie's instructions on how to get to her office came back to him. He could not help but think as he walked along, about all that had happened. Alex Coxe - what a truly useless way to die, he just got sick. Useless? Was his death really any more useless than the others? What did we accomplish? Sam Applewhite - Dawson believed Applewhite saved his life, either by choice or by accident. Joe Tamashiro - the Tasmanian Devil, had he not been such a fierce fighter, Dawson would probably not have made it. He too saved my life. Jim Webb - he died believing that he had escaped. His was the only body that would ever go home to rest.

Dawson had picked him for the mission. His blood is on my hands. Pat Deluca - twenty-three years old. He knew he was going to die! What were his final thoughts..., his Mother, his Father, his girlfriend? The thought of his girlfriend reminded Dawson of what Deluca had given him. Dawson removed the folded paper from its hiding place. He looked at the picture and read the letter. Dawson was under order not to contact any dependants of the team. However, as Dawson looked at the picture of Deluca's son he knew someday he would have to tell the boy about his father. He was more man than any of them had suspected. He also made it possible for me to make it back. He thought. He did it by buying me some time, time he paid for with his own life. When you get old enough, Patrick Junior, Dawson said looking at the picture, I'll tell you about how your father put a new meaning to the word man.

Dawson stopped in front of the big blue Air Photo Intelligence sign Genie had told him to look for. As he walked up the building he stopped and asked an airman where the photo interpreters were located and was directed to another building. By now, his mind was only on Genie. His heart was pounding, he felt like a schoolboy on his way to his first date. Dawson wondered what she would say when she saw him. Maybe I should have called her first, he thought. His mind was flying through time collecting memories, visions. He wondered if she would still feel the same way about him and about how good it would be to hold her in his arms and to fill his lungs with her perfume. When Dawson got to the building a Vietnamese man cutting the grass told him that everyone had gone to a meeting and would not be back for two hours. The old man directed Dawson to a snack bar where he could get something to eat while waiting. The snack bar was full of garrison soldiers complaining about how tough life was at Tan Son Nhut. They complained that the movie didn't change often enough, the bowling alley was too small and the quickie girls cost too much. Dawson knew they were smoking pot. They kept looking at him to see if he was going to say something. He began to get a terrible headache and started sweating heavily. He left without finishing his food. Once outside he decided to take a walk. It was good just to be able to walk along the street and not have to look behind you every step of the way. As time passed, the tension eased and the headache cleared. He returned to Genie's building and rang the bell. A pretty young girl, disguised as an Air Force Officer, opened the door.

"I'm Jack Dawson," he said. "Is Lieutenant Genie Francis here?"

A look of bewilderment came over her and without saying a word she slammed the door in his face. He waited a few seconds then rang the bell again. The door opened again and a Major Colt introduced himself and invited him in.

"You will have to excuse Lieutenant Brown," he said. "She is terribly emotional."

"What is there to be so emotional about?" Dawson asked, but did not receive an answer.

Inside the Major's office, Dawson was offered some coffee and a seat. The Major looked at him briefly, then said, "I'm sorry to have to tell you this Mr. Dawson but ..., Genie is dead!"

Operation Minerva

Dawson's heart exploded in his chest, he felt like his blood was under such pressure that it was going to come out the pores of his skin. His ears rang and he could not breathe. He sat up in the chair and held his head back so he could get some air into his oxygen-starved lungs. The major was talking but Dawson could not hear him. He held his hand up to the Major and motioned for him to stop! He could see the Major's mouth moving but could not hear a word he was saying. Dawson got up and walked around the room taking several deep breaths, then sat down again. He tried to talk but could not force it out. Every time he tried to say something, he felt as though all his guts were going to come flying out of his mouth.

"Genie loved you very much," the Major said. "She always wore Tabu. But, after you left, she stopped. We asked her why and she said Tabu was your favorite perfume and that she wouldn't wear it again until you came back."

The Major went on talking about Genie and how she never stopped talking about 'her Green Beret.'

Dawson finally got control of himself enough to ask the question.

"How did it happen?" He fought back the tears and choked on the words.

"The air field was attacked five nights ago. Genie was at the air field to pick up Lieutenant Sue Brown, the officer who met you at the door. They were walking through the terminal when a rocket exploded just out side the building. Eight people were killed; Genie was one of them. A small piece of shrapnel struck her in the heart and she died instantly. Sue was walking beside her and was not injured. We just now returned from the chapel where we held a service for her to coincide with her funeral today in her home town."

Dawson felt like the room was closing in on him. His headache returned, he started sweating again and his stomach was in a knot. He excused himself, and ran out of the building. Once outside he stopped, leaned against a pole and looked up into the sky. He could no longer stand the pressure inside.

He screamed in agony and cried. "What is it with me God, what have I done?"

People were walking by and staring at him as if he had gone mad. After several minutes, he started walking aimlessly down the street. Later, he found himself standing on a bridge looking at some ducks. Then he remembered that Genie had told him that this was her favorite place. She liked to stand here and feed the ducks. He thought of their last night together, her parachute nightgown, her giggle, her giggle, her contented, knowing, inviting little giggle. As he stood in Genie's favorite spot, he pulled out his knife and looked at its bright steel blade in the sunshine.

"How easy it would be, just one quick thrust and I would be with the team, with Genie."

He placed the point just below his ribcage slightly to the left and tilted the blade up. Then he applied pressure. He needed to feel the pain. The point of the blade broke the skin and blood ran down his shirt; however, he felt nothing.

What would they say to me if I did join them? He thought. Would Genie be happy to see me? Would the team welcome me?

"I wish I had died with you!" he said aloud, looking up at the sky.

He thought again about how easy it would be to drive the knife deeper. Would they be happy to see me or give me hell for wasting my life after they died to save it? He placed the knife back in its sheath. As he looked at his reflection in the water, he wondered how many times this same pool had reflected her image. He picked up six rocks and slowly dropped each one into the pool. With each rock he repeated the name of a friend he had lost. He watched the bubbles as they sank out of sight in the murky water. At that instant a peaceful calmness came over him and he lifted his head up and sniffed the air. He thought for sure he had caught the faint scent of Tabu.

THE END